Survive the Night

ALSO BY RILEY SAGER

Final Girls
The Last Time I Lied
Lock Every Door
Home Before Dark

Survive the Night

Riley Sager

HODDER &
STOUGHTON

First published in Great Britain in 2021 by Hodder & Stoughton
An Hachette UK company

1

Copyright © Todd Ritter 2021

A CIP catalogue record for this title is available from the British Library

Trade Paperback ISBN 978 1 529 37995 2
Paperback ISBN 978 1 529 37994 5
eBook ISBN 978 1 52937996 9

Printed and bound in Great Britain by Clays Ltd, Elcograf S.p.A.

Hodder & Stoughton policy is to use papers that are natural, renewable
and recyclable products and made from wood grown in sustainable
forests. The logging and manufacturing processes are expected to
conform to the environmental regulations of the country of origin.

Hodder & Stoughton Ltd
Carmelite House
50 Victoria Embankment
London EC4Y 0DZ

www.hodder.co.uk

To all those wonderful people out there in the dark

Survive the Night

Fasten your seat belts. It's going to be a bumpy night.
—*All About Eve*

Fade in.

Parking lot.

The middle of night.

The middle of nowhere.

Beginning at the end, like a great film noir. Bill Holden dead in the swimming pool. Fred MacMurray giving his last confession.

Going full circle. Like a noose.

There's a car, a diner, a neon sign in the parking lot fading to streaks in the rearview mirror as the car speeds away. Inside are two people—a young woman in the passenger seat and a man behind the wheel. Both stare through the windshield to the road ahead, uncertain.

About who they are.

About where they're going.

About how they got here, to this precise moment in time. Just before midnight. The final seconds of Tuesday, November 19, 1991.

But Charlie knows what brought them to the cusp of this uncertain new day. As the situation unfolds frame by frame, like film through a projector, she knows exactly how it all happened.

She knows because this isn't a movie.

It's the here and now.

She's the girl in the car.

The man behind the wheel is a killer.

And Charlie understands, with the certainty of someone who's seen this kind of movie a hundred times before, that only one of them will live to see the dawn.

NINE P.M.

INT. DORM ROOM—DAY

Staying isn't an option.

That's why Charlie has agreed to get into a car with a perfect stranger.

She's promised Robbie—promised herself as well—that she'll bolt if anything about the situation strikes her as shady. One can't be too careful. Not these days.

Not after what happened to Maddy.

Charlie has already steeled herself for flight, mentally listing all the scenarios in which she should run. If the car looks battered and/or has tinted windows. If someone else is inside, no matter the excuse. If he seems too eager to depart or, on the flip side, not hurried enough. She's sworn—to Robbie, to herself, to Maddy, whom she still sometimes talks to even though she's now two months in the grave—that a single shiver of apprehension will send her running back to the dorm.

She doubts it will come to that. Because he seems nice. Friendly. Definitely not the type of guy who'd do the things that had been done to Maddy and the others.

Besides, he's not a stranger. Not completely. They'd met once before, in front of the ride board in the campus commons, dwarfed by that wall of flyers from students desperate to get home and those eager to drive them there in exchange for gas money. Charlie had just put up her own flyer—carefully printed, her phone number placed on each meticulously cut tab—when he appeared at her side.

"You're going to Youngstown?" he said, his gaze flicking from her to the flyer and back again.

Charlie hesitated before responding. A post-Maddy habit. She never willingly engaged with people she didn't know. Not until she had a grasp on their intentions. He could have been making small talk. Or trying to pick her up. Unlikely, but not entirely out of the realm of possibility. It was how she met Robbie, after all. She'd been pretty once, before guilt and grief had sunk their claws into her.

"Yeah," she eventually said, after his gaze returned to the ride board, making her decide he was there for the same reason she was. "That where you're heading?"

"Akron," he said.

Hearing that made Charlie stand at attention. Not quite Youngstown, but close enough. A quick stop on the way to his final destination.

"Rider or driver?" she asked.

"Driver. Was hoping to find someone willing to split the cost of gas."

"I could be that someone," she said, letting him look her over, giving him the chance to decide if she was the type of person he'd want to spend hours alone in a car with. She knew what kind of vibe she gave off—an angry dourness that would have made guys like him tell her to smile more if she hadn't looked like she'd punch them for doing so. Doom and gloom hovered over her like a rain cloud.

Charlie studied him right back. He appeared to be a few years older than the typical student, although that could have been a product of his size. He was *big*. Tall, broad-chested, square-jawed. Wearing jeans and an Olyphant University sweatshirt, he looked, Charlie thought, like the hero of a forties campus comedy. Or the villain in an eighties one.

She assumed he was a grad student like Robbie. One of those people who got a taste for college life and decided they never wanted to leave. But he had nice hair, something Charlie still noticed even though she'd let her own grow limp and scraggly. Great smile, too, which he flashed when he said, "Possibly. When were you looking to leave?"

Charlie gestured to her flyer and the four letters placed all-caps in the dead center of the page.

ASAP

He tore a tab from the bottom of the flyer, leaving a gap that brought to Charlie's mind a missing tooth. The thought made her shudder.

The man placed the torn-off tab in his wallet. "I'll see what I can do."

Charlie hadn't expected a response. It was the middle of the week in the middle of November, with Thanksgiving just ten days away. No one was looking to leave campus then. No one but her.

But that night, her phone rang, and a vaguely familiar voice on the other end said, "Hi, it's Josh. From the ride board."

Charlie, who'd been sitting in her dorm staring at the half of room that had once been filled with all things Maddy but now sat lifeless and bare, amused herself by responding, "Hi, Josh from the ride board."

"Hi—" Josh paused, no doubt checking the paper tab in his hand for the name of the girl he was calling. "Charlie. I just wanted to tell you that I can leave tomorrow, but it won't be until late. Nine o'clock. If you want, there's a space in the passenger seat with your name on it."

"I'll take it."

And that was that.

Now tomorrow is today, and Charlie is having one last look at the dorm room she'll most likely never come back to. Her gaze sweeps slowly across the room, making sure to take in every inch of the place she's called home for the past three years. The cluttered desks. The beds piled with pillows. The strand of fairy lights Maddy had put up their first Christmas and never bothered to take down, now in full twinkle.

The golden sunlight of an autumn afternoon streams through the window, giving everything a sepia glow and making Charlie feel both joy and sadness. Nostalgia. That beautiful ache.

Someone enters the room behind her.

Maddy.

Charlie smells her perfume. Chanel No. 5.

"What a dump," Maddy says.

A melancholy smile plays across Charlie's lips. "I think I—"

"*Charlie.*"

INT. DORM ROOM—NIGHT

The sound of Robbie's voice from the open door breaks the spell like a finger snap. In a blink, the room has lost its magic. The desks are bare. The beds are stripped. The fairy lights remain, only they're unplugged and have been that way for months. At the window, Charlie sees not warm sunlight but a stark rectangle of darkness.

As for Maddy, she's long gone. Not even the faintest trace of her perfume remains.

"It's nine," Robbie says. "We should get going."

Charlie stands in the center of the room, still momentarily lost. How strange it is—how utterly jarring—to go from the picture in her mind's eye to harsh reality. There's no happiness left in this room. She sees that now. It's just a white-walled box that contains only memories now soured by tragedy.

Robbie watches her from the doorway. He knows what just happened.

A movie in her mind.

That Robbie's never been bothered by them is one of the things she loves about him. He knows her story, knows her obsessions, understands the rest.

"Did you take your pill today?"

Charlie swallows and nods. "Yeah."

"And you're all packed?" Robbie says, as if she's simply going away for the weekend and not, in all likelihood, forever.

"I think so. It wasn't easy."

She had spent most of the day sorting her things between two piles: take or leave behind. She ended up taking very little. Just two suitcases with all her clothes stuffed inside and a box filled with mementos and her beloved VHS tapes. The rest went into boxes conscientiously placed in the middle of the room, making it easier for the custodian assigned to dispose of it all when they realize she's never coming back.

"You can take more time if you need it," Robbie says. "You don't have to leave tonight. And I can still drive if you're willing to wait until the weekend."

Charlie understands. But to her, waiting—even just a few more days—is as unthinkable as staying.

"I think it's too late to back out now."

She grabs her coat. Well, Maddy's coat. A hand-me-down from her grandmother accidentally left behind when the rest of her belongings were carted away. Charlie found it under Maddy's bed and claimed it as her own. It's vintage—from the fifties—and uncharacteristically dramatic for Charlie, who usually favors anything that makes her blend in with the crowd. Made of bright red wool, the coat has a massive collar shaped like butterfly wings that come together as Charlie buttons it to her chin.

Robbie takes her suitcases, leaving Charlie cradling the box and the JanSport backpack she uses instead of a purse. She doesn't lock the door behind her. Why bother? Her last act before departing is to wipe away the names scrawled in erasable marker on the whiteboard affixed to the door.

Charlie + Maddy

The words leave a smudge of ink on her palm.

They depart quickly and quietly, unnoticed by the other girls on her floor, most of whom are gathered in the TV lounge down the hall. Charlie hears the braying voice of Roseanne Barr, followed by canned laughter. Even though she never understood her dorm's television obsession—why watch TV when movies are so much better?—tonight Charlie welcomes the distraction. Her plan is to skip the goodbyes. Although she used to be good friends with many girls on her floor, that all ended the moment Maddy died. Now it's best to simply vanish. Here one moment, gone the next. Just like Maddy herself.

"This will be good for you," Robbie says as they ride the elevator to the first floor. Charlie notes the hollowness of his voice, making it clear he thinks the opposite. "A little time away is all you need."

In the three days since Charlie announced her intention to leave school, Robbie has remained sweetly in denial about what it means for them as a couple. Despite promises to be true to each other and hastily made plans for Robbie to visit Youngstown over Christmas break, Charlie knows the reality of the situation.

Their relationship is ending.

Not in a both-going-our-separate-ways way. Definitely not in a Rhett Butler "Frankly, my dear, I don't give a damn" way. But Charlie understands that some kind of breakup will be the inevitable result. She'll be two states and four hundred miles away. He'll still be at Olyphant, remaining, to use Maddy's phrase after she'd first met him, a catch. Robbie Wilson, the campus math nerd and assistant swimming coach with the Richard Gere chin and the Brad Pitt abs. Already, girls are circling, eager to take Charlie's place. She can only assume one of them will eventually succeed.

If that's the price she must pay to get out of this place, then so be it. Her only hope is that she won't eventually come to regret it.

EXT. DORM BUILDING—NIGHT

The dorm lobby is empty when they step out of the elevator. So is the snow-dusted quad they cut across on their way to the parking lot. Despite winter's arrival, windows are open in a few of the upper-floor dorms, leaking out the now-familiar sounds of campus life. Laughter. The beep of one of Olyphant's infamously unreliable in-room microwaves. Music played louder than dorm rules allow. Charlie recognizes the song. Siouxsie and the Banshees. "Kiss Them for Me."

Maddy had loved that song.

Once they're out of the quad and at the curb, Robbie drops her suitcases next to a streetlamp—the designated meeting spot.

"I guess this is it," he says.

Charlie braces for another variation of the conversation they've had a dozen times. Is she sure she needs to leave? Is there any possibility she could stick it out until the end of the semester?

Her answer's been the same every time. Yes, she has to go. No, she can't make it to finals. There was a time, shortly after Maddy died, when she thought such a scenario was possible.

Not anymore.

Now Charlie understands with soul-deep certainty that she needs to get the hell out of Dodge.

She's stopped going to class, stopped talking to friends, stopped almost every aspect of her previous life. A constant pumping on the brakes of her existence. Now it's time to start moving again, even if that movement is really just running away.

To his credit, Robbie doesn't make one last-ditch attempt to get her to stay. Charlie suspects she's worn him down. Now all that's left to do is say their goodbyes.

Robbie leans in for a kiss and a tight hug. Wrapped in his embrace, Charlie feels a stab of guilt about her decision to leave, which was caused by another, far different sense of guilt. It's a Russian doll of remorse. Guilt tucked into guilt that she's ruining the only thing that has yet to be ruined.

"I'm sorry," she says, surprised by the hitch in her voice that she's forced to swallow down. "I know this is hard."

"It's been worse for you," Robbie says. "I understand why you need to do this. I should have understood sooner. And what I hope happens is that your time away will be exactly what you need and that when the spring semester rolls around, you'll be ready to come back to me."

Charlie's hit with another pang of guilt as Robbie looks down at her with those huge brown eyes of his. Bambi eyes, Maddy used to call them. So round and soulful that Charlie couldn't help but be mesmerized the first time they met.

Although she suspects that initial meeting was probably mundane, her memory of it is like something out of a classic romantic comedy. It was at the library, she a sophomore strung out on Diet Coke and midterm stress and Robbie a ridiculously handsome first-year grad student simply looking for a place to sit. He chose her table, one that comfortably sat four but had been commandeered by Charlie and all the books she'd spread across it.

"Room for one more?" he said.

Charlie looked up from the Pauline Kael book she was reading, saw those eyes, and promptly froze. "Um, sure."

She didn't clear space for him. Didn't move at all, in fact. She only stared. So much so that Robbie swiped a palm across his cheek and said, "Do I have something on my face?"

She laughed. He sat. They started chatting. About midterms. And college life. And life in general. She learned that Robbie had been an undergrad at Olyphant and chose to remain there for his graduate studies, well on his way to becoming a math professor. Robbie learned that Charlie's parents took her to see *E.T.* three times in the theaters and that she bawled all the way home after each screening.

They ended up talking until the library closed. And talking more after that at an all-night diner off-campus. They were still talking when they strolled up to Charlie's dorm at two a.m. That was when Robbie told her, "Just so you know, I wasn't really looking for a place to sit. I just needed an excuse to talk to you."

"Why?"

"Because you're special," he said. "I could tell the moment I saw you."

Just like that, Charlie was smitten. She liked Robbie's looks, obviously, and how he seemed to be oblivious to them. She liked his sense of humor. And that he didn't care at all about movies, which seemed so refreshingly foreign to her. It was a far cry from the *Godfather*-obsessed man-children who populated most of her film classes.

For a time, things were good between them. Even great. Then Maddy died and Charlie changed, and now there's no going back to being the girl she was that night at the library.

Robbie checks his watch and announces the time. Five past nine. Josh is late. Charlie wonders where that should fall on the worry spectrum.

"You don't need to wait with me," she says.

"I want to," Robbie says.

Charlie knows she should want that, too. It would be normal to want to spend as much time with him as possible before they part. But, to her, normal is wanting to avoid a rushed goodbye in front of an almost complete stranger. Normal is desiring a sad, quiet farewell witnessed by no one else but them. Bogart putting Bergman on the plane at the end of *Casablanca*. Streisand sweeping a hand through Redford's hair in *The Way We Were*.

"It's cold," she says. "You go on back to your apartment. I know you have an early class tomorrow."

"You sure?"

Charlie nods. "I'll be fine. I swear."

"Call me when you get home," Robbie says. "No matter how late it is. And call me from the road, if you see a pay phone. Let me know you're safe."

"We're driving from New Jersey to Ohio. The only danger is dying of boredom."

"That's not what I mean."

Charlie knows, because she's thinking what Robbie's thinking. The thing neither of them wants to articulate because it will ruin this goodbye.

Maddy was killed.

By a stranger.

One who's still out there. Somewhere. Likely waiting to do it again.

"I'll try to call," Charlie says. "I promise."

"Pretend it's one of those movies you were always making me watch," Robbie says. "The ones with the French-sounding name."

"Film noir?" Charlie shakes her head. After a year of dating, has she taught him nothing?

"Yeah, one of those. You're being held captive against your will and the only way to get help is by speaking in code to your worried boyfriend."

"What's the code?" Charlie says, playing along, grateful for the way Robbie's choosing to wrap up this goodbye.

Not sad.

Cinematic.

"'Things took a detour.'"

The way Robbie says it makes Charlie assume he's trying to imitate Bogart, even though it sounds more like Jimmy Stewart to her ears.

"And if everything is fine?"

"'It's smooth sailing, sweetheart.'"

This time he really does sound like Bogart, and hearing it makes Charlie's heart crack open a bit.

"I love you," she says.

"I know."

Charlie can't tell if Robbie's response is an intentional *Star Wars* reference or if it's just a happy accident. Either way, she doesn't care, because now he's kissing her again and hugging her one last time and saying goodbye for real, in a way that's sadder than any movie. The pain in her chest grows—an acute ache Charlie expects will stay with her the entire ride home.

"You're still special, Charlie," Robbie says. "I need you to know that."

Then he's gone and it's only her. Standing alone at the curb with her box and two suitcases, the situation finally feels real.

She's doing it.

She's actually leaving.

In a few hours she'll be home, probably watching a movie with Nana Norma, maybe on her way to returning to the person she used to be.

Charlie opens her backpack and fishes out the orange pill bottle that's been rattling around at the bottom of it since September. Inside the bottle is more orange—tiny tablets that always reminded her of M&M's when she took one. Back when she *did* take them.

She lied to Robbie about that. It's been three days since she gulped one down, even though the psychiatrist who prescribed them promised they'd keep the movies in her mind at bay. And they did. But they also made her both drowsy *and* restless, her body constantly veering between those two extremes. The result was weeks of sleepless nights and lost days. A vampire. That's what the orange pills turned her into.

To counteract that, the psychiatrist also gave Charlie a prescription for little white pills to help her sleep.

Those were worse.

So much worse that she had already gotten rid of them.

Now it's time to say goodbye to the orange ones. She's through with pills of any color.

Charlie steps off the curb and walks a few yards to a storm drain carved into the asphalt. She pours the pills into it, enjoying the twinge of satisfaction she gets from watching them bounce off the metal grate before dropping into the darkness below. The bottle goes into a nearby trash can.

Returning to her box and suitcases, Charlie pulls her red coat tighter around her. The November night is pitched precisely between autumn and winter. The sky is clear and the stars are bright, but there's a sharp chill to the air that makes her shiver. Or maybe the shiver comes from the fact that she's now alone outside while there's a killer on the loose.

Even if she didn't realize that danger on her own, she'd be reminded by the Take Back the Night flyer taped to the streetlamp next to her. The flyers are a direct response to Maddy's murder. As were the candlelit vigils. And guest speakers. And grief counselors who descended onto campus armed with pamphlets and good intentions.

Charlie avoided all of it, preferring to grieve alone. As a result, she also missed out on the sense of fear that's gripped campus for the past two months. She spent most of her time locked in her room and thus had no reason to be scared.

Now, however, she feels a frigid tingle on the back of her neck. Not helping is the list of rules printed on the flyer, most of which she's currently disobeying.

Never go out alone at night.

Always walk in pairs.

Always tell someone where you're going.

Never trust a stranger.

That last one gives Charlie pause. Because as much as she likes to think otherwise, Josh *is* a stranger. Or he will be, if he ever shows up. Charlie doesn't wear a watch and has no clue what time it is. But she suspects it's close to quarter after nine. If he doesn't show up soon, she'll have no choice but to return to the dorm. She probably should have done that already. Hell, according to the Take Back the Night flyer, she shouldn't even be here at all, alone at the curb with suitcases and a box, clearly looking like someone about to leave and who no one would miss for a few days.

Because her need to get away far outweighs her fear, she stays put, watching the entrance to the parking lot. Soon enough, a double-barreled glow appears on the horizon.

Headlights.

They swoop farther into the lot before curving in a wide arc and aiming right at her. She squints against their brightness and looks to the sidewalk, where her shadow stretches like a ghost into the snow-dusted grass behind her. A second later, a car is waiting at the curb. The driver's-side door opens, and Josh climbs out.

"Charlie, hi," he says, speaking the words with a shy smile, as if it were a first date.

"Hey."

"Sorry about the night drive," Josh says. "It couldn't be helped."

"I don't mind."

In the past two months, Charlie's become well-acquainted with the dark. More nights than not, she was wide awake until dawn, thanks in part to her pills, the dorm room aglow from the light of the TV and whatever movie she happened to be watching.

"Well, your chariot awaits," Josh says as he pats the roof of the car. "Not quite a limousine, but it'll get us where we need to go."

Charlie takes a moment to examine the car. The slate-gray Pontiac Grand Am—to her eye, at least—looks far from junky. Exterior freshly washed. No obvious scratches or dents. Definitely no tinted windows. Charlie can see right into the front seat, which is blessedly empty. It's the kind of car her father might drive, if he was still around. Sensible. Hopefully dependable. A car built to blend in with the crowd.

Josh eyes the box and suitcases at her feet. "I didn't think you'd be bringing that much. You plan on being gone awhile?"

"Hopefully not too long," Charlie says, not meaning it but also wondering if she secretly does. And why shouldn't she want that? Doesn't she owe it to Robbie to at least try to come back for the spring semester? Doesn't she owe it to herself?

Even though Maddy's the reason she's doing all this, Charlie knows she'd disapprove.

You're being an idiot, darling. That's what Maddy would have said about her plan to leave campus.

"Is there enough room for it all?" Charlie says.

"Plenty," Josh says as he quickly moves to the back of the car and unlocks the trunk.

Charlie grabs the cardboard box and starts to carry it toward the open trunk. Josh swoops in before she can get near it, taking the box from her arms and leaving Charlie only with her backpack.

"Let me get that for you," he says.

Her arms suddenly unburdened, Charlie spends the next few seconds watching Josh load her things into the trunk. In that short span of time, she notices something strange about the way he's standing. Rather than pack everything from directly behind the car, Josh remains at an angle, his broad back blocking whatever view Charlie might get of the open trunk. Almost as if there's something else inside. Something he doesn't want her to see.

Charlie suspects it's nothing.

She *knows* it's nothing.

People sometimes do weird things. She's the girl who sees movies in her mind, and Josh is the guy who fills his trunk in a weird way. End of story.

But then Josh turns around after slamming the trunk shut and she notices something else about him. Something that, to her mind, is stranger than how he loaded the trunk.

Josh is dressed the same as he was at the ride board.

Exactly the same.

Same jeans. Same sweatshirt. Same nice hair. Yes, they're at a college and everyone dresses like this; it's the unofficial uniform of Olyphant. But Josh wears it uncomfortably, almost like these are not his normal clothes. There is, Charlie realizes, a bit of Central Casting to his look, as if he's been hired as an extra. Generic College Hunk #2.

Josh smiles again, and Charlie notices that it's absolutely perfect. The smile of a matinee idol, intimidating in its full glory. It might be sexy. It might be sinister. Charlie can't decide which.

"We're all set," he says. "Ready to ditch this pop stand?"

Charlie doesn't immediately answer. She's distracted by the idea that these all could be warning signs. The trunk. The clothes. They're exactly the kinds of things she'd sworn would make her turn around and go straight back to her dorm.

It's not too late for that. She could easily inform Josh she's changed her mind and that he should just take her things out of the trunk. Instead, she tells herself to stop being so suspicious. This isn't about Josh. Or what he's wearing. Or how he loads the trunk.

It's about her and the fact that, now that she's on the cusp of leaving, she's suddenly seeking out reasons to stay.

And there *are* reasons. She should get an education. She loves her major. Then there's the simple fact that it would make Robbie happy.

But would she be happy?

Charlie doesn't think so.

She could pretend to be, for Robbie's sake. She could go through the motions, just like she's been doing since September. And maybe—just maybe—the storm cloud she's been living under would eventually lift and she could go back to being a normal college student. Well, semi-normal. Charlie has enough self-awareness to know she'll never be exactly like everyone else. There always has been and always will be an aura of eccentricity about her. And that's okay.

What's not okay, at least to Charlie, is remaining in a place where she's miserable. Where she's reminded daily of a deep, painful loss. Where memories sting and guilt lingers and not a week, day, hour goes by in which she doesn't think, *I shouldn't have left her. I should have stopped him. I should have saved her.*

She looks at Josh, still patiently waiting for an answer.

"As ready as I'll ever be," she says.

INT. GRAND AM—NIGHT

Charlie learned to drive in the car her parents would later die in.

It was her father who taught her, his patience thinning with each lurching spin around the high school parking lot. He insisted Charlie learn how to drive stick because, in his words, "Then you'll be able to drive anything."

But the manual transmission baffled her. Three pedals instead of two, like in her mother's car, and all those steps she had to follow. A dance she didn't know and thought she'd never, ever master.

Left foot clutch.

Right foot brake.

Neutral. Ignition. Accelerate.

It took an entire afternoon of practice before Charlie could drive a single lap around the lot without stalling or grinding the gears in a way that made her father break out in a cold sweat. It took two more weeks before she truly felt comfortable behind the wheel of that maroon Chevy Citation. But once that happened, the rest came quickly to her. The three-point turns and parallel parking and slaloms through traffic cones her father had borrowed from a buddy who worked construction.

She aced her license exam on the first try, unlike her best friend, Jamie, who needed three attempts before she passed. Afterward, Charlie and her father went out for celebratory ice cream, her behind the wheel and him continuing his lessons with advice offered from the passenger seat.

"Never drive more than five miles over the speed limit," he told her. "Cops won't bother you. Not for that."

"And over five?" Charlie asked, taunting him with the idea that she intended to be a speed demon.

Her father gave her one of those *Excuse me?* looks that had become common during her teenage years. "Do you *want* to use that brand-new license of yours?"

"Yes."

"Then stick to the speed limit."

As Charlie shifted the car into second gear, her father seemed to shift, too. He leaned back in his seat and let his gaze roam from the windshield to the passenger-side window.

"Your mother would be livid if she ever found out I told you this," he said, "but sometimes, in real life, you can't avoid speeding. Sometimes your only choice is to drive like hell."

Although Josh doesn't drive like hell, keeping his speed at a legal forty-five miles per hour as they leave campus, it's good enough for Charlie. After two months of stasis, she's finally in motion. No, it won't change what happened. It certainly won't change her role in it. But Charlie hopes this bit of movement is the first step on the long road to acceptance and forgiveness. And when they pass the brightly lit Olyphant University sign on the way out, she allows herself to enjoy the sense of relief that wraps around her like a warm hug.

Or maybe that's just the heater, pumping through slatted vents on the dashboard. After standing in the cold for so long, Charlie feels soothed by the warmth and the fact that the car is as clean inside as it is on the outside. No dirt on the floor or McDonald's wrappers on the front seat, like in Robbie's car. It even smells clean, making Charlie think Josh came straight here from a full-service car wash. She catches traces of shampoo rising from the upholstered seat beneath her. Mixed with it is the strong, not entirely pleasant scent of pine, courtesy of a tree-shaped air freshener dangling from the rearview mirror. It swings as they turn onto the main road that runs parallel to the university, sending a fresh swath of pine stink Charlie's way. She wrinkles her nose at the smell.

Josh notices, because of course he does. Although not a compact car by any means, the front seat of the Grand Am keeps the two of them in close proximity. All that separates them is the center console, inside of which comes the rattle of loose change and plastic tapping plastic. Josh steers with his left hand and shifts with right, his forearm coming within inches of Charlie's.

"Sorry about the air freshener," he says. "It's, uh, potent. I can take it down, if you want."

"It's fine," Charlie says, even though she's not entirely sure it is. Normally, she loves the smell of pine. As a kid, she'd bring her face close to each freshly cut Christmas tree and inhale its scent in lung-filling gulps. But this is something different. Chemicals pretending to be nature. It makes Charlie want to crack open the window. "I'm sure I'll get used to it."

It's a good enough answer for Josh, who nods while staring out the windshield. "I did the math, and I think the drive should take us about six hours, not counting pit stops."

Charlie already knows this, thanks to similar trips home. It takes a half hour to reach Interstate 80, all of it on a local road lined with hobby shops, dentist offices, and travel agencies. Once on the highway, it's about another thirty minutes until they cross the Delaware Water Gap into Pennsylvania. After that comes the Poconos, followed by hours of nothing. Just fields and forests and monotony until they hit Ohio and, soon after that, the exit for Youngstown. When Josh told her they couldn't leave until nine, she resigned herself to not getting home until three a.m. or later. She didn't have much of a choice.

"You're welcome to sleep the whole way, if you want," Josh says.

Sleeping through the drive is not on the table. Josh might seem friendly and nice, but Charlie plans to be conscious during the entire trip.

Always remain alert. Another piece of advice on that Take Back the Night flyer.

"I'll be all right," she says. "I don't mind keeping you company."

"Then I'll be sure to make a coffee stop before we hit the highway."

"Sounds good," Charlie says.

"Good," Josh replies.

And just like that, they run out of things to say. It only took two minutes. Sitting awkwardly in the newfound silence, Charlie wonders if she should say something—anything—to keep the conversation rolling. It's something she's fretted over since Josh agreed to give her a ride—the etiquette of being in a car with an almost stranger.

She knows it's not the same as in the movies, where two strangers confined together in a car find endless things to talk about, usually leading to either romance or murder. But in real life, if you talk too much, you're annoying. If you don't talk enough, you're rude.

The same standards apply to Josh. As she packed, Charlie was both worried he'd be too chatty and worried he'd say nothing at all. Silence between strangers is different from the long periods of quiet she'd experienced with Maddy or Robbie. With someone you know and trust, silence doesn't matter. With a stranger, it could mean anything.

A stranger is just a friend you haven't met yet, Maddy used to say. Ironic, seeing how she was the more judgmental of the two of them. Charlie was merely awkward and shy. It took tenacious prodding to coax her out of her shell. Maddy was the complete opposite. Outgoing and theatrical, which made her quick to tire of those who either didn't share her flair for the dramatic or failed to appreciate it. It's why they were a perfect combo: Maddy performed, and Charlie watched with adoration.

"You're not her friend," Robbie once said in a huff after Maddy had shrugged off plans with them in order to go to a kegger with her theater major friends. "You're her audience."

What Robbie didn't understand—what he *couldn't* understand—was that Charlie knew and didn't care. She was a willing audience to Maddy's antics. It gave her quiet life the drama it otherwise would have lacked, and Charlie loved her for that.

But that's all over now. Maddy's dead. Charlie's retreated from the world. And since she'll never lay eyes on Josh again once they reach Youngstown, she sees no point in turning him from stranger to friend.

Just as she resigns herself to spending the next six hours in awkward, pine-scented silence, Josh pipes up from behind the wheel, suddenly chatty.

"So what's in Youngstown that you're so eager to get back to?"

"My grandmother."

"Neat," Josh says with an amiable nod. "Family visit?"

"I live with her."

Over the years, she's learned that answer requires less explaining than the truth. Telling people that her grandmother technically lives in the house Charlie inherited from her dead parents usually leads to follow-up questions.

"I gotta say, I didn't expect to find someone to share the drive with me," Josh says. "Not many people are leaving campus. Not this time of year. And everyone there seems to own a car. You ever notice that? The parking lots are filled. I'm surprised you don't have a car."

"I don't drive," Charlie says, knowing it sounds like she doesn't know how.

In truth, she doesn't *want* to drive. Not since her parents' accident. The last time she was behind the wheel of a car was the day before they died. When her license expired three months ago, she never bothered to renew it.

Charlie's okay with being a passenger. She has to be. She knows that riding in a car is unavoidable, just like she knows something bad could happen regardless of whether she's behind the wheel or not. Just look at her mother. She was simply along for the ride when Charlie's father steered the car off the highway and into the woods, killing them both instantly.

No one knows what prompted him to drive off the road, even though theories abound. He swerved to miss a deer. He had a heart attack behind the wheel. Something went tragically awry with the steering column.

Accidents happen.

That's what Charlie was told in the weeks following the crash, when it became clear she had no intention of ever driving again. Accidents happen and people die and it's a tragedy, but she shouldn't live in fear of getting behind the wheel of a car.

What no one understood was that dying in a car crash wasn't what frightened Charlie. Culpability—that was her big fear. She didn't want to cause the same pain her father had. If there was an accident and people died, including her, she didn't want to be the one responsible.

The irony is that someone *has* died and Charlie *is* responsible and it didn't involve a car at all.

"Lucky we found each other, I guess," Josh says. "You ever use the ride board before?"

Charlie shakes her head. "First time."

She's never had to before. Nana Norma used to drive her to campus at the start of a semester and pick her up when it was over. After her eyesight started going bad last fall and she, too, stopped driving, Robbie took over. The only reason Charlie's not in his Volvo right now is because he couldn't find someone to cover his TA and coaching duties for the two days it would take for him to drive to Youngstown and back.

"Mine, too," Josh says. "I went to the board thinking it would be a waste of time, and there you were, just putting up your flyer. Charlie. Interesting name you've got there, by the way. Is that short for something?"

"Yes. Charles."

Maddy had loved that answer. Whenever Charlie used it—usually at whatever loud, intimidating mixer she'd been dragged to—Maddy would let out a wicked cackle that made her feel pleased with herself for coming up with it. It was sassy, for Charlie. Like something Barbara Stanwyck would have said in a screwball comedy.

"Your real name is Charles?" Josh says.

"It was a joke," Charlie says, bummed that she's forced to explain it. Barbara Stanwyck never explained things. "Not my name. That really is Charlie, although it's not short for anything. I was named after a character in a movie."

"A boy character?"

"A girl. Who, incidentally, was named after her uncle."

"What's the movie?"

"*Shadow of a Doubt.*"

"Never heard of it."

"Alfred Hitchcock," Charlie says. "Released in 1943. Starring Joseph Cotten and Teresa Wright."

"Is it good?" Josh asks.

"It's *very* good. Which is lucky for me, because who wants to be named after a character in a shitty movie, right?"

Josh gives her a glance, one brow arched, looking either impressed or surprised by her enthusiasm. That raised brow tells Charlie she's talking too much, which only happens when the subject is movies. She could be mute for hours, but if someone mentions a film title, the words pour out. Maddy had once told her that movies were her version of wine coolers. *They really loosen you up*, she said.

Charlie knows it's true, which is why asking people about their favorite movie is the only icebreaker she has. It instantly tells her how much time and energy she should spend on a person. If someone mentions Hitchcock or Ford or Altman or even Argento, they're probably worth talking to. On the flip side, if someone brings up *The Sound of Music*, Charlie knows it's best to just walk away.

But Josh seems okay with her chattiness. Giving a slight nod of agreement, he says, "Not me. It would be like being named after a serial killer or something."

"That's what the movie's about," Charlie says. "There's this girl named Charlie."

"Who's named after her uncle and you're named after her."

"Right. And she idolizes Uncle Charlie, which is why she's so happy when he comes to visit for a few weeks. But Uncle Charlie is acting suspicious, and one thing leads to another until Charlie begins to suspect her uncle is really a serial killer."

"Is he?"

"Yes," Charlie says. "Otherwise it wouldn't be much of a movie."

"Who does he kill?" Josh asks.

"Wealthy widows of a certain age."

"Sounds like one bad dude."

"He is."

"Does he get away with it?"

"No. Charlie stops him."

"I thought so," Josh says. "From the way you talk about her, I assumed she was plucky."

Charlie feels a minor jolt at the word, mostly because she's not sure she's ever heard someone say it in conversation before. She's certain no one has ever used it to describe her. She's been called a lot of things in her life. Weird? Yes. Shy? Yes. Standoffish? Sad, but true. But never plucky. And knowing she's not plucky now makes Charlie feel oddly guilty for not living up to the reputation set by her namesake.

"Is that your thing?" Josh says. "Movies?"

"They're more than just my thing," Charlie says. "Movies are my life. And my major. Film theory."

"Like, learning how to make them?"

"Studying them. Learning how they tick. Understanding what works and what doesn't. *Appreciating* them."

She's said all this before, at one time or another. To Maddy, when they were thrust together in the same dorm room the first day of their freshman year. To Robbie, the night they met in the library. To anyone who would listen, really. Charlie is a disciple, preaching the gospel of cinema.

"But why movies?" Josh asks.

"Because they take our world and improve upon it," Charlie says. "Movies are magical that way. Everything is magnified. The colors are brighter. The shadows are darker. The action more violent and the love affairs more passionate. People break out into song. Or they used to. The emotions—love, hate, fear, laughter—are all bigger. And the people! All those beautiful faces in full close-up. So beautiful it's hard to look away."

She pauses, aware she's been swept up in movie talk. But there's still one more thing she wants to say. She *needs* to say it, because it's true.

"Movies are like life," she finally says. "Only better."

She leaves out another truth, which is that you can get lost in movies. Charlie learned that the day her parents died, when Nana Norma came to stay for good.

The wreck happened on a Saturday morning in mid-July. Her

parents had left early to go to the lawn and garden place two towns over, waking her long enough to say they'd be back by ten.

Charlie didn't think much of it when ten came and went and they still weren't home. Same thing when the grandfather clock in the living room struck eleven. Fifteen minutes later, a cop came to the door. Deputy Anderson. Her friend Katie's dad. She'd slept over at Katie's house once when she was ten, and Mr. Anderson made them pancakes the next morning. It was the first thing Charlie thought of when she saw him on the doorstep. Mr. Anderson standing over the stove, spatula in hand, flipping pancakes as wide as dinner plates.

But then she saw the hat in his hands. And the gray tint to his face. And the uncertain half shuffle he did on the welcome mat, as if forcing his legs not to run away.

Seeing all of that, Charlie knew something horrible had happened.

Deputy Anderson cleared his throat and said, "I'm afraid I have bad news, Charlie."

She barely heard the rest, registering only the most important snippets. Accident. Highway. Killed instantly.

By that time, Mrs. Anderson was there, no doubt brought as backup, pulling Charlie into her arms and saying, "Is there someone we can call, honey? Family?"

Charlie whimpered yes. There was Nana Norma. And then she broke down crying and didn't stop until hours had passed and Nana Norma was there.

Nana Norma used to be an actress. Or had tried to be. As soon as she turned eighteen, she did the whole hop-on-a-bus-to-Hollywood cliché, like a million other small-town girls who'd been told they were pretty or had talent. Nana Norma had both. Charlie's seen the pictures of the beautiful brunette with the Rita Hayworth figure, and she's heard her grandmother singing in the kitchen when she thought no one else was around to hear it.

What young Norma Harrison didn't have was luck. After a year of checking coats, going on auditions, and not getting even a millimeter past the dream stage, she hopped back on that bus and returned to Ohio a little harder and a lot humbled.

But it didn't diminish her love of movies. Or pictures, as she still calls them, like she's a walking, talking *Variety* headline.

"Let's watch a picture," she said to Charlie that first, awkward night, both of them too bowled over with grief to do anything but sit there, silent and shell-shocked.

Charlie hadn't wanted to. At the time, she wasn't much of a movie fan, despite always knowing how she got her name. That was Nana Norma's doing. She had a thing for Hitchcock and instilled that love in Charlie's mother.

"It'll make you feel better," Nana Norma told her. "Trust me."

Charlie relented and joined her on the couch, where they watched old movies all night and into the dawn. The characters talked tough and smoked and drank glass after glass of whiskey. Even the women. There were murders and double-crosses and stolen glances so scorched with lust it made Charlie's cheeks turn red.

Even better was Nana Norma's running commentary, in which Charlie got glimpses of her Hollywood days.

"Nice guy," she said of one actor. "Drank too much."

"Went on a date with him once," she said of another. "Got too handsy for my taste."

When early-morning sun started trickling through the living room blinds, Charlie realized Nana Norma was right. She did feel better. All those churning emotions—the pain, the rage, the sadness so thick she'd thought she'd sink right into it like quicksand—had momentarily left her.

They watched movies until dawn the next night.

And the night after that.

And the one after that.

By the time Charlie realized they were using cinematic fantasy to escape their horrible reality, it was too late. She was hooked.

On the day her parents were buried, everything felt larger than life. The closed coffins side by side at the front of the church sat in a patch of sunlight colored by stained-glass windows. The flowers behind them burst out of their vases in rainbow brightness, contrasting perfectly with the black-clad mourners who fanned themselves in the July heat. When they gathered graveside, the sky was piercingly blue. There was a light breeze, too, on which traveled the sound of a gospel choir. It was all so beautiful, in a way that made Charlie sad but also comforted. She knew that as hard as this was, she was going to get through it.

After the funeral, she asked Nana Norma if she knew the name of the hymn the choir had been singing as her parents' coffins were lowered into the ground.

"What hymn?" Nana Norma had asked. "And what choir?"

That was the moment Charlie knew the reality of her parents' funeral was far different from the one she had experienced. She understood then that her brain had embellished it, turning it into a mental movie. Images on film churning through reels, telling someone else's sad tale, which was how she was able to endure it.

"Have you ever thought about making movies?" Josh says, bringing her back to the moment. "Since you love them so much."

"Not really."

Charlie had considered it only briefly, back when she was trying to decide which schools she should apply to. She suspected there was more gratification in creating something as opposed to taking it apart. But she also feared that knowing the nitty-gritty of making films would ruin the magic of watching them, and since there was already so little magic in her life, she didn't want to risk it. That's especially true now that Maddy's gone.

Gone.

Such an awful word. So absolutely blunt in its finality that Charlie gets sad just thinking it.

Maddy is gone.

Never to return.

And Charlie herself is to blame.

Grief suddenly washes over her, as it's done so many times in the past two months. With it is a sense of guilt so heavy Charlie feels pinned to the passenger seat. Both emotions overwhelm her to the point where she only barely hears Josh say, "Why not? Seems like a sweet gig."

"Lots of gigs are sweet," Charlie says. "Doesn't mean I want any of them."

She looks to her right, checking her reflection in the side mirror outside the window. The dashboard lights illuminate her from below, casting a cool glow on her coat collar, revealing how it matches her shade of lipstick. Not that she can see those matching reds. The night and the moonlight make everything appear monochrome. Not black and white. Nothing that stark. A thousand shades of gray.

"Charlie?"

INT. GRAND AM—NIGHT

Charlie huffs out a breath, blinks her eyes, checks herself in the side mirror, and sees that everything's in color, because of course it would be. It's the real world. But for the briefest of moments, Charlie wasn't living in it. She was somewhere else.

"What just happened there?" Josh says. "You started to answer my question then just stopped."

"I did?"

"Yeah. You completely zoned out."

"Sorry," Charlie says. "I do that sometimes."

Too embarrassed to face Josh, she looks straight ahead. While she was zoned out, to use his phrase, it started snowing. Big, fat flurries that look fake as they drift to the ground. She thinks of soap flakes on sound stages and *It's a Wonderful Life*. Even though the snow isn't covering the road, enough of it clings to the windshield for Josh to hit the wipers, which yawn to life and flick it away.

"Does it happen a lot?" Josh says.

"Every so often." Charlie pauses an awkward beat. "Sometimes I, um, see things."

Josh takes his eyes off the road to give her a look that's more curious than weirded out. "What kind of things?"

"Movies." Another pause. "In my mind."

Charlie doesn't know why she admits this. If she had to guess, she'd chalk it up to the temporary intimacy of their situation. They're two people thrown together in a darkened car, barely making eye contact, ready to spend the next six hours in a shared space and then never see each other again. It makes people talk. It makes them reveal things they might not tell their closest friends. Charlie knows such a thing can happen. She's seen it in the movies.

Maddy was the first person Charlie had told about the movies in her mind. She came clean the third week of their freshman year, when Maddy caught her drifting away for four minutes and twenty-six seconds. She'd timed it. After Charlie told her, Maddy nodded and said, "That's weird. Not gonna lie. Lucky for you, I'm a fan of weird things."

"Movies that you've seen before?" Josh says now.

"New ones. That only I can see."

"Like a daydream?"

"Not quite," Charlie says, knowing that in daydreams the world goes hazy at the edges. This is the opposite. Everything is sharper. Like a movie projected onto the backs of her eyelids. "It's not *The Secret Life of Walter Mitty.*"

"I'm guessing that's a movie."

"Starring Danny Kaye, Virginia Mayo, and Boris Karloff," Charlie says, rattling off the names the same way baseball fans recite player stats. "Loosely based on the short story by James Thurber. It's about this guy named Walter who has this elaborate fantasy life. What happens to me is . . . different."

"Different how?" Josh says.

"Instead of what's really happening, I see a heightened version of the scene. Like my brain is playing tricks on me. I hear conversations that aren't happening and see things that aren't really there. It feels like life—"

"Only better?"

Charlie shakes her head. "More manageable."

She had always thought of it as seeing things in wide-screen. Not everything. Just certain moments. Difficult ones. A Steadicam operator gliding through the rough patches of her life. It wasn't until she was forced to see the psychiatrist who prescribed the little orange pills that Charlie realized what the movies in her mind really were.

Hallucinations.

That was what the psychiatrist called them.

She said it was like having a mental circuit breaker, triggered when Charlie's emotions threaten to overwhelm her. In times of grief or stress or fear, a switch flips in Charlie's brain, replacing reality with something more cinematic and easier to handle.

Charlie knows the one she just experienced was caused by a mix of guilt, sadness, and missing Maddy. One of those emotions would have been enough to handle on her own. She might have even been able to deal with a combination of two of them. But put all three together and—click!—the switch in her brain was flipped and the movie in her mind began.

"You said you hear and see things that might not be there," Josh says. "Are we talking people?"

"Yes," Charlie says. "Sometimes people."

"So you could see something—or someone—that doesn't really exist?" Josh says, fascinated. "Or have an entire conversation that's not real?"

"I could. Someone talks to me, I talk to them, and no one else can hear it because it's all in my head."

"And this just happens without warning?"

"Yep."

"You can't control it?"

"Not really."

"Doesn't that worry you a little bit?"

"It worries me a lot," Charlie says, not daring to say anything more.

The movies in her mind never used to worry her. If anything, she was thankful for them. They made things easier. A balm that soothed the sting of prickly emotions. Besides, they never lasted very long, and they certainly never hurt anyone.

Until one of them did.

Now she'll never forgive herself.

Now she just wants them to go away.

"What kind of movies are we talking about?" Josh says.

"Anything, really. I've seen musicals and dramas and scary movies."

"And what about a minute ago? What kind of movie was going through your head then?"

Charlie rewinds her mind to that image of her in the side mirror. Wearing Maddy's red coat and matching lipstick that's definitely not there in real life, Charlie looked dramatic. But she was no femme fatale. That was always Maddy's role.

And Josh was the handsome but wary man behind the wheel, possibly with a past. The two of them could have been anyone. Lovers on the lam. Siblings only recently reunited. Strangers in the dark who, for reasons unknown even to them, had set out across the country without a plan.

Which, in a way, is the truth.

"Film noir," Charlie says. "Not a classic, though. Something the studios churned out on a weekly basis. A solid B movie."

"That," Josh says, "is oddly specific."

Charlie responds with an embarrassed shrug. "I can't help it. It's how I'm wired."

"What if this, right here and right now, were a movie?" Josh says. "Who would play me?"

"You mean, what actor?"

"Yeah."

"Living or dead?"

"Doesn't matter."

Charlie leans back and raises her hands, fingers straight and thumbs extended, like a director framing a shot. She takes a moment to study Josh. Not just his face, which is undeniably handsome, but also his physical features. He's formidable. A heavy, slightly hulking presence that, combined with his good looks, brings to mind only one person.

"Marlon Brando," she says.

Josh cringes. "Ouch."

"*Young* Marlon Brando," Charlie's quick to add. "*Streetcar* Brando. You know, back when he was hot."

"Oh, so you think I'm hot?" Josh says, puffing out his chest a little bit, pleased.

Charlie blushes. "I didn't mean it like that."

"Too late," Josh says. "Now that you've said it, you can't take it back. I like being that Brando. He's kind of fat and crazy now, though, right?"

"Something for you to look forward to."

"Very funny," Josh says. "And here I was about to be nice and say who *I* think should play you in this imaginary movie of yours."

"Who?"

"Audrey Hepburn."

Charlie continues to blush. She's heard this before, but it was from Maddy, who once told her, "You could look like Audrey, if you wanted to. You've got that wide-eyed, fragile, deer-tiptoeing-into-a-meadow thing going on that guys love."

"Deer don't tiptoe" is what she told Maddy then. What she tells Josh now is, "I'm surprised you know who that is."

"Give me some credit," he says. "I'm not a total lunkhead. Oh, and the proper response would have been to thank me."

"Thank you," Charlie says, feeling another wave of heat on her cheeks.

"I'm about to ask you a personal question," Josh warns.

"More personal than me admitting I see movies in my mind?"

"Not *that* personal," Josh says. "I'm just curious if you have a boyfriend."

Charlie goes still, unsure how to react. Josh is clearly flirting with her, probably because he thinks she was flirting with him, even though it wasn't intentional. She isn't flirtatious, despite being taught by the best. Marilyn Monroe. Lana Turner. Lauren Bacall. She knows that to whistle, you just put your lips together and blow. What eludes her is why anyone would want to try.

Her problem, according to Maddy, was that she spent too much time obsessing over men in the movies to know how to act around them in the real world. Charlie knows there's some truth there. She had no problem getting weak in the knees at the sight of a young Paul Newman but froze when meeting someone a fraction that handsome in real life.

Despite the undeniable chemistry they shared upon meeting, her official first date with Robbie was awkward at best. Charlie felt so much pressure to be anything but her weird, usual self because she thought that was what Robbie wanted. So she tried to compliment him—"I, um, like the pattern of that shirt," she said of the simple, striped oxford he had been wearing—and attempted small talk. She gave up after fifteen minutes. "I think I'm going to go?" she said, phrasing it like a question, seeking his permission to put them both out of their misery.

Robbie surprised her by saying, "Please stay. Listen, I'm bad at this, too."

In that moment, Charlie realized, despite his good looks, Robbie was just as awkward as she was. He rambled on about equations the same way Charlie did movies. He was quick to smile and even quicker to blush. And his movements were often hesitant, as if he seemed not entirely at ease in his skin. All turned out to be good attributes for a boyfriend to have. Robbie was easygoing in every way. He agreed to whatever movie she wanted to see, never pressured her for sex, and when they did start having it, he always told her it was great, even when she knew it sometimes wasn't.

If anything bothered Charlie, it was the fact that, deep down, she knew Robbie was out of her league. Dorkiness aside, he was still a golden boy. Handsome. Athletic. Smart. His father was an engineer and his mother a doctor. Both were still alive, which was more than Charlie could say. She felt inferior in every regard. An ugly duckling who would never turn into a swan.

Her insecurity was easier to deal with when Maddy was alive. She'd always made Charlie feel, if not normal, then at least like a fellow outcast. It provided balance. Robbie's normalcy on one side, Maddy's Auntie Mame–like eccentricity on the other, and Charlie firmly in the middle. Without Maddy, things no longer worked. And no matter how hard Robbie tried to ease her grief, guilt, and self-hatred, Charlie knew it was only a matter of time before he'd realize she wasn't worthy of such attention.

When she decided to leave school, Charlie told herself she would be doing Robbie a favor. Deep down, though, she knows she's also hastening the inevitable: breaking Robbie's heart before he gets a chance to shatter hers.

"Yes and no," Charlie says, finally giving the vaguest of answers to Josh's question. "I mean, yes, I do. Technically. But I also don't know what the future holds. Or if the two of us even have a future."

"I've been there myself," Josh says.

"And you?"

"Single as can be."

"It's hard meeting people," Charlie says.

"I've found that not to be true," Josh says. "Meeting people is easy. Keeping them around is the hard part."

Through the windshield, the snowfall outside looks even bigger and faster in the Grand Am's headlights. Like stars flying by at warp speed.

"Punch it, Chewie," Charlie says.

Josh brings the windshield wipers up another notch. "I get that reference."

"It's nice to know that you have, indeed, seen at least one movie."

"I've seen plenty of movies."

"Define 'plenty.'"

"More than you think." Josh straightens in the driver's seat and pats the steering wheel. "Hit me with another quote. Bet I can name the movie it's from."

Charlie decides to go easy on him at first, tossing out an appropriately accented "I'll be back."

"*Terminator*," Josh says. "And quit giving me the obvious ones. I'm not as movie illiterate as you think."

"Fine." She pauses, thinking. "'You're gonna need a bigger boat.'"

"That would be *Jaws*," Josh says, adding a smug "I've seen that movie twice."

"Twice?" Charlie says with mock surprise.

"And how many times have you seen it, Siskel and Ebert?"

"Twenty."

Josh lets out a low whistle. "Why would you watch the same movie twenty times?"

"It's a masterpiece," Charlie says. "The real question is why *wouldn't* you watch it twenty times?"

"Because life is too short."

That had been another of Maddy's favorite phrases, used whenever she needed to cajole Charlie into doing something she didn't want to do. *Life is too short to* not *go to this party*, she'd say. So Charlie would go and Maddy would get lost in the crowd, and more often than not, Charlie would wind up back in their dorm room, watching movies.

"I want to give you a quote," Josh says.

"I'll guarantee I'll guess it."

"I'd be disappointed if you didn't." Josh clears his throat. "'We all go a little mad sometimes.'"

The way Josh says it hits Charlie like electricity. A tiny zap at the base of her spine. She's heard that line quoted a thousand times before, and always with too much emphasis, too much over-the-top creepiness. But Josh delivers the line exactly the way Anthony Perkins did—calm, matter-of-fact, like it's no big deal to admit madness.

"Did I stump you?" Josh says.

"*Psycho,*" Charlie replies. "Alfred Hitchcock. Nineteen sixty."

"How many times have you seen that one?"

"Too many to count."

It had been among Charlie's favorite Hitchcock films, watched as frequently as *Rear Window* and *Vertigo* and *North by Northwest.* She hasn't seen it since Maddy's murder, and might not do so ever again. She's not sure she can handle the shower scene and its frenzied cuts and screeching violins, even though she knows the blood was chocolate sauce and the stabbing sounds were casaba melons and that Hitch never once showed a blade piercing flesh. None of that matters. Not when she thinks about Maddy's fate.

"You seem to love your major," Josh says.

"I do."

"Then why are you dropping out of school?"

"Who says I'm dropping out?" Charlie says, irritated. At Josh for being so presumptuous. At herself for being so transparent.

"Those suitcases and box in the trunk. No one packs that much just to go home for a short visit. Especially on a Tuesday in the middle of the semester. That tells me there's a story behind all this."

"There is," Charlie says, her irritation growing. "And it's none of your business."

"But you are dropping out, right?" Josh says. "I haven't heard you deny it."

Charlie slumps in her seat and looks out the window, which has fogged up thanks to the car's heater and her incessant movie talk. She runs a finger along the glass, creating a clear streak.

"I don't know what I'm doing," she says. "Taking a break, I guess."

"College life too much for you?"

"No." Charlie pauses, changes her answer. "Yes."

Until two months ago, she had loved being at Olyphant. It wasn't the fanciest school. Certainly not the Ivy League. And not like NYU or Bennington or any of the other places she'd once dreamed of attending. There wasn't enough money for that, and Charlie hadn't been a good enough student to earn a scholarship. She'd been awarded some cash, yes. But nothing close to a full ride.

She settled on Olyphant because it was one of the few schools she and Nana Norma *could* afford. A small liberal arts college in New Jersey. The film department decent, if not notable. She had planned on working hard, keeping her head down, graduating with a degree that would set her up nicely for grad school somewhere bigger, better, and more prestigious. She thought she'd eventually become a professor at a school similar to Olyphant, teaching film studies to the next generation of cinephiles.

What she hadn't planned on was Madeline Forrester swanning into their dorm room that first day of college on a gust of cigarette smoke and Chanel No. 5. She was beautiful. That was the first thing Charlie noticed. Pale and blond and voluptuous, with a heart-shaped face that reminded her of Vivien Leigh in *Gone with the Wind*. Yet she seemed slightly worn around the edges. An intriguing exhaustion. Like a hungover debutante dragging herself home the morning after a cotillion.

Framed in the doorway, teetering on three-inch heels, she surveyed their shared room and declared, "What a dump!"

Charlie got the reference—Maddy was impersonating Liz Taylor in *Who's Afraid of Virginia Woolf?* impersonating Bette Davis in

Beyond the Forest—and her whole body fizzed like a jostled bottle of champagne. She'd just met a kindred spirit.

"I think I adore you," she blurted.

Maddy fanned herself. "As well you should."

Her style was easy to adore. Maddy talked fast, using a clipped Yankee accent purposefully meant to invoke Katharine Hepburn. Rather than the clothes favored by every other girl on campus— stone-washed jeans, white Keds, GAP sweatshirts under denim jackets—she dressed like a fifties socialite. Pastel cocktail dresses. White gloves. Pillbox hats with delicate veils. She even owned a mink stole, bought secondhand at a yard sale, its fur shabby and matted in spots. At parties, she'd smoke using a cigarette holder, waving it around like Cruella de Vil. Affectations, all. Yet Maddy got away with them because she never took them seriously. There was always a twinkle in her eye that made it clear she knew how ridiculous she could be.

On the surface, they seemed like an odd pair. The glamour girl and her blandly pretty roommate giggling on their way to the dining hall. But Charlie knew they were more alike than it seemed. Maddy grew up in the Poconos, firmly lower middle class, her childhood home a beige ranch house on the outskirts of a small town.

She was extremely close to her grandmother, from whom she claimed to have inherited her wildly dramatic streak. Mee-Maw was what she called her, which Charlie always thought was weird, even though Nana Norma isn't exactly normal. Maddy spent the first four years of her life being raised by her grandmother as her deadbeat dad roamed the northwest in an endless quest to avoid paying child support and her mother drifted in and out of various rehabs.

Even after her mom got clean, Maddy stayed close to her mee-maw, calling her every Sunday just to check in. Sometimes when she was staggeringly hungover. Other times as she got ready to go out. Charlie noticed because it always made her feel guilty that she rarely called Nana Norma just to check in. She only called when she needed something, and hearing Maddy ask her grandmother how she was doing usually caused Charlie to picture Nana Norma home alone on the couch, lit by the flicker of whatever black-and-white movie was on the TV.

Movies were another thing Maddy and Charlie had in common. They watched hundreds together, with Maddy commenting on the action the same way Nana Norma did.

"God, has there ever been a man more beautiful than Monty Clift?"

Or "I would kill for a body like Rita Hayworth's."

Or "Sure, Vincente Minnelli was gay, but you wouldn't know it from the way he filmed Judy Garland."

Like Charlie, Maddy thrived on escapism, living in a fantasy world of her making. It was up to others to decide if they wanted to join her there. Charlie went willingly.

"You can tell me what happened, if you want." Josh gives her a sympathetic look, trying to put her at ease. "I'm not going to tell anyone. And, hell, it's not like we're going to be seeing each other after this. There's no need for secrets in this car."

Charlie's tempted to tell him everything. The darkness, the close quarters, the warmth—all of it sustains her confessional mood. Then there's the fact that she hasn't really talked about it. She's said some things, of course. To Robbie. To Nana Norma. To the psychiatrist she was forced to see. But never the whole story.

"You ever do a bad thing?" she says, easing herself into the topic, seeing if it feels right. "Something so bad you know you'll never, ever forgive yourself?"

"Badness is in the eye of the beholder," Josh says.

He turns away from the windshield long enough for Charlie to see the look on his face. He's smiling again. That perfect movie-star grin. Only this time it doesn't reach his eyes, which are devoid of any mirth. There's nothing there but darkness.

Charlie knows it's just a trick of the light. Or lack thereof. She assumes her eyes look equally as black and mysterious. But something about Josh's dark eyes and bright smile rids her of the urge to confess. It no longer feels right. Not here. Not to this man she doesn't know.

"What about you?" she says, trying to change the subject. "What's your story?"

"What makes you think I have one?"

"You're also leaving in the middle of the semester. Which means you're also dropping out."

"I'm not a student," Josh says.

"I thought you were."

He'd told her he was a student, hadn't he? Or maybe she'd inferred that because of the Olyphant sweatshirt he'd been wearing when they met. The same one, Charlie reminds herself, he's wearing right now.

Josh, apparently sensing her unease, clarifies. "I work at the university. Worked, I guess I should say. I quit today."

Charlie continues to study him, realizing just how much older than her he really is. Ten years, at least. Maybe fifteen.

"Were you a professor or something?"

"A little less upscale," Josh says. "I worked in the facilities department. Custodial work, mostly. Just one of those guys mopping the hallways, invisible to the rest of you. You might have seen me and not even realized it."

Because he seems to expect it, Charlie searches her memory for sightings prior to yesterday, when they met at the ride board. She's not surprised when she can't summon one. In the past two months, she hasn't ventured too far outside the dorm and dining hall.

"How long did you work there?"

"Four years."

"Why'd you quit?"

"My dad's not well," Josh says. "Had a stroke a few days ago."

"Oh," Charlie says. "I'm so sorry."

"There's nothing to be sorry about. Shit happens."

"He'll be okay, though? Right?"

"I don't know," Josh says, his tone justifiably melancholy. "I hope so. We won't know for a few weeks. There's no one else to take care of him, which means it's back to Toledo for me."

Charlie's whole body suddenly tenses.

"Akron," she says. "You told me you were from Akron."

"I did?"

"Yes. When we met at the ride board."

Because it was a possible means of escape, she remembers everything about that moment. And she's certain Josh specifically told her he was going to Akron. *After* he learned she needed to get to Youngstown.

She replays that first conversation in her head. Him sidling up beside her, checking her flyer, seeing her destination clearly typed across the page.

Could Josh have lied about where he was going? If so, why?

Charlie can only think of one reason—to get her to agree to get into a car with him.

The thought makes her nervous. Tiny drops of dread spread across her clenched shoulders. It feels like rain. The first few drops before the storm.

"*Now* I remember," Josh says, shaking his head, as if he can't believe his absentmindedness. "I see why you're confused. I forgot that I told you I'm *driving* to Akron. That's where my aunt lives. I'm picking her up and taking her with me to my dad's place in Toledo."

It's a simple enough explanation. On the surface, there's nothing sinister about it. But the dread doesn't fully leave Charlie. A small bit remains, wedged like a blade between her ribs.

"I wasn't trying to be misleading," Josh says. "I swear. I'm sorry if that's how it seems."

He sounds sincere. He looks it, too. When the car passes under the tangerine glow of a streetlight, it illuminates his face, including his eyes. The darkness Charlie saw earlier is gone. In its place is a glint of warmth, of apology, of hurt for being so misunderstood. Seeing it makes her feel guilty for being so suspicious. His dad just had a stroke, for God's sake, and here she is doubting him.

"It's fine," Charlie says. "I was being—"

She struggles for the best description. Unnecessarily worried? Downright paranoid? Both?

She knows it's not what Josh has said or the way he's dressed or how he put things in the trunk that's made her so jumpy. Her nervousness lies in the fact that because something awful happened to Maddy, Charlie thinks it could also happen to her.

Yet there's more to it than that. The bedrock truth, as Nana Norma would say. A truth that's beneath the surface, buried deep. A foundation upon which all the lies we tell ourselves is built.

And for Charlie, the bedrock truth is that she thinks she *deserves* to have something awful happen to her.

But it won't. Not here, anyway. Not now. Not in a car with someone who seems to be a decent guy and is just trying to make conversation during what would otherwise be a boring drive.

Again, Josh seems to know every single thing she's thinking, because he says, "I get it, you know. Why you're so nervous."

"I'm not nervous," Charlie says.

"You are," Josh says. "And it's okay. Listen, I think I know who you are. I thought your name seemed familiar when we met at the ride board, but I didn't realize why until just now."

Charlie says nothing, hoping that will somehow make Josh stop talking, that he'll just get the hint and drop it.

Instead, he shifts his gaze from her to the road, then back again, and says, "You're that girl, right?"

Charlie sinks back in the passenger seat, the base of her skull against the headrest. A light pain pulses where they connect. The stirrings of a headache. Confession time is here whether she's ready for it or not.

"I am," she says. "I'm that girl. The one who let her roommate get murdered."

INT. GRAND AM—NIGHT

Charlie hadn't wanted to go out that night. That was her excuse for why she did what she did. Back when she had an excuse. Before she came to understand that her actions were inexcusable.

It was a Thursday night, she had an early film class the next morning, and she in no way, shape, or form wanted to head out to a bar at ten o'clock to see a second-rate Cure cover band. But Maddy insisted she go, even after Charlie had begged off several times.

"It won't be any fun without you," she said. "No one else but you gets how much I love them."

"You are aware it's not really the Cure, right?" Charlie told her. "It's just some guys who've learned to play 'Lovesong' in their parents' garage."

"They're really good. I swear. Please, Charlie, just come. Life's too short to stay cooped up in here."

"Fine," Charlie said, sighing the word. "Even though I'm tired. And you know how irritable I get when I'm tired."

Maddy playfully threw a pillow across the room at her. "You become an absolute monster."

The band didn't take the stage until almost eleven, coming out in Goth garb so over-the-top it bordered on the ridiculous. The front man, aiming for Robert Smith realness, had powdered his face with white pancake makeup. Charlie told Maddy it made him look like Edward Scissorhands.

"Rude," Maddy said. "But true."

Three songs into their set, Maddy started dancing with some wannabe Bon Jovi in torn jeans and a black T-shirt. Two songs after that, they were backed against the bar, swapping saliva. And Charlie, who was tired, hungry, and not nearly drunk enough to stay, had had enough.

"Hey, I'm leaving," she said after tapping Maddy on the shoulder.

"What?" Maddy squeezed out from beneath the random guy kissing her and grabbed Charlie's arm. "You can't go!"

"I can," Charlie said. "And I am."

Maddy clung to her as she made her way out of the bar, pushing through a dance floor packed with frat boys in baseball caps and sorority girls in belly tees and preppies and stoners and flannel-wearing deadbeats with stringy bleached hair. Unlike Maddy, they didn't care who was playing. They were just there to get plastered. And Charlie, well, she just wanted to curl up in bed with a movie.

"Hey, what's going on?" Maddy said once they were outside the bar, huddled together in a back alley that stank of vomit and beer. "We were having fun."

"*You* were having fun," Charlie said. "I was just . . . there."

Maddy reached into her handbag—a glittery rectangle of silver sequins she'd found at Goodwill—and fumbled for her cigarettes. "That's all on you, darling."

Charlie disagreed. By her estimation, this was the hundredth time Maddy had dragged her to a bar or a kegger or a theater department after party only to ditch her as soon as they arrived, leaving Charlie to stand around awkwardly asking her fellow introverts if they'd ever seen *The Magnificent Ambersons*.

"It wouldn't be if you'd just let me stay home."

"I'm trying to help you."

"By ignoring me?"

"By forcing you out of your comfort zone," Maddy said, giving up the search for a smoke and stuffing the handbag under her arm. "There's more to life than movies, Charlie. If it weren't for me or Robbie or the other girls in the dorm, you'd never talk to anyone, like, ever."

"That's not true," Charlie said, even as she began to wonder if maybe it was. She couldn't remember the last time she exchanged more than cursory small talk with someone outside of class or the insular world of their dorm. Realizing that Maddy was right only made her more angry. "I could talk to a ton of people, if I wanted to."

"And that's your problem," Maddy said. "You don't want to. Which is why I'm always the one trying to force you into it."

"Maybe I don't want to be forced."

Maddy coughed out a sarcastic laugh. "That's pretty fucking obvious."

"Then quit trying," Charlie said. "Friends are supposed to support each other, not change them."

God knew she could have tried to change Maddy. The flightiness. The drama. The clothes that were more like costumes. Things so dated and preposterous that sometimes people rolled their eyes when she entered a room. But Charlie didn't try to change those things. Because she loved them. She loved *Maddy*. And sometimes—like that night—she questioned if Maddy felt the same way.

"I'm not trying to change you," Maddy said. "I just want you to live a little."

"And I want to go the hell home."

Charlie tried to walk away, but Maddy latched on to her arm again, pleading. "Please don't go. You're right. I brought you here, then ditched you, and I'm sorry. Let's go back inside, have a drink, and dance our asses off. I won't leave your side. I promise. Just stay."

Maybe Charlie would have stayed if Maddy hadn't said what

came next. She was ready to forgive and forget as she always did. But then Maddy took a deep breath and said, "You know I don't like walking home alone."

Charlie flinched—truly flinched—when she heard it. Because it meant Maddy still made it all about her, like she always did. This wasn't about her enjoying Charlie's company or having fun together. She simply wanted someone to walk her drunk ass home when the party was over. It made Charlie think that maybe Robbie was right. Maybe Maddy didn't think of her as a friend. Maybe she *was* only an audience member. One of many. One who was enough of a pushover to let Maddy get away with whatever bullshit she decided to pull on any given night.

Except that night.

Charlie refused to let that happen.

"I'm walking home now," she said. "You can join me or not."

Maddy pretended to consider it. She took a tentative step in Charlie's direction, a hand raised ever so slightly, as if reaching out for her. But then someone left the bar and music blasted out the open door into the alley. A rackety version of "Just Like Heaven." Hearing it, Maddy turned her gaze to the bar, and Charlie knew she'd made her decision.

"You're an awful friend," she told Maddy. "I hope you know that."

Charlie turned and marched away, not even pausing as Maddy called out, "Charlie, wait!"

"Fuck off," Charlie said.

It ended up being the last thing she ever said to Maddy.

But that wasn't the worst part of the night.

Far from it.

The worst came twenty steps later, when Charlie turned around, hoping to see that, despite the fight and the "Fuck off," Maddy was right behind her, struggling to catch up. Instead, Charlie saw her still outside the bar, her cigarettes finally freed from her purse, standing with a man who'd seemingly come out of nowhere.

Charlie couldn't see him clearly. His back was partly turned to her, and his head was lowered. The only part of his body visible to her was his left hand, which was cupped around the small flame of Maddy's lighter. Everything else about him was shadow, from his shoes to his hat.

That hat—a basic fedora that all men used to wear until suddenly they didn't—tipped Charlie off that something about the scene wasn't right. It was 1991. No one wore a fedora anymore. Also, everything was too stark, too stylized. A single shaft of white light slanted between Maddy and the man in the fedora, splitting them into two distinct halves: Maddy glowing in the light, the man swathed in darkness.

It was, Charlie realized, a movie in her mind, brought about by her fight with Maddy.

Rather than watch the scene return to normal, which is what she should have done, Charlie turned around and kept walking.

She didn't look back.

When Maddy didn't return to the dorm that night, Charlie had assumed she'd hooked up with someone from the bar. Fake Bon Jovi, maybe. Or the guy in the fedora. If he existed at all. Charlie had her doubts.

Worry didn't set in until noon, when Charlie returned from class to find the dorm room still untouched by Maddy's presence. Charlie couldn't help but think of the day her parents died. How she had remained unconcerned as time slipped by, oblivious to the fact that she had become an orphan. Refusing to let history repeat itself, Charlie spent the rest of the day going from dorm room to dorm room, asking everyone in the building if they'd seen Maddy. No one had. Charlie's next move was to call Maddy's mother and stepfather, asking if they'd heard from her. They hadn't. Finally, at midnight, exactly twenty-four hours since she'd last seen her, Charlie called the police and reported Maddy missing.

She was found early the next morning.

A cyclist had discovered her on his daily ride, drawn by an unusual sparkle in the middle of a field nine miles outside of town. It was Maddy's purse, its sequins glinting in the morning sun.

Maddy lay next to it, facedown in the dirt, dead for at least a day.

At first, everyone—the police, the town, the university—had hoped it was a normal murder, as if such a thing existed. Foul play that could easily be solved. A jealous ex-boyfriend. An obsessive classmate. Something that made sense.

But there were the multiple stab wounds to contend with. And the fact that her wrists and ankles had been bound with rope. And the missing tooth, an upper canine that dental records indicated hadn't been missing before she disappeared.

It was the tooth that led police to conclude the worst: Maddy was another victim of a man who had struck twice before.

The Campus Killer.

Charlie grudgingly admired the authorities' restraint in the nickname. *The Silence of the Lambs* had hit theaters seven months earlier, entering Buffalo Bill and Hannibal the Cannibal into the pop cultural lexicon. Instead of going for something in that same morbidly catchy vein, the police opted for simplicity.

He was a killer.

He prowled Olyphant University's campus.

He snatched women and tied them up and yanked out a tooth after stabbing them to death. That was attention-grabbing enough for most people—and the general public didn't even know about the missing teeth. Only the victims' families were told that gruesome detail. Charlie had found out simply because she was the first person the police talked to after finding Maddy's body, and they needed to know immediately if she'd been missing a tooth. The detectives begged her not to tell anyone else, and she hadn't. Not even Robbie. She understood it was something the cops needed to keep to themselves to differentiate between a random stabbing and the work of the Campus Killer.

Charlie had learned the nickname the day she arrived at Olyphant. The Campus Killer had struck a month earlier, sending the whole university into a panicked frenzy, even though the victim was a townie and not a student. Her freshman orientation included a lesson in self-defense. Rape whistles were distributed with ID cards. On campus, girls never walked alone. They moved in packs—great, unwieldy groups of nervous giggles and shining hair.

During campus-sponsored mixers or late-night chats in the dorm lounge, the murders were talked about in hushed tones, like urban legends whispered around a campfire. Everyone knew the names of the victims. Everyone claimed to have some tangential connection. A shared class. A friend of a friend. A glimpse on the street two nights before they were killed.

Angela Dunleavy was the first, murdered four years earlier on a rainy night in March. She was a senior who worked part-time at a bar downtown. One of those places that made its waitresses wear tight T-shirts in the hope the college boys would leave bigger tips. She went missing shortly after last call and was found the next morning in a patch of woods on the edge of campus, bearing the then-novel signs of the Campus Killer's handiwork.

Tied up.

Stabbed.

Tooth pulled.

There were no leads, no suspects. Just a horrific murder that police had stupidly assumed was a onetime thing.

Until the second victim was found a year and a half later. Taylor Morrison. The townie killed a month before Charlie's freshman year, her body dumped on the side of a maintenance road two miles away. She worked in a bookstore two blocks from Olyphant, which was close enough to campus for her death to be lumped in with Angela Dunleavy's.

When a year passed without another murder, people started to breathe a little easier. After two years, the rape whistles stopped but the self-defense classes remained. By the start of Charlie's junior year, no one roamed campus in groups and the Campus Killer was barely mentioned.

Then Maddy was murdered, and the vicious cycle began anew. Only this time Charlie was part of it. A supporting player to Maddy's morbid starring role. She talked to so many people in the days following the murder. Local detectives. State police. Even two FBI agents. A pair of women dressed nearly identically in silk blouses and black blazers, their hair pulled back in severe ponytails.

Charlie told them everything.

She and Maddy had gone to a bar to hear a cover band. No, she wasn't yet twenty-one, an admission that caused her not a second's hesitation. Maddy was dead. Her killer was still out there. No one gave a shit about her fake ID. Yes, she and Maddy had argued outside the bar. Yes, she had walked away even though Maddy had begged her to stay. And, yes, the last two words she uttered to her best friend were indeed "fuck off," a realization that, when it hit, sent Charlie running to the police station bathroom to throw up in the sink.

It got worse when she returned to those tough-chick FBI agents and learned everything they knew about Maddy's final moments.

That no one could remember seeing Maddy back in the bar after Charlie left.

That two people exiting the bar five minutes after Charlie saw Maddy leaving the alley with a man, although they didn't know for sure because he had already rounded a corner, giving only a glimpse of white sneaker.

That based on her time of death, authorities believed the man Maddy followed out of the alley was the same person who killed her.

"I saw him," Charlie said, stunned by the realization that what she'd seen hadn't entirely been a movie in her mind.

The FBI agents straightened in their chairs.

"What did he look like?" one of them asked.

"I don't know."

"But you saw him."

"I saw *someone*. But it might not have been the man Maddy left with."

One of the agents gave her a look hot enough to peel wallpaper. "You either saw someone or you didn't."

"I did see someone." Charlie's voice was weak. Her head spun. Nausea continued to churn in her stomach. "But I also didn't."

She had no idea if the person she saw looked anything like his real-life counterpart. The movies in her mind sometimes warped things until they were no longer recognizable. It was entirely possible that the man she'd seen was cobbled together by her imagination using pieces of a dozen different leading men. Part Mitchum, part Lancaster, part Burton.

Charlie had to spend an hour explaining the movies in her mind. How they worked. When they happened. How very often the things she saw weren't really there, including men in dark alleys. Even after all that, the agents insisted she sit down with a sketch artist, hoping that describing what she saw would somehow jolt her into remembering what had really been there.

When that didn't work, they tried hypnosis.

After that, too, failed, Charlie was sent to a psychiatrist.

What followed was reluctant talk about Maddy's murder, her parents' deaths, the movies in her mind. Then came the prescription for the little orange pills, which Charlie was told would make them go away.

The psychiatrist stressed that Maddy's death wasn't Charlie's fault. That each person's brain is different. That it works in unusual ways. It does what it does, and Charlie shouldn't blame herself for what happened.

Charlie disagreed. She had known that night that what she saw outside the bar was a movie in her mind. She could have waited until it passed, revealing the true picture. Or she could have returned to Maddy, apologized, and demanded they walk home together.

Instead, she simply turned and walked away.

In the process, she both failed to save Maddy's life and avoided gleaning any identifying details about the man who murdered her.

Looked at from that perspective, all of it was Charlie's fault.

Time passed.

Days and weeks and months.

Charlie eventually cut herself off from everyone but Robbie and Nana Norma. She didn't even have the mental strength to attend Maddy's funeral, a fact that didn't sit well with everyone else in the dorm, who chartered two buses to shuttle them to Middle-of-Nowhere, Pennsylvania, for the service. Right up to the moment of departure, there'd been needling and disbelief and guilt trips from the girls on her floor.

I can't believe you're not going.

She was your best friend.

I know it'll be hard on you, but this will give you a chance to say goodbye. You'll regret it if you don't go.

Only Maddy would have understood her reasons. She knew about Charlie's parents and the double funeral that had rewired her brain just so she'd be able to cope with it. Maddy wouldn't have wanted her to go through that again.

So Charlie stayed behind. A decision she definitely doesn't regret. Her preference was to remember Maddy alive and laughing and being her usual dramatic self. She wanted her memories to be of Maddy dressing like Liza in *Cabaret* to go to a statistics class. Or of last Halloween, when the two of them went to a costume party as the Gabor sisters and everyone assumed they were Madonna in *Dick Tracy*, even though both of them spoke with exaggerated Hungarian accents. Charlie certainly didn't want to remember Maddy as some lifeless shell in a casket, her face tinted orange by too much mortician makeup.

But the bedrock truth is that not attending Maddy's funeral was an act of cowardice on her part. Quite simply, she couldn't face

Maddy's family and their justifiable anger. The phone call had been enough—that tear-streaked confrontation with Maddy's mother, who had lashed out with a vengeance only a grieving woman could possess.

"You saw him. That's what the police are saying. That you saw the man who killed my daughter but can't remember what he looked like."

"I can't," Charlie said, sobbing.

"Well, you fucking need to remember," Maddy's mother said. "You owe it to us. You owe it to Maddy. You left her behind, Charlie. The two of you were out together, and you left without her. You were her friend. You were supposed to be there for her. But you abandoned her with that man. Now my daughter is dead and you can't even bring yourself to remember anything about him. What kind of friend does that? What kind of *person* does that? An awful one. That's who. You're truly awful, Charlie."

Charlie hadn't voiced anything in her defense. Why bother when everything Mrs. Forrester said was true? She *had* abandoned Maddy. First in life, when Charlie turned away from her outside the bar, and then again in death, when she couldn't remember a single identifying feature about the man who killed her. In her mind, Maddy's mother was right—she truly was an awful person.

So Charlie spent the day of Maddy's funeral alone watching Disney movies, one right after the after. She didn't eat. She didn't sleep. She simply sat on the dorm room floor surrounded by white plastic VHS cases.

Robbie, who did attend the funeral, told Charlie that maybe she should have gone. That it wasn't so bad. That the casket was closed, a family friend had sung "Somewhere" from *West Side Story*, and that the only moment of drama happened graveside as Maddy was lowered into the ground. That's when Maddy's grandmother, overcome with grief, tilted her head back and screamed into the blue September sky.

"I think it would have helped you," he said.

Charlie didn't want or need that kind of help. Besides, she knew that, in time, she'd be okay. A heart can only grieve for so long. That was what Nana Norma told her a few months after her parents died. Charlie knew it to be true. She still missed her parents. Not a day went by when she didn't think of them. But her grief, which at the time had felt so heavy she thought she'd be crushed by its weight, had transformed into something easier to bear. She had assumed the same would happen with Maddy.

It didn't. The pain she felt continued to be as heart-shattering as the day she learned Maddy was dead. And she couldn't take it anymore. Not the grief. Not the guilt. Not the squinty-eyed looks of pity cast her way during the rare occasions she went to class. Which is why she's leaving Olyphant. Even though she knows fleeing the scene of her crime won't make her feel any less guilty, Charlie nevertheless hopes being back home with Nana Norma, lost in a haze of old movies and chocolate chip cookies, will somehow make it easier to deal with.

"Yeah, I thought that was you," Josh says after Charlie's brutal assessment of herself. "I read about what happened in the paper. Do you want to, I don't know, talk about it?"

Charlie turns toward the passenger-side window, now fogged up again. "There's nothing to talk about."

"You're dropping out of college because of it, so, yeah, I think there is."

Charlie sniffs. "Maybe I don't *want* to talk about."

"I'm going to anyway," Josh says. "First, I'm sorry for your loss. It's a horrible thing that happened. And a horrible thing you went through and are still going through. What was your friend's name again? Tammy?"

"Maddy," Charlie says. "Short for Madeline."

"Right. Just like Charlie is short for Charles."

Josh gives her a look, pleased with himself for steering them back to an earlier joke. Charlie's stony expression doesn't change, and Josh moves on.

"They never caught the guy who did it, right?" he says.

"No."

Charlie shivers slightly at the acknowledgment that, thanks to her, the man who killed Maddy hasn't been caught, may never be caught, may spend the rest of his fucking life reveling in how he'd gotten away with murder not once but three times.

That the police know of.

So far.

The idea that the Campus Killer could—and most likely will—strike again prompts another fearful shiver.

"Does it worry you that they never caught him?"

"It makes me angry," Charlie says.

After the initial shock and grief had worn off, Charlie turned to anger pretty quickly. She spent all those sleepless nights seething over the fact that Maddy was dead and her killer wasn't and how utterly wrong that was. Sometimes she'd spend all night pacing the room, envisioning B-movie scenarios in which she took her revenge. In these mental movies, the Campus Killer was always the dark, human-shaped blank she'd seen outside the bar, onto which she inflicted every act of violence she could think of.

Shooting. Strangling. Beheading.

One night, the movie in her mind had her stabbing the Campus Killer in the chest and plucking out his heart, which glistened on the tip of her knife, still beating. But when she looked down at the body, it wasn't a human-shaped blank she saw. It was someone she knew all too well.

Herself.

After that one, Charlie started planning her escape.

"I think I'd be worried," Josh says. "I mean, he's still out there. Somewhere. He might have seen you, right? He might know who you are and try to come for you next."

Charlie shivers again, this one more intense than the others. A shudder. One she feels all the way down to her core. Because Josh is right. The Campus Killer probably did see her. Maybe he even knows who she is. And although Charlie saw him, too, she wouldn't know it was him even if he was sitting right next to her.

"That's not why I'm leaving school," she says.

"So it's a guilty conscience, then."

Charlie says nothing, allowing Josh to add, "I think you're being too hard on yourself."

"I don't."

"But you are. It's not like it was your fault."

"I *saw* him," Charlie says. "Yet I can't identify him. Which *does* make it my fault. Even if I could identify him, there's still the fact that I abandoned Maddy. If I had stayed with her, none of this would have happened."

"I don't blame you for any of that. I'm not judging you. I guess you think others do—"

"I know they do," Charlie says, thinking about that call with Maddy's mother, how afterward she'd felt hollow. How she still feels as empty as a football, to quote Jimmy Stewart in *Rear Window*.

"Why? Were people mean to you?"

"No."

If anything, everyone was suffocatingly kind. All those weepy-eyed girls coming to her door with food and cards and flowers. There were invitations to trade dorm rooms, to go on group outings ("There's safety in numbers!"), to join a prayer circle. Charlie declined them all. She didn't want their sympathy. She didn't deserve it.

"Then maybe you should stop beating yourself up over something you couldn't control."

Charlie's heard it all before, from literally everyone except Maddy's family. And she's tired of it. Tired of being told what to feel, that it wasn't her fault, that she needs to forgive herself. So tired of it all that a lump of anger explodes in her chest like a firecracker—white-hot and shimmering. Fueled by its burn, she whips away from the window and, practically snarling at Josh, yells, "And maybe you should shut the fuck up about something that has nothing to do with you!"

The outburst surprises Josh, who's so startled he sends the car shuddering off the road for a few jarring seconds. Not surprised is Charlie, who always suspected such an explosion would arrive at some point. She just didn't think it would be in a car with a man she doesn't know, her voice booming through the pine-scented interior. Now that it's happened, she's left breathless, shaken, and completely ashamed of herself. She slumps back in her seat, suddenly exhausted.

"I'm sorry," she says. "I was—"

"Holding that in for a long time." Josh's voice is a monotone. His expression is blank. Charlie wonders if he's feeling hurt or angry or frightened. All are justifiable. If their roles were reversed, she'd be wondering what kind of crazy person she'd just let into her car.

"I didn't mean—"

Josh stops her with a raised hand. "Let's just not talk about it."

"That's probably for the best."

No one says anything for the next few minutes. Plunged into silence, they both keep their eyes on the road. The snow has stopped. A sudden ceasing. Almost as if her outburst had frightened it away. Charlie knows that's stupid to think. It was just a brief November squall, here and gone in minutes, yet she feels guilty all the same.

The car is still quiet when they pass a sign indicating that the entrance ramp to Interstate 80 is two miles ahead. Immediately after that is another sign, this one for 7-Eleven.

The last convenience store before they hit the highway.

If the two of them make it that far. After the way she's acted,

Charlie wouldn't blame Josh for dumping her on the side of the road and speeding away. Instead, he pulls into the empty 7-Eleven lot, parks near the front door, and cuts the engine.

"I'm getting coffee," he says. "You want some?"

Charlie notes his tone. Cordial but cool.

"Yes," she says, speaking the same way, as if she's talking to a professor she doesn't like. "Please."

"How do you take it?"

"Milk and two sugars," Charlie says, reaching for her backpack on the floor.

"This one's on me," Josh says. "I'll be right back."

He slides out of the car and hurries into the 7-Eleven. Through the store's giant front window, Charlie sees him nod hello to the cashier—a kid in a flannel shirt and green knit cap. Behind him, a tiny TV near the ceiling broadcasts the news. President Bush is on the screen, doing an interview with Barbara Walters, as his white-haired wife—a second Barbara—sits beside him. Josh gives the TV a passing glance before moving toward the coffee station.

Charlie knows she should go in with him. It would be the polite thing to do. A signal, however meager, that she's an active, willing part of this journey. But she doesn't know how to do that. There's no cinematic frame of reference for her to follow. As far as she knows, there's not a heralded I-let-my-best-friend-get-murdered-and-now-I-can't-function-like-a-normal-human-being movie out there that she hasn't seen yet.

So she remains in the car, the seat belt still strapped tight across her chest as she tries to pull herself together. She worries she's going to spend the entirety of the trip like this—nervous and flighty, her emotions as prickly as a ball of barbed wire. It makes her question her decision to leave Olyphant. Not the why of it. She's certain about that part. What she doubts is *how* she chose to leave. Maybe it would have been better to wait until Robbie could drive her and not ride with a stranger who, if she keeps this up, really might drop her off in the middle of nowhere. Maybe, despite her urgent desire to leave, she's just not ready to make this journey without someone she knows.

Outside the car, a pay phone sits a few feet from the convenience store's front door. Charlie starts to search her backpack for loose change, wondering if she should call Robbie and ask him to take her back to campus. She can even try to make light of the situation, using the code he gave her.

Things took a detour.

Yes, they have. In all manner of ways. Now all she wants is for Robbie to take her back to Olyphant. It's not that far of a drive. Only thirty minutes. And when they get there, she'll wait—simply wait—until Thanksgiving.

Then she can go home, try to put all this behind her.

Mind made up and armed with change, Charlie unfastens the seat belt, which retracts with a startling click. When she opens the passenger-side door, the car's interior light flicks on, bathing her in a sickly yellow glow. She starts to slide out of the car but stops herself when another car pulls into the parking lot. A beige Dodge Omni packed with teenagers. Inside, music pulses, muffled by windows rattling to the beat. The car screeches to a stop two spaces away from Josh's Grand Am, and a girl immediately pops out of the passenger side. Inside the car, someone shouts for her to grab a bag of Corn Nuts. The girl bows and says, "Yes, my darling dearest."

She's young—seventeen at most—but drunk. Charlie can tell by the way she shuffles to the curb on high-heeled boots, hampered further by her skintight minidress. Seeing her gives Charlie a painful twinge. Memories of Maddy, also drunk. The girl even looks a bit like her, with her blond hair and pretty face. And while her clothes aren't remotely similar—Maddy would never have worn something so current—their attitudes seem to match. Bold and messy and loud.

Charlie supposes there's a Maddy in every town, in every state.

A whole army of brash blond girls who get drunk and do sweeping bows in parking lots and serve their best friends birthday breakfasts of champagne and cake, as Maddy used to do for Charlie each March. The thought pleases her—until she realizes there's now a town without one.

Making it worse is the music spilling out the Omni's still-open passenger door.

The Cure.

"Just Like Heaven."

The same song that was thrumming inside the bar when Charlie spoke those horrible last words to Maddy.

You're an awful friend. I hope you know that.

Followed by the final two, lobbed over her shoulder like a grenade.

Fuck off.

Charlie recoils back into the car and slams the door shut. All desire to return to Olyphant, even if just for the next ten days, is gone. If this was some kind of sign that she should continue moving forward, Charlie's noticed it loud and clear. So loud that she covers her hands with her ears to muffle the music, removing them only after not-quite-Maddy gets back into the car with an ice-blue Slurpee, a pack of Marlboro Lights, and a bag of Corn Nuts for her friend.

Josh exits the 7-Eleven as the Omni pulls out of the parking lot. He pushes through the door balancing two jumbo coffees, one stacked atop the other. He uses his chin to steady them, his wallet a buffer between it and the plastic lid of the top cup. When he steps off the curb, the cups bobble and his wallet slides out from under his chin. It hits the asphalt with a splat.

This time, Charlie doesn't need a cinematic example to understand she must get out of the car and help. So she does, chirping "I'll get it" before Josh can kneel to pick up the wallet.

"Thanks," he says. "Can you also get the door?"

"Sure."

Charlie scoops up the wallet and stuffs it in her coat pocket before rushing back to the car and opening the driver's-side door. Josh then hands her a coffee cup so big she has to hold it with both hands as she slides into the passenger seat. Back inside the car, both of them cradle their steaming cups. Charlie takes a few small, scalding sips to show her appreciation.

"Thank you for the coffee," she says after another demonstrative sip.

"It was no problem."

"And I'm sorry about earlier."

"It's fine," Josh says. "We're both dealing with shit right now. Emotions are a little raw. Everything's cool. Ready to go?"

Charlie gives the pay phone outside the store a brief, disinterested glance and takes another sip of coffee. "Yeah. Let's roll."

It's not until Josh has started the car and is backing it out of the parking spot that Charlie notices the lump in her coat pocket. Josh's wallet, all but forgotten. She holds it up and says, "What do you want me to do with this?"

"Just set it on the dashboard for now."

Charlie does, the wallet sliding a few inches as Josh turns the Grand Am onto the main road. It slides again a few seconds later when they veer to the right, hitting the entrance ramp to the interstate. It keeps on sliding as Josh shifts into second gear—a sudden jolt of speed. The wallet drops off the dashboard and into Charlie's lap, flapping open like bat wings taking flight.

The first thing she sees are credit cards tucked into individual slats that obscure everything but the tops of Visa and American Express logos. On the other side of the wallet, snug behind a plastic sleeve, is Josh's driver's license.

His license photo is enviably good, the shitty DMV camera somehow managing to highlight his best assets. The jawline. The smile. The great hair. The picture on Charlie's license makes her look like a stoned zombie—a secondary reason she chose not to get it renewed.

Charlie's about to close the wallet when she notices something strange.

Josh's driver's license is issued by the state of Pennsylvania. Not Ohio, which would make sense, considering that's where he's from. Even more logical would be a New Jersey license, seeing how Josh told her he's worked at Olyphant for the past four years.

But Pennsylvania? That just seems wrong. Even if he lived there before moving to Ohio with his father, it would have expired like her own.

Charlie's gaze darts to the date when the license was issued.

May 1991.

As current as you can get.

Then she sees the name printed at the bottom of the license and all the air leaves her lungs.

It says Jake.

Not Josh or Joshua or any other variation of the name.

Jake Collins.

Charlie snaps the wallet shut and tosses it back on the dashboard. A sinking feeling overwhelms her, as if the car is coming apart and at any second her heels will start scraping asphalt. Her gaze flicks to the road ahead, just in case such a scenario is actually happening and she needs to know what to expect. Ahead of them is a dark ribbon of highway stretching toward the horizon.

They've reached Interstate 80.

The road that will take them out of New Jersey, all the way across Pennsylvania, and into Ohio.

And Charlie has no idea who the man driving her there really is.

TEN P.M.

INT. GRAND AM—NIGHT

Charlie keeps her gaze fixed on the highway ahead. There are other cars on it, but not many. Certainly not as many as she thought there'd be. Taillights glow red in the distance—too far away to provide any comfort. The same goes for headlights behind them. A quick glance in the side mirror reveals only one car on their tail. Charlie estimates it's a quarter mile away. Maybe more.

It only reinforces the feeling that she's alone.

In a car.

With a stranger.

"It's quiet in here."

Charlie's so distracted by the highway and the license and the wallet sitting on the dashboard that at first she doesn't hear Josh.

Or Jake.

Or whoever he is.

It's only when he says her name—a curt, curious "Charlie?"—that she snaps out of it and turns his way.

"What did you say?" she says, studying Josh, double-checking to make sure it really is his picture on that driver's license, even though there's no reason he'd be carrying another man's license. No *good* reason, that is. No legal one.

"I said it's quiet in here." Josh flashes his killer smile, inadvertently confirming for Charlie that, yes, he is the man pictured on that license. Few people have a smile like that. "Were you watching a movie?"

Charlie doesn't know what to do. Once again, her film knowledge—a guidepost for most of her mundane actions—has failed her when she needs it most. She thinks about *Shadow of a Doubt* and that other Charlie, her namesake. What would she do in this situation?

She wouldn't be stupid, that's for sure.

She'd be smart. She'd be plucky.

That was good old Movie Charlie.

And being plucky means being brave and facing the situation head on. It doesn't mean throwing open the passenger-side door and flinging herself out of the car, injuries be damned, which is Real Charlie's first instinct. Her fingers have wrapped around the door handle, even though she doesn't remember moving them there. She forces her hand into her lap.

Another thing Movie Charlie wouldn't do is let Josh know *she* knows he might be lying to her, which goes against common sense. Most people, if stuck in this scenario, would just flat-out ask if his name is really Jake Collins.

That's what Maddy would have done.

But Maddy's dead now, maybe because she did exactly that. Called some guy out. Got him angry. Made him want to hurt her.

And not just any guy.

The Campus Killer.

So Charlie stays silent, even though the question is perched on the tip of her tongue, ready to springboard into the air. She starts to wash it away with a splash of coffee but decides against it before taking a sip. If Josh isn't who he says he is, she's certainly not going to drink more from the coffee cup he just handed her. Never accept a drink from someone suspicious. That's Common Sense for Women 101.

"I'm just thinking," she says.

It's the truth. She *is* thinking. About the license in Josh's wallet. About what it means. About why she hopes there's a simple, rational, non-scary reason behind it.

"Is it the coffee?" Josh says. "Did I mess up? Too much sugar?"

"No, it's fine. It's great, actually."

Charlie pretends to take a long, satisfied swig. As she does, a thought hits her.

Maybe Josh's driver's license is fake. There's nothing suspicious about that. After all, Charlie herself has a fake ID, procured freshman year through the friend of a friend of a guy Maddy knew from one of her theater classes. It's the one the police didn't care about.

But unlike her, Josh doesn't need a fake ID. He's clearly over twenty-one, which makes Charlie wonder why he has it. Sentimental reasons, maybe. Yet that still doesn't make sense. Even if she understood the idea of keeping a fake ID from your youth, which she doesn't, it doesn't explain why Josh carries it in the spot in his wallet reserved for his real driver's license. Then there's the date Charlie saw. It's current. There's no way a fake ID from five, maybe even ten years ago would sport that date. Also, Josh looked the same age in the license photo as he does now. Unless he's a vampire, something else is going on here.

"Mind if I play some music?" Josh says.

"Yes."

"So that's a no on the music?"

"No. On the no, I mean." Charlie hears the anxiety in her voice. She's flustered. Knowing Movie Charlie never got that way, she takes a breath and says, "What I mean is yes, play some music. Whatever you want."

"You're my guest," Josh says. "What do you like? And please don't say Paula Abdul. Or, worse, Amy Grant."

Charlie, who saves all her strong opinions for films, doesn't know what music she likes. She always listened to whatever Maddy was playing, which meant moody alternative pop. The Cure, of course, but also New Order, Depeche Mode, a little R.E.M. Charlie stole one of Maddy's mixtapes just before her stepfather arrived to collect her things from the dorm. She occasionally listened to it and pretended Maddy was in the room with her.

"I have no preference," she says. "Truly."

"Driver's choice, then."

Josh flips open the console separating them. When the lid bumps Charlie's arm, she recoils, startled.

"Wow, you're jumpy," Josh says.

Yes. Yes, she is. And it's showing, which needs to stop immediately. Charlie gives him a tight-lipped smile and says, "I wasn't expecting it, that's all. My bad."

"No worries."

He pulls a plastic cassette case from the console. The cover sleeve shows a naked baby submerged in water, swimming toward a dollar bill on a fishhook. Charlie's seen the image before. One of the RAs in her dorm has a poster of it on her wall.

Josh pops the cassette into the car's tape deck and presses play. An aggressive guitar riff fills the car, followed by a blitz of drums and, hot on its heels, an explosion of sound. Then everything settles into a drumbeat as quick and steady as a runner's post-sprint heart rate.

Charlie knows the song. "Smells Like Teen Spirit." She'd heard it several times thumping through the wall of the dorm room next door. But now, unmuffled, it feels like a primal roar, urging her to scream along.

"I love these guys," Josh says. "They're awesome."

While Charlie wouldn't go that far, she appreciates how the music fills the car, eliminating the need to talk. Now she can just sit here and continue to think about Josh/Jake/Whoever and his driver's license.

Sure enough, another theory presents itself: Josh isn't a legal resident and needs a fake license to drive. That would explain the date. And the picture. And maybe even why it's a Pennsylvania license and not from New Jersey or Ohio.

Charlie thinks back to an hour ago, when Josh picked her up. She didn't look at the Grand Am's license plate. It never occurred to her to do so. She was too focused on checking the rest of the car for signs she should turn around and leave. If she had and seen Pennsylvania plates, then she'd know for certain Josh is lying about his name.

But she didn't look. Not then and not when he was inside the 7-Eleven. Until they stop again—which could be hours—the only way to find out where the car is registered is to check his insurance and registration cards.

Which, Charlie realizes, could be anywhere. Her parents kept theirs in the glove compartment. Nana Norma keeps hers in her purse. And Maddy, who drove an ugly orange Volkswagen Beetle she'd dubbed Pumpkin, stashed hers behind the driver's-side visor.

Charlie eyes the closed door of the glove compartment, mere inches from her knees. She can't open it. Not right now. Not without making Josh wonder why she felt compelled to start rifling through it. The same goes for his wallet, which now sits stubbornly on the dashboard, not moving a millimeter.

Right now, she has no other option but to sit quietly as Josh taps the steering wheel in time to the music. Watching him makes Charlie think back to the driving lessons with her father and how he'd toss out questions as she tried to parallel park or enact a three-point turn. *What's the speed limit in a school zone when students are arriving? When driving in fog, should your headlights be at high beam or low beam? Always come to a complete stop at a yield sign: true or false?*

Charlie knew the answers. She'd all but memorized her driver's ed manual. But with most of her brain concentrating on driving, the correct responses eluded her. She messed up. Or got flustered. Or tossed out an answer she knew was wrong just because she felt compelled to say something.

She knows Josh is lying to her. At least, she assumes he is. All she needs is proof. And while she might not be able to root around in his wallet and glove compartment, she *can* ask questions while he's distracted and hope the truth emerges.

That sounds like something else Movie Charlie would do. Toss out a few innocent-sounding questions. Ones that won't make Josh suspect her motives. They might lead to nothing. But they can't hurt. It's certainly better than just sitting here.

"I just realized something," she says, talking over the music. "I don't know your last name."

"Really? I never told you?"

"Nope."

Josh takes a sip of coffee, his eyes never leaving the road. Charlie wonders if not glancing her way is a sign of disinterest or a sign he knows what she's thinking and doesn't want to add fuel to her suspicion.

"I don't think you ever told me yours," he says.

"It's Jordan," Charlie says.

"Mine's Baxter."

Josh Baxter.

Charlie takes in the name, stoic, even as a small bubble of disappointment pops in her chest. She truly hoped he'd say Collins, which would then make her think that Josh was some sort of nickname. Maybe a middle name he preferred over his first one, like the girl in her dorm whose unfortunate first name was Bunny but demanded everyone use her middle name, Megan. It wouldn't have explained everything, but at least it would have calmed her some.

Now she's the opposite of calm, simmering with dread that she's really on to something.

"Did you always live in Akron?"

"I grew up in Toledo, remember?"

Damn. She'd hoped he would be easy to trip up. If Josh *can* be tripped up. Charlie remains aware that he might not be lying. That there might be a silly, simple explanation for why the license in his wallet says the complete opposite of what he's telling her now.

"That's right," she says. "Toledo. Your uncle lives in Akron."

"My aunt," Josh says. "My uncle died five years ago."

"Since you grew up in Ohio, what brought you to Olyphant?"

"I just ended up there. You know how it is. You get a job. Stay a while. Move on to something else. A couple years go by and you do it again."

Charlie notes the vagueness of his answer, assumes it was that way on purpose, moves on.

"Did you like it there, though? Being a groundskeeper?"

"Janitor," Josh says.

Charlie nods, disappointed that she again failed to trip him up. She needs to do better.

"Are you sad to be leaving?"

"I guess so," Josh says. "I haven't really thought about it. When your dad needs you, you go, right?"

"How long do you think you'll be home?"

"I don't know. It depends on how quickly he recovers. If that's even possible." Josh's voice breaks. Just a little. A tiny crack in his otherwise smooth tone. "I was told he's in pretty rough shape."

Another vague answer, although this time Charlie's not as quick to assume it's intentional. Josh sounds sincere. Enough to give her a twinge of guilt for doubting everything he's told her. She considers the possibility he's telling the truth. If so, what does that make her? Paranoid? Heartless?

No, it makes her cautious. After what happened to Maddy, she has every right to be that way. Which is why she resumes her line of questioning.

"I'm sorry to hear that," she says. "What happened to him again? Heart attack?"

"Stroke," Josh says. "I just told you that, like, fifteen minutes ago. Boy, you have a terrible memory."

He looks at Charlie for the first time since the conversation began, and she notices a shimmer of suspicion cross his face. He's on to her.

Maybe.

He could also be wondering why she's suddenly asking so many questions. Or why she can't seem to remember any of his answers. It makes Charlie add another item to her list of things to do, joining "be smart" and "be brave."

Be careful.

"Smells Like Teen Spirit" ends, replaced with another song Charlie's heard only through the dorm room wall. She waits a few beats before saying, "Sorry about all the questions. I'll stop, if you want me to."

"I don't mind," Josh says, a hollow ring in his voice telling Charlie that might not be the truth. He might mind quite a bit.

"I'm just curious," she adds. "I've only seen Olyphant as a student. I think it's interesting to get a picture of the place from the side of someone who worked there."

"Even though you're not going back?"

"I might be," Charlie says. "At some point."

"Well, I can't say it's all that interesting from the other side."

"I don't remember seeing a lot of janitors around," she says. "What kind of hours did you work? Nights? Weekends?"

"Sometimes. Also days. My hours were all over the map."

"And you worked in classrooms?"

"And offices. Everywhere, really."

Josh turns away from the road again to give her another maybe-suspicious-maybe-not look. It's more than just his answers that are vague, Charlie realizes. It's his whole persona. Everything about Josh is hard to read.

Now she needs to use it to her advantage.

"What was your favorite building to work in?" she says.

"My favorite?"

"Yeah," Charlie says. "Everyone has a favorite building on campus. Mine is Madison Hall."

Josh squints, uncertain. "Is that the one—"

"With the thing on top?" Charlie says. "Yeah."

"That's right," Josh says, nodding along. "I like that one, too."

Charlie waits a beat. Considering her options. Weighing which is smarter, braver, more careful. Finally, she says, "There is no Madison Hall on campus. I was just messing with you."

Josh rolls with it, as she hoped he would. Slapping a hand to his cheek, he smiles and says, "No wonder I was confused! You were so convincing, yet I kept thinking, *Is she making this up? I've never heard of Madison Hall.*"

And there it is. She tricked him at last, a fact that provides Charlie with no sense of happiness. The opposite happens. She feels worse knowing that her fears are if not proven, at least justified. Josh is lying to her. At least about working at Olyphant University. And probably about everything else as well.

Because there *is* a Madison Hall on campus. Right in the center of it. A massive, multicolumn structure that hosts graduations, concerts, and performances. Every student knows of its existence. Which means every employee would, too. Even a janitor.

This leads Charlie to an unnerving conclusion. One that creates the same lump of worry in her gut she got as soon as she saw his license.

Josh doesn't work at Olyphant.

He never has.

And if he's not a student and he's not an employee, then who is he?

And why was he hanging around the ride board in the campus commons?

And—the biggest, scariest question—what, if anything, does he want with Charlie?

INT. GRAND AM—NIGHT

Josh shifts the car into a lower gear as they reach an incline. The beginning of a hilly area that will take them over a ridge and then down through the Delaware Water Gap and into Pennsylvania. With the change in elevation comes fog, wisps of which begin to envelope the Grand Am the higher it climbs. Soon the car is surrounded. Charlie looks out the windshield and sees only thick, gray swirls ahead of them. A glance in the side mirror shows the same thing behind them. Any cars that might be in the vicinity are lost in the mist. A sense of isolation settles over Charlie, drifting around her like the fog.

It's just her and Josh.

All alone.

The song ends and another begins, startling Charlie, who'd stopped noticing the music. She had been too busy thinking. Wondering about Josh. Who he is. What he wants. Lost in her own mental fog, during which her right hand had once again found its way to the door handle at her side. This time, Charlie lets it stay there.

The new song has a slinky bass riff that slightly reminds Charlie of the surf guitar rock her parents listened to constantly. She knows the title of the song, though she's not sure how.

"Come as You Are."

Josh shuts off the stereo, and the car is plunged into silence.

"Let's play," Josh says.

"Play what?" Charlie replies, trying hard to keep from sounding as nervous as she feels.

"Twenty Questions. If we're going to play the game, we should do it right."

Charlie continues to study the side mirror, hoping a car will speed into view behind them. She'd feel better with another set of headlights in sight and not just a muted glow in the distance. It would mean there's someone else nearby if things go bad. She's seen enough movies to know how situations can change for the worse in a split second. And she's had enough life experience to back that up.

Not that she's certain Josh wants to do her harm. When it comes to the man sitting a mere foot away, nothing is certain. But it's a possibility. Enough of one that she slides a little closer to the passenger door, trying to put an additional inch between them. Enough to keep her checking the side mirror, looking in vain for those headlights. Enough for the same six words to keep repeating through her head like a good-luck chant.

Be smart. Be brave. Be careful.

"I wasn't really playing a game," she says.

"Seemed like it to me." Josh gives a little shrug, the lift of his shoulder cut short by his grip on the steering wheel. "Seeing how you were messing with me just now. I mean, I assume that's why you did it. Because we're playing a game."

Charlie makes another minuscule edge toward the door. "I didn't mean anything by it."

"Oh, I know," Josh says. "I'm not mad. I get it. We're stuck in this car together. Running out of things to say. Why not ask some questions and kid around a bit. So now it's my turn. Twenty Questions. You ready?"

"I'm really not in the mood right now."

"Humor me," Josh says, cajoling. "Pretty please?"

Charlie relents. It's the right thing to do. Play along, keep him occupied, hope the fog clears and more cars start to surround them.

"Fine," she says, forcing a polite smile. "Let's play."

"Great. I'm thinking of an object. You've got twenty questions to figure out what it is. Go."

Charlie knows the game. She played it on road trips with her parents, back when she was a little girl and they used to drive everywhere. Kings Island and Cedar Point, which were every-summer destinations. But also places outside of Ohio. Niagara Falls. Mount Rushmore. Disney World. Charlie spent every drive slumped in the back seat, sweltering because her father claimed that using the air conditioner wasted gas. When she inevitably got too bored and whiny, her mother would say, "Twenty questions, Charlie. Go."

There was a standard question she'd always ask first. One designed to narrow things down immediately. Only now, at the start of a very different game, she can't remember it to save her life. That lump of worry she still feels in her gut tells her Josh isn't playing this just to amuse himself.

There are stakes involved.

Ones much higher than when she was a kid.

"You going to ask a question?" Josh says.

"Yeah. Just give me another second."

Charlie closes her eyes and pictures those road trips like grainy home movies. Her father behind the wheel in ridiculous oversize sunglasses that clipped over his regular glasses. Her mother in the front seat with the window down, her hair trailing behind her. Her in the back seat, her sweaty legs sticking to Naugahyde, opening her mouth to speak.

The memory works. The mandatory first question pops into her head, fully formed.

"Is it bigger than a bread box?" she says.

Josh shakes his head. "Negative. One question down. Nineteen to go."

Charlie's memory hums like a film projector, quickly giving her the second question she'd always ask.

"Is it alive?"

"Interesting," Josh says. "I'm going to say no, but someone smarter than me might say yes."

Charlie considers his response, thinking hard, knowing that if she does, it might push aside all the other thoughts slithering through her brain. Scary thoughts. Ones she doesn't want to think about. So she focuses on the game, pretending it really is just a game even though she knows it's not.

Not for her.

"Is it associated with something alive?"

"Yes."

"So it's part of something."

"Yes," Josh says. "And I consider that a question even though it wasn't phrased as one. That wouldn't pass muster on *Jeopardy!*"

"Animal or vegetable?"

It's another one of the standard questions she'd ask her parents on those long-ago road trips. Even though it was technically two questions, her mother always let it slide. Josh, on the other hand, calls her out on it.

"You know I can only give you yes or no answers. Care to rephrase?"

Charlie no longer tries to think about the games she played with her parents in that hot, sticky car with its perpetual McDonald's smell. She worries the current game will ruin those memories. She doubts she'll ever willingly play Twenty Questions again. Even if Josh turns out to be harmless. A very big if.

"Is it vegetable?" Charlie says, ridding her brain of images of her father's clip-on sunglasses and her mother's wind-blown hair. Instead, she pictures plants and all the things attached to them. Leaves and branches. Thorns and berries.

"No."

"It's animal, then."

"Yes," Josh says, the answer narrowing things down but not a whole lot.

"Is this animal common?"

"Very."

"Is it wild or tame?"

"That's two questions again, Charlie."

"Sorry."

Charlie's voice goes small, and she winces upon hearing it. How weak she sounds. How scared. And she can't sound weak or scared. She can't, under any circumstance, let Josh know she suspects he's up to no good. If she remains calm—if she continues to be smart, brave, careful—there's a chance nothing bad will happen.

"I'll rephrase," she says, forcing some steel into her voice. "Is this animal wild?"

"It can be. The wildest."

Josh smirks as he says it. A knowing, winking, bordering-on-smarmy upturn of his lips that tells Charlie more than any spoken answer could.

"You're talking about humans, right?" she says.

"I am."

"And is this object you're thinking of part of the body?"

"You're good at this game, you know that? You've only asked—" Josh pauses to count the fingers on his right hand, the digits flexing. "Ten questions and you're so close already."

Charlie's not sure if that's a good or bad thing. It's hard to tell without knowing the stakes. But since Josh seems to be in no hurry to do anything but continue to play the game, Charlie decides it's best to do just that.

Keep him occupied.

Keep him happy and calm and driving until they reach a place where they can stop and Charlie can get out of the car and never get back in again.

That's another thing she's decided. To do what she's starting to fear she should have done back at the 7-Eleven just before the highway—tell Josh she's changed her mind, leave the car, get her things from the trunk, and let him drive away without her. She doesn't care if she's overreacting and Josh is just some harmless weirdo who only wants to drive her to Youngstown. It's better to be safe than sorry. And right now, safe is a place outside of this car.

"Is this body part useful?"

"Oh, it's *very* useful," Josh says, again with the knowing smirk. This time, though, its accompanied by a lift of the eyebrows that suggests something both sexual and sinister. Seeing it makes Charlie shift in her seat.

It occurs to her—just now, when it's far too late, and not back when she was still safely at Olyphant—that Josh could be a sexual predator. Someone who lures college girls into his car, rapes them, dumps them on the side of the road. Then he drives off to a different university and the process begins anew. Josh is certainly physically capable of it. His size was one of the first things Charlie noticed about him.

The worried lump in her stomach expands, rising upward into her chest, pushing against her lungs. Her rib cage tightens. So much so that she takes a deep breath, just to prove to herself that she still can.

"Do all humans have it?" she asks, silently pleading that Josh says yes and she can stop tallying all the pornographic possibilities he might be thinking of.

"We do," Josh says, more straightforward this time, as if he's realized he's crossed some invisible line he didn't intend to breach. Not that it makes Charlie feel any better. Now that the idea of Josh being a rapist is in her head, she can't shake it.

Her fingers have never left the door handle. She flexes them against it. A test. Seeing how long it might take to pull the handle and fling the door open, if it should come to that.

She desperately hopes it doesn't come to that.

"Is this body part located above the waist?"

"As a matter of fact, it is," Josh says.

"Is it above the neck?"

"Yes."

"Is it something we're born with?"

Josh appears thoughtful, taking a moment to squint at the thinning fog outside the windshield. Charlie does the same, relieved to see not only the lightening of the gray outside but a set of taillights glowing not too far in front of them. She checks the side mirror, and her relief grows. There's a car behind them now, headlights cutting through the dissipating gloom. Another pair of headlights joins it. Then another.

Charlie's hit with a faint shimmer of hope. Maybe one of the cars will try to pass them. Maybe she can flag down the driver.

"It's funny you should ask that," Josh says, still gazing out the windshield. "Because we're not."

In an instant, all of Charlie's hopefulness disappears. Because she knows the object Josh is thinking of—a realization that makes it feel as if all the blood has drained from her body. Ice water pours in to replace it, leaving Charlie motionless and numb.

"You know the answer, don't you?" Josh says.

Charlie nods, too unnerved to speak.

"Then say it, smarty-pants."

Charlie swallows and forces herself to speak, willing the words onto her tongue and into the stifling air of the car.

"Is it a tooth?"

"It is." Josh smiles, proud of himself. "Very good. You solved it in sixteen questions."

"What made you pick that object?"

"I don't know. It just came to me." A stricken look crosses Josh's face. "Oh, shit. I'm so sorry, Charlie. I wasn't thinking. No wonder you look like you've just seen a ghost. It's because of your friend. That guy pulled out one of her teeth after killing her, didn't he?"

Charlie shakes her head, wanting him to stop talking. Needing him to stop. The urge to shut him up is so great that she'd lunge into the driver's seat and clamp a hand over his mouth if there was a way to do it without them running off the road. Because the more he talks, the worse the situation becomes.

Still, she has another question. One she must ask. She needs to hear Josh's answer. She wants to believe what he says, even though every ice-cold nerve in her body tells her she won't.

"How did you know about the tooth?"

"I read about it in the newspaper."

"It wasn't in the papers," Charlie says.

"I'm positive I read it there," Josh says.

He's lying. The police wouldn't have made her swear not to tell anyone about Maddy's missing tooth if they planned on giving that information to the press, and Charlie assumes she would have heard about it if they had.

She runs through all the ways Josh could know about the missing tooth, the least scary being that he's somehow related to Maddy and heard it from her mother. But that makes no sense. If Josh was a family member, it's likely Charlie would have known about him when Maddy was alive. Even if Maddy hadn't mentioned him—and she loved to talk about her family—there's no reason why Josh wouldn't have brought up the connection immediately.

Next, Charlie considers the idea that Josh could be a cop. Or used to be one. Again, it's unlikely. Any cop familiar with Maddy's case would also know Charlie had been her roommate.

That leaves one last possible reason Josh knows about the tooth.

One so scary it makes Charlie simultaneously want to scream, throw up, and leap from the moving car.

Josh knows about Maddy's missing tooth because he's the one who took it from her.

Which would make him worse than anything Charlie had previously thought of.

It would make him the Campus Killer.

INT. GRAND AM—NIGHT

Charlie remains motionless in the passenger seat, thinking the unthinkable.

She might be in a car with the man who killed Maddy.

A man who might also plan on killing her.

A man who had flat-out warned her such a scenario could happen.

Charlie stares out the windshield, her gaze fixed on the yellow beams of the headlights chasing away the last bits of fog as she recalls what Josh had told her earlier.

He's still out there.

He might know who you are.

He might try to come for you next.

Charlie clings to the second word of that thought.

Might.

She has no proof Josh is the Campus Killer. Only a vague suspicion based on something he said.

No.

More than something.

Several things. All of them adding up to a suspicion that's more than vague. Charlie already knows Josh has lied to her—and is continuing to do so. The amount of lies he's told since leaving Olyphant probably outnumbers truth ten to one.

But that doesn't mean he's a killer.

It especially doesn't mean he's the man who killed Maddy.

This isn't a movie. This isn't *Shadow of a Doubt*. Just because she's trying to think like Movie Charlie doesn't mean they share the same situation. Movies are fake, after all. Something she intrinsically knows but always forgets when the lights dim and the projector whirs and Technicolor fills the screen. That's why Charlie loves them so much. They're a bit of magic brightening a reality that's cold and gray and dull.

Mundane.

That's the best way to describe daily existence, with its endless parade of drudgeries and disappointments. In real life, people don't break into song. They don't battle space monsters. And they certainly don't unwittingly get into cars with serial killers.

"You're pretty quiet over there, Charlie," Josh says.

Charlie struggles to summon a response. She doesn't want Josh to know she's suspicious or afraid. If movies have taught her anything, it's that predators can sense fear.

"I guess I am."

"You're not mad at me, are you? For the tooth thing? You know I didn't mean anything by it. It wasn't intentional."

"I know."

"So we're good?" Josh says.

"We're good," Charlie says, even as she mentally lists all the things that are definitely *not* good about Josh, starting with the fact that Josh isn't his real name. And how he lied about working at Olyphant. And how he knew about the Campus Killer yanking out Maddy's tooth after stabbing her to death.

Charlie sneaks a glance at Josh, searching for any similarities

between him and the dark figure she saw in the alley the night
Maddy died. Anything she comes up with is vague at best. Maybe
they're the same height. Maybe they share a broadness of the shoulders. But it's all conjecture. The truth is that there's no way for
Charlie to know if they're one and the same.

The inside of the car has become unbearably hot, even as Charlie
herself remains freezing cold. It's a clash of extreme temperatures
that makes her think she's going to melt away any moment now.
Her skin sliding off. Her organs turning to gel. A disappearing.
The only things left behind a steaming pile of bones.

And teeth, of course.

Charlie suspects there's a reason Josh's game of Twenty Questions led to that. It's possible he was trying to tell her who he is and
what he's done. A roundabout confession. Or perhaps a warning.

It's also possible he meant nothing by it, although Charlie has
her doubts. The odds of him settling on a tooth as the answer are
as slim as her accepting a ride from the man who killed Maddy.

Yet those are the only two options. Either Josh is a harmless liar
who so far has managed to say and do all the wrong things, or he's
the man who brutally murdered her best friend and two other
women. Charlie can think of no other scenario between those unlikely poles.

Faced with such uncertainty, she understands one thing and one
thing only.

She needs to get out of this car.

Immediately.

It doesn't matter if Josh poses no real threat. The alternative—
that he does—is too risky to consider. It's best to err on the side of
caution. To be smart, to be brave, to be careful.

Staying in this car with Josh isn't any of those things.

They've descended into the Delaware Valley, a few miles from
the Pennsylvania border. The fog is completely gone now, revealing

a night sky pulsing with starlight, a river to their left, and three lanes of blacktop stretching toward the horizon in front of them.

Charlie remains focused on the highway ahead, unable to bring herself to look at Josh for even a second. Yet she remains hyper-aware of his presence, mere inches away. The sheer bulk of him. The way his presence fills the car. The steady rhythm of his breath. There's no way to ignore him.

There's no way to escape him, either, short of throwing herself out of the car, an idea Charlie keeps returning to again and again. Her right hand continues to grip the door handle, her fingers tight around it, ready to spring into action.

Charlie would do it, too, if she was certain such a leap wouldn't kill her. But it definitely could. She guesses she has a fifty percent chance of survival. Maybe less, considering there are now more cars on the road. Charlie counts four behind them. Four vehicles that might not be able to veer out of the way if she does jump, their tires rumbling over her body like it was a speed bump.

It would be different if they were in the right lane, where Charlie could attempt to fling herself onto the road's shoulder, where grass would slightly soften her landing. But Josh has steered the Grand Am into the center lane, his driving as even as his breathing. Keeping the car tightly inside the lane lines. Going an acceptable three miles over the speed limit. Doing nothing to draw the attention of other motorists.

One of the cars behind them changes lanes, moving into the right one. Its shift in position leaves a speck of brightness in the side mirror outside Charlie's window.

Headlights.

Getting larger.

Charlie twists in her seat to get a better look at the car coming up on the right. The driver clearly intends to pass them eventually, even though it's technically only legal to pass on the left. As the car keeps coming, Charlie spots something on top of its roof—a light bar stretching from one side of the car to the other. She then sees the words that have been applied to the vehicle's body, right over the front tire.

STATE TROOPER

Charlie's heart gallops. A state trooper is pulling up beside them. Almost as if she willed him into existence. Now all she needs to do is get the trooper's attention without Josh seeing.

Charlie presses her forehead against the window, the glass cool against her skin.

"You okay, Charlie?" Josh says.

"I'm fine."

"You don't look fine."

"Just a little carsick."

A warm breath rides the sibilant second half of the word. It hits the window, creating a tiny circle of fog on the glass. Charlie stares at it, not blinking until it fades.

She speaks again.

"Don't worry. I'm not going to puke or anything. It always passes."

The window fogs again, this time in a slightly larger patch. Charlie counts off the seconds until it disappears.

One.

Two.

Three.

Four.

Five.

Six.

Seven.

Eight.

Nine.

Josh notices the trooper, too, because he taps the brakes a moment, bringing them below the speed limit.

"You sure?" he says.

"I'm sure."

A fresh bloom of fog spreads onto the window. Charlie counts again.

Another nine seconds.

Not a lot of time. But possibly enough.

She runs a finger along the glass, moving it in a pattern, tracing letters that don't exist.

Yet.

Charlie turns toward Josh, making sure his eyes are still on the road. Then it's back to the window, her forehead meeting glass, looking backward to track the state trooper's progress. When the police car's front bumper runs parallel to the Grand Am's back one, she gets to work.

"I'm feeling better already," she says. "Cooling my forehead helps."

The twin huffs from those last two words create a circle of fog twice the size of the previous ones. The countdown begins.

Nine.

Charlie does another quick check of Josh.

Eight.

She returns to the window.

Seven.

She twists her body, blocking Josh's view.

Six.

She presses the tip of her index finger to the glass and begins to write.

Five.

The first letter is three quick lines in the fog.

Four.

Another letter, this time one long line followed by three short bursts.

Three.

And another—two quick slashes.

Two.

The final letter. A slash and a swoop.

One.

The fog vanishes, taking with it the word she'd managed to scrawl.

HELP

"You ever get that way?" she asks Josh. "Carsick?"

The circle of fog reappears on the window, as does the word "HELP," written backward so it can be read clearly by the trooper when he drives past them.

As the police car gains on them, Josh gives the brakes another brief tap. The reduction in speed brings the two vehicles in line. They travel side by side a moment, Charlie's hopeful heart thumping even harder when she spies the trooper behind the wheel. He looks tough. A bulldog with a buzz cut. And all Charlie needs to get his attention is to breathe.

If that doesn't work, she'll scream.

So loud he'll be able to hear her through two panes of glass.

Then the trooper will switch on those beautiful red and white lights and Josh will have no choice but to pull over and Charlie will run. She doesn't care if Josh turns out to be harmless and she looks stupid. At that moment, all she wants is to be out of this car, free from Josh and all the doubt and uncertainty he carries with him.

Charlie inhales, gathering her breath, hoping for a cloud of fog on the glass that will last ten seconds, maybe longer.

She exhales.

The window fogs, obscuring the image of the trooper in the next car over as the word she drew starts to form.

HELP

Josh hits the brakes again. Harder this time. Enough for Charlie to feel momentum tug her against the seat belt as she watches the trooper pull ahead of them. A moment later, the state police car has passed them completely. Charlie's heart, so wild seconds earlier, all but stops as the trooper keeps moving, his patrol car getting smaller with each passing second.

She's missed her chance.

All because Josh tapped the brakes.

Did he do that on purpose?

More doubt.

Enough to heighten Charlie's desire to get out of the car by any means possible.

Her hand drops back to the door handle and gives it a squeeze. God help her, she's going to have to jump.

Right now.

The good news is that the highway has narrowed to two lanes—likely the reason the state trooper passed them on the right. He was running out of road. And maybe Josh knew that, hence the tapping of the brakes that foiled her plan.

Charlie sneaks a glance at the speedometer.

Now that the trooper is a Matchbox car on the horizon, Josh has increased his speed to sixty miles an hour.

Fast.

Too fast for the road ahead, which runs next to the Delaware River, hugging the mountainside in a series of tight turns.

And definitely too fast for her to leap from the car like she now knows she must do. Even if she could survive the jump unscathed—which she can't; not at this speed—there's now nowhere to go. On

Josh's side of the highway is more highway, a low stone wall, then river. Charlie's side is nothing but mountain, rising high into the night sky, its trees and crags barely visible.

Charlie had always liked this stretch of road, for both its wild beauty and its incongruity. With its peaks and pines and wide expanse of curving river, it reminded her of something more likely to be found out west and not on the border between New Jersey and Pennsylvania. When passing through with Nana Norma or Robbie behind the wheel, she'd roll down the window, take in the fresh air, revel in the scenery she found beautiful in any season.

But that was always in daylight. She's never traveled through this canyon at night until now. It changes things, the darkness. It makes the familiar foreign. The innocent suspicious.

She wonders if it's the same with Josh, if it's merely the presence of night that's making her suspicious of everything he does and says and implies. Maybe all of this would feel different and less threatening in the light of day.

Charlie doesn't think so.

Josh's actions would be shady no matter the time.

He doesn't acknowledge it when Charlie makes another check of the speedometer and sees they haven't slowed. He hasn't shown any interest in her at all since the state trooper appeared behind them. Yet he's watching her all the same. Charlie can feel it. A prickle of heat coming from the driver's side as he navigates another curve. As they speed through the bend, the pine air freshener swings from the rearview mirror like a corpse on the gallows.

Charlie tightens her grip on the door handle, partly to steady herself as the Grand Am careens through another hairpin curve and partly in case she decides to risk it and jump anyway, even though that would be tantamount to suicide. The mountainside is so close to the car—a presence as unnerving as Josh and likely more dangerous. Chunks of stone litter the road's narrow shoulder.

The remains of boulders that have fallen from the hillside and crashed to earth.

That's what her skull would look like if she jumped.

Broken bits of bone strewn among the rocks.

Within seconds, they've reached the bridge that spans the Delaware River, and leaping onto the side of the road isn't even an option. There's no side of the road to jump to. Just a thin strip of gravel-studded blacktop and concrete bridge railing. Beyond that, dozens of feet below, is dark water.

Jumping now *would* be suicide.

But there's light ahead. A beacon Charlie had completely forgotten about until this moment.

A toll plaza.

Six lanes of booths blocking the entire westbound highway just on the other side of the bridge.

Josh will have no choice but to slow down.

And when he does, Charlie will make her move.

As the Grand Am continues across the bridge and the toll plaza lights get brighter, Charlie runs through the motions in her head. An action movie of her making.

Wait for Josh to slow the car.

Fling the door open before he brings it to a complete stop.

Then run.

Out of the car.

Into the next toll lane.

Then the next and the next and the next.

She'll run screaming and not cease until another car stops for her or a tollbooth operator grabs her or she reaches some place that's safe. There are other roads nearby. Ones with houses and businesses and onlookers who'll hopefully come to her rescue.

The toll plaza is closer now, their lane crossed by one of those flimsy wooden gates that serve as symbols more than anything else. A car could smash right through it, something Charlie fears Josh might try to do. But then he taps the brakes and the speedometer plummets from sixty-five to forty-five to twenty-five.

Charlie squeezes the door handle.

Waiting.

Waiting.

Waiting as the car slows to fifteen, ten, five.

Now, a voice in Charlie's head shouts. It might be her mother's voice. It might be Maddy's. Most likely it's a combination of the two, their message loud and clear. *Run now.*

Charlie's body tightens. Getting ready. Preparing for the sprint.

Run! Maddy and her mother keep screaming in her skull. *Now!*

Another voice joins them.

Josh.

Speaking calmly from the driver's seat.

"Charlie?"

INT. GRAND AM—NIGHT

Charlie hears music.

The opening chords of a song she thought they already started listening to.

Nirvana.

"Come as You Are."

"That must have been one hell of a movie," Josh says.

Shock stills Charlie's hand. She finds herself turning to face Josh, even though she knows she should be doing the opposite.

Opening the door.

Running to safety.

But what Josh just said holds her in place, forcing her to ask, "What do you mean?"

"A movie in your mind," Josh says. "You just had one. I could tell."

He brings the Grand Am to a full stop at the tollbooth. He then reaches across the console, his arm invading Charlie's side of the car, and for a split second she thinks he's about to reveal his true nature.

One she started to suspect minutes and miles ago.

She flinches, waiting.

But all Josh does is retrieve his wallet from the dashboard. If he notices Charlie's reaction—and how could he have missed it?—he doesn't show it. He simply plucks a five-dollar bill from the wallet, rolls down the window, and nods to the toll collector, a stout woman stifling a yawn.

"You look as tired as I feel," Josh says, oozing charm as he hands her the five and palms the change. "Hope you got some strong coffee on you."

"I do," the toll collector says. "I'm gonna need it."

Josh stuffs the cash back into his wallet, arranging it. He then shoves the wallet into his back left pocket. Charlie watches him do it, her body buzzing with uncertainty. What was Josh talking about? There was no movie in her mind.

Right?

Charlie's fingers flex against the door handle, urging the rest of her to just pull it, just get out, just get away. She can't bring herself to do it. She needs to know what Josh meant.

"Shift just starting?" he asks the toll collector.

"Yeah. Long night ahead."

"Hope it goes quick for you."

As Josh rolls up the window, Charlie's hit with a desperate need to yell to the toll collector for help. Her mouth drops open, but she doesn't know what to say. Josh just said she experienced a movie in her mind, and she has no idea why or what it could mean. And now it's too late, because the window is shut and the car's in motion again. The Grand Am passes the gate and leaves the toll plaza, its lights receding in the rearview mirror as the car picks up speed.

Fifteen miles per hour. Twenty-five. Thirty-five.

It's not until they hit fifty-five that curiosity gets the best of Charlie. She clears her throat, trying to rid the fear that coats her tongue like drying paint, and says, "What were you talking about back there?"

"You went to the movies," Josh says. "Your eyes were open, but you were totally zoned out."

But that doesn't make any sense. When Charlie sees a movie in her mind, the second it's over she understands it was all in her mind's eye. That it wasn't real, even though it felt like it. It feels like being nudged awake when you fall asleep in class. Disorienting only for the tiny sliver of time it takes to understand what happened.

She's never, not once, thought that what she experienced was still real after the fact.

"For how long?" she says.

"Awhile, I guess."

Charlie scans the dashboard, hoping to see a clock that might tell her what Josh can't—or won't. But there isn't a clock on the dashboard. No surprise there. Maddy's car didn't have a clock, either. Only fancier cars do, like the tan Mercedes Nana Norma inherited from one of her elderly boyfriends who'd passed away two summers ago.

"I need you to be more specific than that," she says.

"Why does it matter?"

It matters because she has no idea what really happened and what was just a dark, twisted fantasy occurring only in her mind. One that still might be occurring, although Charlie has her doubts. She assumes she'd have snapped out of it by now. Then there's the fact that everything currently feels depressingly real. The movies in her mind are usually stylized. Life amplified. This has the dullness of reality.

"Just give me a time," she says.

She finds herself hoping Josh will give her an outlandish figure. One long enough to erase every unsettling thing she's experienced during the drive. It could easily happen. A long drive. Nothing to see out the window but night. Boredom settling in, just like it did when she was a kid. Her thoughts drifting, turning the drab reality of a car trip into something exciting, something new.

"Five minutes," Josh says, sounding like he picked that number simply because he thinks it will please her.

"You sure?"

"Maybe six. Or longer. I honestly don't know."

Charlie wonders if Josh is being vague on purpose. That he knows he slipped up by mentioning the tooth and is now trying to cover it by confusing her. Then again, it's also possible he truly doesn't know how long she was lost in her own head and is trying to be helpful.

"You have to have *some* idea of how long it lasted," she says. "I was sitting next to you the entire time."

"I don't get why you're asking me all these questions," Josh says, growing annoyed. "It's been nonstop ever since we hit the highway. If I'd known this would become an interrogation, I wouldn't have offered you a ride."

This is, in its own backhanded way, helpful. Charlie hopes that through Josh's experience of the drive she'll get a better idea of her own.

"So I *did* ask you all those questions?" she says.

"Yes. About my dad and where I grew up and my damn work schedule."

Since that part was real, so was everything that came before it. Including her seeing Josh's driver's license, which prompted all those questions in the first place. That particular worry hasn't changed.

It still exists.

It's still potentially dangerous.

As if to underscore that thought, Josh says, "Are you scared of me, Charlie? I get the feeling I make you nervous. Can't say I blame you. Considering what happened to your friend and all. In fact, I'd be surprised if you weren't nervous. You don't know me. Not really. Don't know what I'm capable of doing."

Charlie eyes him from the other side of the car. His expression reveals nothing. It's just a blank slate facing an open road. She hates how unreadable he is. So maddeningly opaque. Yet she's jealous, too. She longs to know how he does it. How it seems so easy for him to hide his emotions when it feels like her every thought and feeling are visible, like an image projected onto a movie screen.

"Yes," she says. Since he clearly suspects it, there's no point in denying it. "You make me nervous."

"Why?"

Because her best friend was murdered and she thinks Josh is the man who did it and if she can't even trust her mind, then she sure as hell isn't going to trust him. He's lied to her, after all. This uncertainty about the movie in her mind doesn't change that.

"Because I know you're lying," she blurts out. "I know your name isn't Josh Baxter. I saw your driver's license."

Josh furrows his brow. "I honestly don't know what you're talking about, Charlie."

"I saw it, Josh. Or should I start calling you Jake?"

The furrow across Josh's forehead grows deeper—a ridge of confusion stretching from temple to temple. "Who's Jake?"

"Your real name," Charlie says. "Which I saw on your real driver's license. When your wallet fell off the dashboard, it flopped open and there it was. Jake Collins."

Josh laughs. A low, incredulous chuckle.

"Is that what you really think? That I've been lying about my name?"

"And other things," Charlie says, finally releasing the suspicion she'd been holding back since Josh first steered them onto the highway. "You didn't work at Olyphant. Because if you did, you'd know that there really is a Madison Hall there."

Josh grows quiet, which Charlie takes as a sign he knows he's been busted about at least one untruth.

"You're right," he finally says. "I never worked at the university. I never went there, either. I made all of that up. For the past four years I've been working at the Radio Shack just off campus. We passed it as we were leaving."

Charlie nods, taking it in. Truth at last. A small, tiny, inconsequential bit of it.

"Obvious question," she says. "Why did you lie about that?"

"Would you have agreed to get in a car with me if I told you the truth?"

"No," Charlie says, not needing to even think about it. Of course she wouldn't have. No student in their right mind would ride with some random stranger not associated with the university. "Another obvious question: Why did you need to lure someone into your car?"

"I didn't lure you," Josh says.

Charlie shoots him a look. "Well, I sure as fuck feel lured."

"I didn't want to be alone. Is that a good enough answer for you? My dad had a stroke, and I felt helpless and sad and didn't want to drive to Ohio with nothing but all those bad thoughts to keep me company. So I put on this stupid sweatshirt, went to the ride board, and looked for someone to ride with me."

Josh's voice has grown quiet, almost sad. When he looks at Charlie, his expression matches his tone. Enough that guilt starts to gain a tiny foothold in Charlie's heart. As someone going through her own share of pain, she even understands why he did it. Grief and sadness are horrible places to dwell in alone.

Was it deceitful?

Yes.

Was it creepy?

Hell yes.

But it doesn't mean Josh is dangerous. It doesn't mean he wants to do Charlie harm.

"You could have just told me that from the start," she says.

"You wouldn't have believed me," Josh says. "It seems to me like you don't believe a word I've said."

"You haven't given me any reason to," Charlie says. "I know your real name, remember."

"I *gave* you my real name."

Using only one hand to steer, Josh pulls the wallet from his back pocket. He hands it to Charlie, who looks at it like it's something venomous. A snake ready to strike.

"Go on," he urges. "See for yourself."

Charlie takes the wallet, holding it by a corner between her thumb and forefinger, as if she still expects it to bite. She places it in her lap, hesitant. She already knows what she's going to see. A Pennsylvania driver's license with Josh's picture and the name Jake Collins.

But when she opens the wallet, she finds no such thing. Inside, snug behind its clear plastic sleeve, is a license different from the one she saw. The picture's the same—Josh's perfect genetics still shining through. But the license itself is a New Jersey one. And printed across the bottom, in letters clear as day, is the name Josh Baxter.

"Now are you convinced?" he says.

"I don't understand."

"I do," Josh says.

Charlie knows what he's implying—that it was another movie in her mind.

"No," she says. "I know what I saw."

"What you *think* you saw," Josh says.

Charlie stares at the license in her lap, not blinking, as if that might somehow change it back to the one she saw earlier. Or thought she saw, to put Josh's spin on it. As she keeps staring, Charlie realizes how ridiculous it is to *want* Josh to be lying about his name. But the alternative is far more frightening. Because if she's wrong about the license—and, on the surface, it looks like she's *very* wrong—then she could be wrong about everything that's happened since she got into the car.

Charlie's head starts to spin—a full-fledged Tilt-a-Whirl that only gets faster the longer she looks at Josh's license. She slaps the wallet shut, opens the center console, and drops it inside.

"Come as You Are," which had still been blasting from the stereo, ends and another song begins. The sudden change in music hits a switch in Charlie's brain.

Josh turned off the stereo right before he started his increasingly uncomfortable game of Twenty Questions. But the stereo was playing when Charlie emerged from the alleged movie in her mind. That makes it likely everything she experienced while the stereo was off might not have happened.

Including the answer to Josh's game.

A tooth.

Could that also have just been in her head? Could the one thing that made her think Josh is the Campus Killer not be real?

"Did we play Twenty Questions?" she says.

Josh, about to take a drink from his cup of coffee, stops mid-sip. "What?"

"The game. Twenty Questions."

"I know what it is, Charlie."

"So did we play it? After you shut off the stereo?"

Charlie presses the stop button on the car stereo, as if Josh needs a demonstration to fully understand. The sudden quiet in the car is discomfiting. It makes her realize just how long Josh waits before answering. Is that because he has no idea what she's referring to? Or is it because he knows exactly what she means and is debating whether to lie about it?

"I never turned off the stereo," Josh says.

"You did. You turned off the music and we played Twenty Questions. I asked. You answered. And I need—" Charlie's voice catches on the word, dragging it out, making it clear just how important this is to her. "I need to know if that actually happened."

"Why?"

Because the answer would tell her if she might be trapped in a car with a serial killer, that's why. Only Charlie can't say that to Josh. If he knew what she was thinking, then he'd undoubtedly lie. Yes, there's a chance he could lie even without knowing her suspicions, but Charlie's not going to make that decision for him.

"Please just tell me," she says. "Did we play Twenty Questions?"

Josh's answer comes startlingly fast. No waiting this time. Just an instant "No" tossed at her like a lit firecracker.

The answer she wanted yet dreaded.

"Positive?" she says.

"Yes, Charlie. I'm absolutely certain we didn't play Twenty Questions."

Charlie sits with that a moment, letting it seep into her brain like one of those little orange pills she used to take. And should still be taking. Because without them, there's nothing stopping the movies in her mind from taking over. From not knowing what is reality and what is an illusion. A fucked-up form of Hollywood magic.

No seeing Josh's real name on his real driver's license.

No state trooper riding up beside them to rescue her like a cowboy in a John Ford flick.

No huffing hot breath onto the window. Or writing "HELP" on the fogged glass. Or plotting a daring leap from the moving car.

Is such a thing even possible? Could she have gotten so lost in her own specific brand of make-believe that it's started to bleed into reality?

That's never happened before.

Until now, Charlie had thought of the movies in her mind as brief moments. Small windows of time in which fantasy eclipses harsh reality. No different from the way cinematographers used to rub Vaseline on the camera's lens to give the leading lady a gauzy glow.

And when one ends, Charlie knows it's over. Her body snaps back to the present—the equivalent of the credits rolling and the theater lights coming up.

But the past hour was more like a fever dream. Real and surreal and *alive.*

The idea that some of her memories, her past, her *life* might not have occurred the way she assumes they did is almost as unnerving as thinking she's in a car with a serial killer. It's so concerning that she's reluctant to believe it. Why should she trust Josh over her own mind?

So she's back where she started. Wanting to believe Josh but also unwilling to. And as the Grand Am continues down the highway, heading farther into the uncertain night, Charlie is conscious of four things.

None of it might have happened. Or all of it might have happened.

One of them would make Josh completely harmless. The other might mean he's the Campus Killer.

And Charlie has no idea which one is the truth.

INT. GRAND AM—NIGHT

"Mind if I turn the music back on?"

Josh's voice cuts through Charlie's thoughts, jerking her out of the deep mental well into which she'd fallen. She looks at Josh. She looks at his finger, poised above the stereo's play button. She wonders if she just experienced another movie in her mind and that none of the past ten minutes actually happened.

"What was the last thing you said to me?"

"Mind if I turn the music back on," Josh says, this time without the questioning inflection.

"Before that."

"That we hadn't played Twenty Questions."

Charlie nods. Good. It wasn't a movie in her mind. Unless it's still going on. Thinking such things makes her feel simultaneously drunk and also in need of a strong drink. Part of her wants to tell Josh to pull off at the next exit, where she can put her fake ID to good use at the first bar they pass.

Instead, she'll settle for a rest stop, which, according to a highway sign they're just now passing, sits a mile up the road.

"I need to go to the bathroom," she says, eyeing the sign as it slides past the passenger window.

"Now?"

"Yes. Now. It was all that coffee," she says, even though she hasn't had a sip since first seeing Josh's driver's license.

What she really wants is to get out of the car and get away from Josh. Just for a moment. She needs to be alone with the crisp night air on her face, hoping that will bring some clarity. Because right now she has nothing. "I'll be quick."

"Fine," Josh says, letting out a weary sigh exactly like the ones her dad would sometimes make during those long-ago road trips. "I wouldn't mind stretching my legs myself."

When the off-ramp comes into view, Josh hits the right turn signal and slides off the highway. Ahead of them, the building housing the restrooms sits squat and silent. It's a sad, ungainly single-story rectangle of beige bricks with doors and a roof painted shit brown.

The parking lot is empty, save for a car driving away as they pull in, its taillights winking red. Charlie's heart sinks as she watches it depart. She had hoped the place would be crowded, providing peace of mind while she stops to regroup. An empty rest stop provides no such comfort. Right now, Josh could slit her throat, yank her tooth, and drive away without anyone knowing.

If he's the Campus Killer, that is.

Something else Charlie's not completely certain about. She doubts the Campus Killer would park directly beneath one of the parking lot's streetlamps, as Josh does now.

It could be a sign that she should trust him.

Or it could be him trying to trick her into giving him that trust.

Sitting in the parked car under the cone of light coming from the streetlamp, Charlie knows she needs to stop thinking this way. All this doubt—her mind veering wildly between two very different scenarios—will only get worse the longer the night goes on. She needs to pick a lane and act accordingly.

To help with that decision, Charlie does what she should have done the moment Josh pulled up to her dorm: check the Grand Am's license plate. She gets out of the car and stands behind it, pretending to stretch. Rolling her head and swinging her arms, she sneaks a look at the license plate.

New Jersey.

That's at least one check in the Trust Josh column.

"I'll be right back," Charlie tells him, even though it's not a given. It's entirely possible she might decide to never enter that car again. There's also the possibility Josh might kill her before she gets the chance to make that decision.

Charlie quickens her pace as she walks to the restrooms. It's unnervingly quiet here, not to mention secluded. Behind her, about a hundred yards from the parking lot, is the interstate. Up ahead, looming darkly behind the facilities, is a forest of unknown size and density.

Just outside the door to the restrooms is a pay phone. Charlie pauses in front of it, knowing it's still not too late to call Robbie. Which is what she should have done at the 7-Eleven before they hit the highway. Charlie knows that now. She regrets, with an intensity that aches, not picking up the phone and saying those four magical words.

Things took a detour.

Charlie's about to reach for the phone when she notices a piece of masking tape stuck over the coin slot. She grabs the receiver anyway, lifting it from its cradle. There's no dial tone. Just her luck.

It isn't until after she slams the phone back into place that Charlie realizes Josh could be watching her. She's still outside the building, in full view of anyone in the parking lot. She shoots a quick, cautious glance toward the Grand Am. Josh is there, outside the car now, stretching his arms to the sky while rolling his neck. He hasn't seen a thing.

Good.

Charlie steps into the building, finding the inside as depressing as the outside. The walls are gray. The floor is dirty. The lights overhead buzz out a wan, yellow glow. Vending machines line the wall to the left, offering three choices: snacks, sodas, hot beverages. To the right are the bathrooms, men's room by the door, ladies' room toward the back.

Hanging on the wall between them is a large map showing the state of Pennsylvania, with wide slices of New Jersey and Ohio on either side. Charlie's entire route home is visible—the long red line of Interstate 80 slithering its way across the Keystone State. And they've barely made it past the border, as evidenced by a tiny white arrow marking their current location. On top of the arrow, in minuscule red letters, it reads YOU ARE HERE.

"Don't be too sure of that," Charlie mutters, aware that she could still be in the Grand Am, lost in another mental movie.

Hell, why stop there? There's nothing to keep her from thinking that the entire night's all a movie in her mind. She could snap out of it and find herself back at Olyphant. Or, even better, back in September, waking up the morning after marching away from that bar and awful Cure cover band to see Maddy still asleep on the other side of the room, the past two months nothing but a horrible nightmare.

Charlie closes her eyes, hoping for that exact scenario. She waits, her body still, trying to will that version of events into existence. But when her eyes open, she's in the same spot, facing the map and its white arrow, which now feels like a taunt.

YOU ARE HERE.

Fuck.

If the map says it, then it must be true. It's about the only thing she can trust.

INT. REST STOP BATHROOM—NIGHT

Disheartened, Charlie pushes into the ladies' room. It's dim inside, thanks to the fact that only one row of lights seems to be working. The result is a rectangle of brightness centered near the sinks while the stalls on the other side of the bathroom sit in shadow. It also smells awful. A mix of urine and industrial cleaner that makes her gag.

Using a hand to cover her nose and mouth, Charlie retreats to one of the stalls on the dim side of the bathroom. The last one in the row, farthest away from the door. She backs herself inside and sits on the toilet, trying to think, trying to come up with some kind of plan.

She could wait. That's certainly an option. She could stay in this bathroom, inside this stall, and not emerge until someone else arrives at the rest stop, which they're bound to do soon. Another vehicle could be pulling into the parking lot this very second. Charlie could ask them for help and beg for a ride to the nearest police station. If they ask why, she could tell them the truth—that the man she's with sort of, kind of, could be a serial killer.

Not a very convincing argument.

And that's what has Charlie so on edge. If she knew with certainty that Josh was dangerous, she'd be barricading the bathroom door or running for the highway or hiding in the woods.

But nothing about the situation is certain. She could be wrong about Josh. It could all be a huge misunderstanding. Her fanciful imagination running at full gallop because her life has been a guilt-ridden train wreck for two months.

Someone knocks on the bathroom door. A single, sharp rap that startles Charlie so much that she gasps when she hears it.

Josh.

Charlie doesn't think a woman would knock. It's the ladies' room. She would just walk right in. Which is exactly what happens next. Charlie hears the creak of the door opening, followed by the sound of footsteps on the sticky tile floor.

The bathroom's lone working light starts to flicker, on the cusp of joining the others. There's a moment of pure darkness, followed by staccato buzzes of light that continue in a strobe-like pattern.

Charlie hears a rap on the first stall in the row, as if Josh is checking to see if someone's inside. After another quick rap, the door is opened with a rough shove. Rather than going in, he moves to the second stall, raps on the door, pushes it open.

He's on the hunt.

For her.

Two stalls away, Charlie pulls her legs onto the toilet seat so Josh won't be able to see them under the door. If she stays like this, completely silent and still, then maybe Josh will think she's not in here, that she's left without him noticing, that she simply disappeared.

Then he'll go away.

Josh is at the third stall now. Right next to Charlie's. The flickering lights splatter his shadow across the floor in uneven bursts that make it hard to track his precise location. It's there for a slice of a second, then gone, then back again, only slightly closer this time.

Charlie stares at the floor, watching the stutter-start progress of the shadow as the door to the stall next door is thrown open. She clamps a hand over her mouth, trying to mute the sound of her breathing. A useless act. She fears her heartbeat alone will give her away, pounding like a drum in her chest.

Josh is now in front of her stall, his strobing shadow stretching under the door and into the stall itself, as if it's trying to grab Charlie.

There's a rap on the door.

Then another.

So hard it rattles the door and makes Charlie realize, with nerve-scalding horror, that she never turned the latch.

She makes a desperate grab for the lock, but it's too late. The door swings inward, revealing Charlie crouched on top of the toilet, caught in the disco glow of the faulty lights. Standing on the other side of the now-open door is a woman. Mid-twenties. Too-tight stone-washed jeans. Bleached-blond hair with a strip of brown at the roots. She lets out a startled yelp as she jumps away from the stall.

"Shit," the woman says. "I thought it was empty."

Charlie remains crouched on the toilet like something feral. No wonder the woman scuttles to the sinks on the other side of the bathroom. The wide mirror above them reflects the strobing flash of the overhead fixture, making it look like she's moving in slow motion.

"I'm sorry I scared you," Charlie says.

The woman locks eyes with her. "Looks like I scared you more."

"I thought you were someone else." Charlie steps down from the toilet, still uncertain. "Why were you checking all the stalls?"

"Because this is a rest stop late at night and I'm alone and I'm not an idiot."

The woman pauses, leaving the harsh remainder of the sentence unspoken.

Like you.

The bathroom light continues to strobe. No wonder Charlie was frightened. It's very slasher flick. Very Wes Craven. The result is that the woman is now scared of her, as if she's the danger here. When Charlie steps out of the stall, the woman flinches.

"Did you see a guy out in the parking lot?" Charlie says. "Next to the Grand Am?"

"Yeah." The woman, still backed against the sink, eyes the stall behind her. Charlie can tell she has to use it but is now wondering if she can wait until the next rest stop. "You with him?"

Charlie risks another step toward her. "I'm not sure I want to be. Is it possible— I mean, could you, please, give me a ride?"

"I'm only going to Bloomsburg," the woman says.

Charlie doesn't know where that is. She doesn't care, as long as it's not here.

"I don't mind," she says, trying to sound accommodating but edging closer to desperation. "You can drop me off somewhere and I'll find a ride the rest of the way home."

"Why can't your boyfriend take you?"

"He's not—"

My boyfriend.

That's what Charlie wants to say.

But before she can get the words out, the bathroom door opens again and in saunters Maddy.

"Hello, darling," she says.

Charlie watches her cross the room to the sinks, as clear and present and real as the woman in the stone-washed jeans. Maddy's better dressed, of course. Fuchsia dress, black heels, a strand of pearls double-looped around her neck.

Maddy stands at the sinks, oblivious to the other woman in the room. Gazing at her reflection in the mirror, she puckers her lips before applying crimson lipstick.

"You look wretched," she says to Charlie, smacking her lips, now red as blood. "But my coat looks fab on you."

Charlie fingers the buttons on the coat. Big black ones that make her seem impossibly small. A little girl playing dress-up.

"What are you doing here?"

"Freshening up," Maddy says, as if that's a perfectly logical excuse to return from the dead. "Also, I needed to tell you something."

Charlie doesn't want to ask what that something is. But she does anyway. She needs to.

"Tell me what?"

"That you shouldn't have abandoned me," Maddy says.

Then she grabs Charlie by the hair and slams her face against the edge of the sink.

INT. REST STOP BATHROOM—NIGHT

Charlie jerks back to life, her body spasming, as if her head really had been smashed into the sink's edge. She can still hear the ghastly sound the impact made. Bone banging off porcelain.

But there was no sound like that.

Not one that could be heard by the other woman in the bathroom. And there is only one other woman here. Maddy's gone. Where she once stood is just a patch of grimy tile caught in the unremitting flash of the overhead light.

Next to it, the woman in the stone-washed jeans says, "Hey. Are you okay?"

Charlie's not sure how to answer that one. She just saw her dead best friend in the bathroom of an interstate rest stop. Of course she's not fucking okay. But the woman didn't see Maddy. As always, the movie in her mind played to an audience of one.

"No," Charlie says, conceding the obvious truth.

"Have you been drinking?"

"*No.*"

Charlie says it the way a drunk person would. Too loud. Too

emphatic. Overcompensating in a way that makes it obviously not true, although in Charlie's case it is. But she knows that's not the vibe she's giving off and tries to course correct.

"I just need to get home."

Charlie moves to the woman. Quickly. Closing the gap between them in three big strides, which only makes things worse. The woman shrinks away, even though she's backed all the way up against the sink with nowhere to go.

"I can't take you."

"Please." Charlie reaches out to grab her sleeve, prepared to tug and beg, but thinks better of it. "I know that this is going to sound weird. But that guy out there? I'm not sure I trust him."

"Why not?"

"There's a chance that he might have killed people."

Instead of surprise, the woman gives Charlie a wary look. As if this was exactly what she expected and is now disappointed to be so unsurprised.

"Might?" she says. "You don't know?"

"I told you it was going to sound weird."

The woman huffs. "You weren't lying."

"And no, I don't know if he killed someone," Charlie says. "But the fact that I think he might have—even a tiny, little bit—means I shouldn't get back in the car with him, right? That I should be worried?"

The woman, done with it all, including the idea of using the stall she'd been eyeing, pushes past Charlie and heads to the door.

"If you ask me," she says, "he should be worried about *you* getting back in that car. Whatever shit you've been drinking, I suggest switching to water. Or coffee."

The woman pushes through the door and, just like that, is gone. Alone again in the foul-smelling bathroom, Charlie looks around, checking for any signs Maddy might still be there. The faint idea that she could still be around—that what Charlie had seen was something beyond a mental movie—proves to her just how un-moored from reality she's become.

She goes to one of the sinks and stares at her reflection in the mottled mirror above it. Each flash of the overhead light brightens her skin, washing out her complexion, as if she were ill. Or maybe, Charlie thinks, maybe it's not the light. Maybe this is how she really looks. Sapped of color, turned pale by uncertainty.

No wonder that woman fled the bathroom. If Charlie saw some-one looking the way she does, saying the things she said, she'd leave, too. And she'd likely think the same things the woman thought of her.

That she's drunk. Or crazy.

But she's uncertain. And anxious. And no longer capable of trusting what she sees. That's what she should have told the woman instead of saying she didn't trust Josh. She should have flat-out stated that it was herself she didn't trust.

Tired of staring at her reflection, Charlie splashes cold water on her face, not that it helps, and hurries to the door. She wants to leave the bathroom before Maddy has another chance to reappear. But Charlie knows that no matter how fast she leaves, there's a chance Maddy will show up somewhere else. Or that she'll think something's happening when it's actually not. Or that another movie in her mind will spring up out of nowhere and she won't even be aware it's happening.

For all she knows, it's happening right now.

Movie after movie after movie. Like they're on the bill at a mall cineplex so tightly scheduled the ushers don't even have time to sweep up the spilled popcorn between shows.

The frequency of these visions worries Charlie. For the first time in her life, she thinks it could be a sign she's slipping deeper into psychosis and that one of these times she'll never snap out of it. She's heard of such things happening. Women who disappear into their own worlds, lost in a land of make-believe.

Maybe she's already there.

Charlie pauses before opening the bathroom door. She needs to compose herself a moment before returning to Josh and the Grand Am, which she has to do. She went into the bathroom knowing she needed to make a decision.

It turns out the decision was made for her.

If she can't trust herself, then she needs to trust Josh.

EXT. REST STOP PARKING LOT—NIGHT

He was still stretching when the woman arrived. Arms over his head, fingers laced, trying to ease out some of the tension tightening his neck and shoulders. Then the car arrived. An Oldsmobile with a lousy muffler and a tailpipe that looked like it was about to fall off.

The car parked on the other end of the lot, under a streetlamp exactly like the one where the Grand Am sits. The woman got out and gave him a nervous glance before hurrying up the sidewalk to the restrooms.

She needn't have worried. She's not his type.

Charlie, on the other hand, is very much his type, which poses a problem.

Another problem: that the woman in the Oldsmobile entered the restroom five minutes ago. Now he's concerned she and Charlie have got to talking. He shouldn't have let Charlie go off alone like that. He should have followed her inside and pretended to peruse the vending machines while she went to the bathroom.

There's a lot he should have done tonight. Starting with keeping his damn mouth shut.

Twenty Questions was a mistake. He realizes that now. But Charlie was asking so many questions and he was getting annoyed and he thought it would be amusing to make a game of it. But making his object a tooth, well, that wasn't the smartest move. Curiosity made him do it. He wanted to see Charlie's reaction when she figured it out. He should have known it would set her off a little, make her suspicious. Now she and the Oldsmobile chick are in that bathroom, talking about God knows what.

That's all his fault. He's man enough to admit it.

Until tonight, everything had been easy. Staggeringly easy. An easy he wouldn't have thought possible if he hadn't experienced it firsthand. He'd been on campus less than an hour before finding her. When he showed up sporting a university sweatshirt to try to fit in, he thought it would take days to track her down and a bit of old-fashioned force to get her into his car.

Instead, all it took was a Diet Coke in the campus commons. There he was, sipping his soda and scoping out the crowd, when she appeared at the ride board with her sad little flyer. It only got easier from there. Lie about going to Akron, flash her a smile, let her size him up and think she knew exactly what type of guy he was. It's a gift, his looks. The only valuable thing his father ever gave him. He's handsome, but not memorably so. A blank slate onto which people project whatever they want. And Charlie, he could tell, just wanted someone trustworthy to drive her home. She practically jumped into his car.

So incredibly easy.

He should have known things would eventually go wrong after that. That always seems to be the way. Sure, he messed up with Twenty Questions. But shit luck is to blame for everything else that happened tonight. So instead of cruising to their destination—which isn't Ohio; not even close—Charlie's with a stranger, maybe right now sharing her suspicions.

And she *is* suspicious. She got that way as soon as his wallet flopped open in her lap. He knows she saw his driver's license because she got all nervous immediately after.

Honestly, the only thing that's gone his way tonight is Charlie's mental state. He knew she'd be a little messed up. After what she went through, it would be weird if she wasn't. But this—this was unexpected.

Movies in her mind?

Talk about serendipity.

It allowed him to get out of the sticky situation caused by that game of Twenty Questions. Again, his fault. But he recovered quickly. He's good at thinking on his feet. He has to be.

When he saw that Charlie was about to jump from the car at the toll plaza, he decided to turn the stereo back on, restart the song, and pretend everything in the previous ten minutes—Twenty Questions, the mention of the tooth, those tense taps on the brakes when that damn state trooper came up behind them—hadn't really happened.

It was a wild, ridiculous idea. More of a Hail Mary pass than a rational plan. Yet he thinks Charlie really might have bought it. Thank God for small miracles, as his mom used to say.

Opening the Grand Am's driver's-side door, he slides behind the wheel and opens the center console. Inside, sitting among the empty plastic case for the Nirvana cassette, a scattering of loose change, and a pack of Juicy Fruit gum with one stick remaining, is his wallet. He grabs it and flips it open, coming face-to-face with his New Jersey license, which bears the same fake name as his New York and Delaware ones. He slides it out of its plastic sleeve, revealing another license behind it.

Pennsylvania.

Jake Collins.

He'd managed to switch them at the toll plaza. While chatting up the woman in the booth, piling on the charm, he had his wallet in hand, swapping out the real license with the fake one. Then he made sure Charlie saw it, hoping that, combined with her own fragile mental state, she'd believe everything else he told her.

And she did.

Possibly.

He's still worried about what might be going down in that bathroom, what Charlie might be saying to the Oldsmobile chick, what he might need to do because of it.

He gets out of the car, opens the trunk, and shoves aside Charlie's box and suitcases. He's certain that when she finds out where they're really going, Charlie will regret packing so much.

With her belongings out of the way, he grabs the things he wanted to keep her from seeing when he loaded her stuff into the trunk.

His own boxes.

One is cardboard, inside of which are license plates from New York, Delaware, and Pennsylvania. Unlike his driver's license, he remembered to switch those before heading off to pick up Charlie. He assumed she'd freak out if she didn't see a New Jersey plate on the car. Turns out she never even looked.

Beneath the license plates are several loops of rope in various lengths. Stuffed into a corner of the box is a white cloth that's longer than a handkerchief but shorter than a towel.

His trusty gag.

Next to the cardboard box is a metal tool kit. The same one his piece-of-shit dad kept in the garage when he was a kid. Now his dad is dead and the toolbox is his. He opens it and sifts through everything inside, pushing aside the claw hammer, the screwdrivers with their chisel-sharp tips, the pair of pliers.

Finally, he finds what he's looking for.

A set of handcuffs, the keys to which hang on the keychain in his pocket, and a knife. The knife isn't big. It's definitely not a hunting knife, although there's one of those sitting somewhere inside the toolbox.

This is a classic Swiss Army Knife. Suitable for every occasion and easy to hide.

He takes the cuffs and the knife and shuts the trunk. Before heading to the restrooms, he slides the knife into one front pocket of his jeans and the handcuffs into the other.

He doesn't want to use them.

But he will if he has to.

ELEVEN P.M.

INT. REST STOP BUILDING—NIGHT

Josh is there when Charlie leaves the bathroom.

Right there.

Inches from the door, his hand raised in a knock that never happens.

Charlie shrinks back, startled. A replay of the blond woman in the bathroom when she found Charlie in the stall.

"A woman outside said I should check on you. She said you're shit-faced." Josh pauses, thrusting his hands deep into his pockets. "So I have to ask. Are you, um, shit-faced?"

Charlie shakes her head, wishing she were. That, at least, would explain what's happening inside her head. But instead of drunk, she feels unmoored. Caught on a tide dragging her out to sea, even though she's paddling as hard as she can toward shore.

"It was just a misunderstanding," she says.

Josh responds with a curious head tilt. "A movie misunder-standing?"

"Of course."

They step outside, and Charlie sees that it's started snowing again. More flurries. As wispy as dust. Josh stops to catch one on his tongue, which is how Charlie knows the snow is real and not just her own personal snow globe à la *Citizen Kane.*

The fact that she's not even capable of discerning the weather on her own tells Charlie she's made the right decision. Yes, she has her suspicions about Josh, but they fade with each step taken toward the parking lot. He's still catching snowflakes, for God's sake, his tongue hanging out like a dog's. That's not something killers do. Kids do that. *Nice* people do that.

And Charlie's leaning into the idea that Josh could be nice, once you see past the lies he told her. Lies that he clearly regrets. Because before they climb back into the Grand Am, Josh looks at Charlie across the snow-dappled roof of the car and says, "I'm really sorry, by the way. I shouldn't have lied earlier. I should have been up front with you about everything, starting with when we met at the ride board. You have every right to not trust me."

"I do trust you," Charlie says, even though she doesn't. Not implicitly. The simple truth is that right now she trusts herself less.

As for Josh's lies, she chalks those up to loneliness and not malice. Charlie understands being lonely, having cut herself off from everyone but Robbie and Nana Norma. So she and Josh might as well be lonely together.

"We're good, then?" Josh says.

"I guess," Charlie says, which is about as honest an answer as she can muster.

"Then let's go."

Charlie gets into the car. Even if she does have lingering reservations, there are no other options. The one other car at the rest stop, an Oldsmobile idling on the far end of the parking lot, belongs to the woman Charlie encountered in the bathroom. She stands next to the car, smoking a cigarette, watching them leave.

As they pass, Charlie notices the concerned look on the woman's face, appearing and receding in a plume of smoke. It makes her wonder what else the woman told Josh while she was still in the bathroom. Did she mention Charlie's distrust? If not, does she now regret it? Should Charlie regret getting back into this car?

She tells herself no. That everything is fine. That she should follow the woman's advice and have some coffee to clear her head. Then she'll settle in for a long, uneventful trip home.

Josh apparently has other ideas.

"So what kind of movie was it?" he says. "Must have been a doozy if that woman thought you were on the sauce."

Charlie can still picture Maddy standing before the mirror, putting on that lipstick as bright as blood. Even worse, she can still hear her voice.

You shouldn't have abandoned me.

"I don't want to talk about it," she says.

"Must have been a bad one," Josh says.

"It was."

Charlie wants to forget all about it. And she certainly has no intention of rehashing it with Josh.

"Be honest now," he says. "Was it really that bad? Or do you not want to tell me because you still don't trust me?"

"I trust people I know."

"Then get to know me." A genial smile creeps across Josh's face. "Maybe we really should play Twenty Questions."

Charlie doesn't smile back. She's still too unnerved by the fact that she imagined an entire game of Twenty Questions. That a movie in her mind lasted that long. That a whole chunk of time was lost.

"I'd rather not," she says.

"Then let's do one question each," Josh suggests. "I ask you something, and then you ask me something."

"You already know enough about me."

"You haven't told me about your parents."

"What about them?" Charlie says.

"They died in a car accident, right?"

Charlie's jolted by the question. To mask her unease, she takes a sip of coffee and focuses on the snow hitting the windshield. "How did you know that?"

"I didn't," Josh says. "I just assumed it."

"Fine. How did you *assume* that?"

"Because you mentioned that you live with your grandmother, which tells me your parents are no longer alive. You also said you don't drive, which I assumed was a choice and not because you're physically incapable of it. Putting all that together, I came to the conclusion that you don't drive because your parents were killed in a car accident. Turns out I was right."

A prickle of annoyance joins Charlie's sense of unease. That's a lot of assumptions on his part. That they're all true doesn't make it feel any less intrusive.

"By that logic, I'm going to assume that since you haven't mentioned your mother, it means she's dead, too."

"She might be," Josh says. "I don't know. She left when I was eight. I haven't seen or heard from her since."

Charlie doesn't know what to say to that, so she says nothing.

"It was Halloween," Josh says. "I remember because I dressed up as Batman that year. And it was a real costume, too. Not one of those cheap masks and plastic capes you get at the drugstore. My mother spent weeks making it for me. She was good with a sewing machine, I'll give her that. She made a great costume. I was so excited to show it off, you know? I couldn't wait for people to see me as Batman."

"Why all this excitement about Batman?"

"Because he was the coolest."

"Batman?" Charlie says, incredulous. She's seen both the cheesy sixties TV show and the dark, dour Tim Burton movie. Neither of those Batmen struck her as particularly cool.

"To an eight-year-old, yeah," Josh says. "Especially one who felt a little weird and awkward and whose parents wouldn't stop fighting."

His voice grows soft, confessional.

"When I'd see my dad start drinking and my mom get that disapproving look in her eyes, I knew it was only a matter of time before a fight broke out. So whenever that happened, I'd grab some Batman comic, crawl under the covers, and pretend I was inside that comic book, moving from panel to panel. It didn't matter if I was scared that the Joker or the Riddler was trying to get me. It was better than being in that house with those people screaming at each other downstairs."

"They were like movies in your mind," Charlie says.

"I guess so," Josh says. "My version of it, yeah. So I was desperate to actually *be* Batman for a night. I put the costume on and my dad took me out trick-or-treating and I got more candy that year than I ever had before. And I knew it was because of that costume. Because of how great it looked. When we got home, my arms were tired from carrying all that candy."

Josh gives a small, sad chuckle.

"And my mother, well, she was gone. While we were out, she'd collected a few things, threw them in a suitcase, and left. She wrote a note. 'I'm sorry.' That's all it said. No explanation. No way to contact her. Just that meager apology. It was like she had just vanished. And I know, that's what all deaths feel like. The person is there and then they're not and you have to adjust to life without them. But what made it so hard was that my mother *chose* to leave. She planned to go that way—without a goodbye. I know because of the costume. She'd never spent that much time on one before, and I think it's because she had already made up her mind that she was going to leave. And so she put all her love and attention into that one stupid Batman costume, because she knew it would be the last thing she ever did for me."

He stops talking, letting his story—that long, sad tale—linger in the car like smoke.

"Do you still miss her?" Charlie says.

"Sometimes. Do you still miss your parents?"

Charlie nods. "And I miss Maddy."

What she doesn't say, because she'd never admit it to anyone, is that she misses Maddy more than her parents. It's not something she's proud of. She certainly doesn't feel good about feeling this way, but it's the truth. She is very much her parents' daughter. Her father was quiet and prone to introspection, and so is she. Her mother, just like Charlie, was an enthusiastic movie lover, courtesy of Nana Norma. Charlie has her father's hazel eyes and her mother's pert nose, and she sees them every time she looks in the mirror. They are always with her, which goes a long way toward lessening the pain of losing them.

But Maddy was something different. As foreign and exotic to Charlie as a tropical flower growing in the desert. Bright and beautiful and rare. It's why her loss stings more and why Charlie feels so guilty about it. She'll never meet another Maddy.

"Why did you tell me that story?" she asks Josh.

"Because I wanted you to get to know me."

"So I'd trust you?"

"Maybe," Josh says. "Did it work?"

"Maybe," Charlie replies.

Josh hits the wipers, swiping away the gathering snow, and shifts the car into a lower gear, helping it climb the slow but steady rise of the highway.

Charlie's familiar with this stretch of road.

The Poconos.

The place where Maddy had been born and raised.

The place from which she hoped to escape.

They pass a faded billboard advertising one of those big honeymoon resorts that had been all the rage in the fifties and sixties.

This one is decidedly rustic. With timber-studded walls and a roof of green slate, it resembles a massive log cabin. Mountain Oasis Lodge, it's called. Or used to be. A conspicuous white banner with black print has been slapped over the image of the lodge.

ENJOY OUR LAST SEASON!

Judging by the state of the banner—frayed at the corners and faded, though not quite as much as the rest of the billboard—Charlie assumes the resort's last season ended several summers ago.

Maddy's grandmother had worked at a place like that until it went belly-up in the late eighties. Maddy had regaled her with stories of visiting her grandmother at work—running through empty ballrooms, sneaking into vacant rooms, sprawling across round beds with mirrored ceilings and scrambling inside bathtubs shaped like giant hearts.

Tawdry.

That's how Maddy described the place. "It tried so hard to be sexy, but it was, like, the worst, cheapest kind of sexy. The hotel version of crotchless panties."

It hadn't always been like this, Charlie knew. Maddy had also told her about the Poconos that existed a couple of generations before they were born. Back then, movie stars often motored the short distance from New York for a few days of fishing, hiking, and boating, rubbing elbows with working-class couples from Philadelphia, Scranton, Levittown. Maddy had shown her a picture of her grandmother posing poolside with Bob Hope.

"She met Bing Crosby, too," Maddy said. "Not together, though. Now that would have been the cat's meow."

Charlie sighs and looks out the window, at the trees skating by in gray blurs.

Like ghosts.

It makes her think of all the people who've died on this highway.

People like her parents. Killed in explosions of glass. Torched in fiery wrecks. Crushed under tons of twisted metal. Now their spirits are stuck here, haunting the side of the road, forever forced to watch others drive by to destinations they failed to reach.

She sighs again, loud enough for Josh to say, "You getting carsick again?"

"No. I'm just—"

Charlie's voice seizes up, the words clogged in her throat like a hard candy that's been swallowed.

She never told Josh she felt carsick.

Not for real.

That was during a movie in her mind, one she only half-remembers now that she knows it didn't really happen. The state trooper coming up on their right. Charlie's covert breaths fogging the window. Her index finger slicing across the glass.

But if it didn't really happen—if it was all in her head—how does Josh know about it?

Charlie's mind starts whirling, clicking like an old movie projector. It spins out a thought. One that should have arrived much sooner.

"Come as You Are" had just started playing before she dropped into that long, vivid mental movie and was still playing when she woke from it.

That makes sense. Charlie had once read that dreams that feel like hours can pass in mere minutes, and she assumes the same is true for movies in her mind. The song started, the movie unspooled in her thoughts, and when it was over, "Come as You Are" was still playing.

But when Charlie snapped out of the alleged movie in her mind, it was still the beginning of the song that she had heard. That definitely doesn't make sense, especially since Josh told her she'd been zoned out for more than five minutes.

Then there's the distance they traveled during that time. On the

map at the rest stop, it would have been about the width of her index finger, which meant it was miles when blown up to full scale.
Far more ground than can be covered during the course of a single
song, let alone a few seconds.

Which means the music hadn't been continuous.

Josh had indeed turned off the stereo.

Charlie watched him do it. It hadn't all been in her head, like he
led her to believe. It was real. It *happened.*

And if that was real, then what immediately followed might also
be real. Including Twenty Questions.

Let's play, Josh had said.

Those questions might not have been just her thoughts. They
might not have been only dialogue in her mind.

There's a chance that she truly *spoke* them. Which means there's
also a chance Josh answered them until she winnowed it down to a
single object that on the surface is so innocent but turns out to be
terrifying with the proper context.

A tooth.

"You're just what?" Josh says, reminding Charlie that she never
finished her sentence.

"Tired," she says. "So tired."

The word clouds the window. Just a tad. In that wisp of fog on
the glass, Charlie can make out the edge of what appears to be a
letter.

Her eyes go wide.

In shock.

In fear.

Her heart does the opposite. It contracts, shrinking into her
chest the way a turtle retreats into its shell, trying to avoid the
threat it senses is coming. But Charlie knows it's too late. The
threat is already here.

She confirms it by saying three more words heavy on the sibilant syllables.

"Just so exhausted."

The fog on the window grows. An expanding gray circle.

Inside it, clearly scrawled by her unsteady finger, is a single word. Written backward. Readable to someone on the outside looking in.

HELP

INT. GRAND AM—NIGHT

Charlie stares at the word, her right eye twitching, as if it no longer wants to look at it. It's the twitch that tells her this isn't a movie in her mind.

That doesn't keep her from wishing, hoping, praying, begging that she's wrong. If there's one single right time to have what she's experiencing not be real, now is that moment. But the snow is still smacking the windshield and the wipers are still moving and Josh is still behind the wheel and the fog on the window is still receding and the word is still clinging to the glass and Charlie knows that all of it is real.

It's *always* been real.

Josh lied to her. About everything.

And she let him. Hell, she helped him do it. By doubting her own mind. By appearing so obviously fragile. By making him think he could do and say anything and she'd believe it. It's literally the plot of a movie.

Gaslight.

Even though she's seen it several times, it still didn't stop her from completely falling for it in real life. She'd be furious if she wasn't so scared. But anger takes a back seat to fear. Because there's only one reason Charlie can think of for why Josh would do such a thing.

He's the Campus Killer.

Not could be. Not may be.

He simply *is*. Charlie has no doubt about that now. Her gut, which so far tonight has been a better guide than her brain, tells her he has to be. He knows about the tooth, which right there is enough to convict him in her mind. Then there's the fact that he told her he's lived near Olyphant for the past four years, which is how long the Campus Killer's been at large.

Angela Dunleavy. Four years ago.

Taylor Morrison. Two and a half years ago.

Madeline Forrester. Two months ago.

Stabbed. Killed. A pulled tooth their killer's trophy.

Charlie has no illusion that he won't try to do the same to her. He will. It's the reason she's here. This is no gob-smacking coincidence. It was intentional on Josh's part. He sought her out.

He might try to come for you next.

And so he has.

Even worse is how Charlie made it so easy for him. All he needed to do was show up at the ride board, flash that movie-star smile, and offer to drive her away from her pain and guilt. Charlie did the rest.

She considers the possibility that it would have happened anyway. That eventually she would have ended up in this precise situation no matter what she did. Earlier she thought that she deserved such a scenario. Maybe fate agreed and had this all planned out. Payback for failing to save Maddy.

What's important now isn't how it happened, or why. It's that Charlie needs to find a way out of the situation. If there is a way out. She suspects this is what a mouse must feel as the trap starts to snap shut. Too late to run. Too late to change your actions. Far too late to undo your own undoing. Just a grim acceptance right before the crunch.

"You're quiet again," Josh says, acting all innocent. As if nothing is wrong. As if he's not a complete monster. "You sure you're not getting carsick?"

Charlie feels sick, although it's not from the car. But she doesn't mind letting Josh think that. It's better than him thinking she knows all the horrible things he's done. That she's terrified by that knowledge. That it has her so scared she's shocked she hasn't puked.

Yet a wild, dangerous part of her wants to tell him she knows who he is and what he's done. Clearly, Josh is toying with her. The lies. The music. The flirting. It's all because he enjoys playing with her emotions. Why not come clean now and deny him that satisfaction?

Because then there'll be nothing left to do but kill her.

Charlie fears—with a quivering depth she didn't know was possible—that the reason Josh lured her into his car and onto the highway is because it makes it easier for him. All he needs to do is swerve onto the side of the road, slit her throat, and shove her out of the car. He wouldn't even have to turn off the engine. And by the time someone noticed Charlie bleeding to death on the rumble strip, Josh would be miles away.

The scared, sensible part of her knows it's best not to reveal anything.

The smartest, bravest, most careful course of action is to pretend she doesn't know a thing. Maybe he won't try to harm her until he's certain she knows who he really is. Maybe he's patient and vowed to wait as long as it takes. Maybe Charlie can pretend long enough to get away.

But where?

That's the problem.

There's no place to get away to. They're in the middle of the

Poconos, with no other cars in sight. The Grand Am speeds down the center lane of the highway, going seventy in spite of the snow. Charlie knows she can't leap from the car, no matter that her hand is back on the door handle and her legs are now twitching as much as her eye and that even her shrunken, terrified heart seems to beg her to do it with every frantic beat.

She tells herself Josh can't hurt her when they're going this fast.

She tells herself that she's safe as long as the car's in motion.

She tells herself that when the Grand Am starts to slow—and it will at some point; it has to—she'll hop out and run like she should have done back at the toll plaza.

"Did you hear me?" Josh says, insistent. "I asked if you're sure you're not getting carsick."

Charlie sits completely still. She should say something. No, she *needs* to say something. But her tongue sits dead inside her mouth, useless. After a few more seconds of struggle, she's able to croak out a word.

"Yes."

"I don't believe you."

She almost snorts out a bitter laugh. The feeling is mutual. But then Josh says, "Let's get off the highway," and the laugh withers in the back of Charlie's throat.

"Why?" she says.

"To look for a place to eat."

"I'm not hungry."

"I am," Josh says. "And I think some food will do you good."

Charlie knows it's all a ruse and that it's time for the inevitable. The moment they've been leading up to since she first got into the car.

An exit ramp appears, and Josh slides the car into the right lane. Charlie tells herself to stay calm.

Don't let him know she knows.

If she can do that, then maybe she'll be okay.

But Charlie's not sure she *can* do that. Not with the Grand Am sliding off the exit ramp and onto a road far different from the interstate. Once they get past the competing gas stations and a shuttered Burger King clustered near the off-ramp, it becomes just two lanes of blacktop slicing through mountain woods, dark as far as the eye can see. The road is devoid of other cars. It's just them and the woods and the dark night and the snowfall trickling to a halt.

Charlie tenses when she sees a street sign bearing the name of the road for which they traded the highway.

Dead River Road.

Not the name of a place anyone would willingly go. It sounds to Charlie like the name of a place people try to avoid. A place frequented only by the lost or unsuspecting.

But Josh doesn't seem lost. He seems to know exactly where they're going, steering the car confidently through the forest, the sweep of the headlights brightening the trees that hug the side of the road. Charlie assumes this is because he has a spot already picked out. He's done his research.

She knows now is the time to act and she should finally make a leap from the car. But fear, that heavy, unwieldy thing, keeps her pinned in place.

Charlie wonders if Maddy was in this same situation two months ago. She hopes not. She hopes Maddy had no idea what was about to happen to her. That the last moments of her life were as grand and vivacious as she was.

"We should turn around," Charlie says, her voice robotic because she's trying to keep her fear from peeking through. "There's nothing here."

"There is," Josh says. "I saw a sign for a place back on the highway."

The only sign Charlie remembers seeing is the billboard for that now-defunct lodge.

"It's late," she says. "The place is probably closed."

Josh remains focused on the road, driving with his fingers tight around the wheel and his forearms rigid. "It might still be open."

Charlie keeps disagreeing, because it's all she can do at the moment, even though it's clear Josh isn't going to listen to her.

"It's so late and we've wasted so much time and I just want to go home."

Her voice breaks on the last word. A bit of sadness slicing through it.

Home.

Nana Norma is there right now, probably waiting up for her. Charlie pictures her on the couch in a robe and nightgown, nursing a bourbon, her eyeglasses reflecting a Busby Berkeley musical playing on the TV. The thought makes her heart crack just like her voice.

Arriving on the heels of that desperate ache is an urge to fight. A surprise to Charlie, who'd spent so much of this drive thinking only of flight.

But fighting might be her only choice.

Hurt Josh before he can hurt her.

Charlie looks down at the backpack at her feet. Inside are things that would normally be found in a purse. Her wallet, spare change, tissues, and chewing gum. Gone is the pepper spray Nana Norma had given her when she left for Olyphant. Charlie lost that more than a year ago and never thought to replace it. All that leaves for self-defense is her keys, which jingle at the bottom of the backpack as Charlie picks it up.

She unzips the bag and reaches inside, feeling for the keys. They aren't much. Certainly not as good as pepper spray. But if she holds them with the keys poking out from between her fingers, Freddy Krueger–style, she might be able to fight off an attack from Josh.

Not that Josh looks remotely close to attacking. Calm behind the wheel, he points to the horizon, where the sky is lightened by a soft electric glow. Within seconds, a diner comes into view. One so traditional Charlie thinks it could be mistaken for part of a film set.

Chrome siding runs below the diner's wide front windows, beyond which are red booths and blue tables. A sign hangs on the front door—red-on-black letters telling them that, yes, they're open. There's another sign on the roof. Neon. It spells out the name of the place. The Skyline Grille. The "e" on the end flickers slightly, like even it knows it's unnecessary.

"Told you there was a place open," Josh says as he steers the Grand Am into the parking lot. "You need to trust people more, Charlie."

Charlie gives a wary nod, knowing the opposite is true. Trust is what got her into this situation. A heaping dose of suspicion would have helped her avoid it entirely.

As Josh pulls into a parking spot, Charlie sizes up the situation. It leaves her stumped. For reasons Charlie can't begin to understand, Josh brought her to a place where help is within reach.

"Ready to eat?" he says. "I don't know about you, but I'm starving."

They get out of the car, Josh a few feet ahead of her. As they cross the parking lot, Charlie cradles her backpack and ponders what to do next. It would make sense to end things immediately. Just burst into the diner and scream that Josh is trying to kill her, that he's killed before, that he'll keep doing it until someone stops him.

There are three other cars in the parking lot. A black Ford pickup, a boxy compact car, and a powder-blue Cadillac deVille with a dent in the driver's-side door. She wonders if the driver of at least one of them is capable of restraining Josh. He's a big guy. Strong. It'll take someone equally as big and strong to subdue him, and Charlie doubts the drivers of the compact car and the Cadillac are up to the task. That leaves the pickup driver.

If he believes her.

Charlie knows full well that bursting into the diner shouting about serial killers will likely make people think she's the troublesome one. They'll assume she's drunk or crazy or a combination of the two, just like the woman in the rest stop bathroom. Charlie remembers the way that woman looked at her. So skeptical, so unwilling to help. There's nothing to suggest the staff and patrons of the Skyline Grille won't be the same way. She's sure she has the same desperate, deranged look she had at the rest stop. That might make it hard to convince someone to help. People don't want to believe that a fellow human being is capable of such vicious cruelty. They want to think everyone they meet is just like them.

Nice.

That's what Charlie thought about Josh when they met at the ride board. Hell, it's what she thought at the rest stop, when he caught a snowflake on his tongue and she decided getting into the car with him—again—was the wisest course of action.

She was wrong.

Just like she could be wrong that someone in the diner won't believe her.

But if no one does—if they look at her the same way the woman in the rest stop bathroom did—then all Charlie will have accomplished is tipping off Josh that she knows what kind of person he is.

Not nice. Even though he's doing something nice right now by holding the diner's front door open for her.

As she walks toward the door, she sees that a better option—a smarter, braver, more careful one—sits outside the diner, by the side of the building, a few feet from the front right corner.

A pay phone. Hopefully in working order.

Charlie can excuse herself, come outside, and call the police, who'll have to believe her. That's their job. Some cop will be dispatched to the diner, and Charlie will be outside waiting, ready to tell them everything she knows about Josh. If they still think she's lying and Josh fools them just like he fooled her, she'll make a scene. Let them think she's drunk or crazy. A jail cell and a drunk and disorderly charge are far better than what Josh has planned.

She's made up her mind.

Pay phone it is.

All she needs to do now is get away from Josh long enough to use it.

INT. DINER—NIGHT

The diner is mostly empty. Just a waitress, an unseen cook in the back, and a couple in a booth by the window. The couple—a man and woman in their late twenties—have a boozy weariness to them, which won't be much help to her.

Neither will the waitress, who looks to be well past sixty. She's got high hair, coral lipstick, and age-spotted arms that poke like sticks from the sleeves of her mint-green uniform.

"Sit anywhere you want," she says as she rearranges the pies inside a glass dessert case near the door. "I'll be there in a jiff."

Charlie makes a move to the left side of the diner, where the couple sits, hoping to snag the booth next to theirs. Safety in numbers. But the woman chooses that moment to let out a drunken cackle, sending Josh to a corner booth on the opposite end of the diner, next to a jukebox pushed against the wall. Charlie has no choice but to join him.

She leaves her coat on after sliding into the booth across from Josh. Since she'll be going right back outside to make a phone call, she sees no point in removing it. There's the added bonus that, like a bullfighter's cape, its bright red has attracted the attention of others in the diner. Normally, Charlie hates feeling conspicuous, but now she appreciates the attention. If all eyes are on her, then Josh will have to be on his best behavior.

That moment of something working in her favor lasts only a few seconds. Because as soon as she's situated, Charlie looks out the window and her heart sinks into her stomach, which sinks to the diner floor.

The pay phone is right outside.

Just on the other side of the glass.

In full view of Josh.

Inches from him.

Charlie takes a breath, trying to stay calm. Maybe she should change her mind and make a scene anyway. She does another quick sizing up of the rest of the diner. The couple in the opposite corner is shrugging on coats and slipping on gloves, clearly preparing to leave. The woman—the drunker of the two—gets her hair caught in her scarf and barks out another laugh.

"You okay to drive, hon?" the waitress says as they pass her on their way out.

"We're fine," the man says.

"Suit yourself," the waitress says. Under her breath, she adds, "But if you wrap your damn car around a tree, don't say I didn't warn you."

Charlie watches the waitress watch the couple climb into the compact car parked outside and pull away. She respects the way the woman is looking out for others. That flinty concern might be needed if Charlie decides to abandon the phone call idea and straight-up ask for help.

The waitress closes the dessert case and flips a switch. It lights up like a window display at Christmas, the three levels of pies inside slowly rotating. Grabbing two menus, the waitress then makes her way to their table.

She looks familiar, but in a way Charlie can't place. Like a character actress she sees on a TV show and then spends the rest of the
night trying to think of what else she's been in. Charlie assumes it's
because she's a walking, talking stereotype of a movie waitress,
right down to the pencil tucked behind her ear.

Still, she makes note of her name tag.

Marge.

"What can I get you kids to drink?" she says with a noticeable
smoker's rasp.

Josh orders a Coke and a coffee. Charlie orders a cup of hot tea.

"Scalding-hot, please," she says, thinking ahead, picturing a scenario in which she has to throw it in Josh's face in order to make a
quick escape.

Marge, clearly a pro, doesn't need to jot it down. "Hot as Hades,"
she says. "Coming right up."

She leaves them to peruse the menu, which is encased in a plastic
sleeve that reminds Charlie of the license in Josh's wallet. Although
she suspects it's really Jake's wallet. Like their game of Twenty
Questions, she no longer thinks it was a movie-in-her-mind situation. It's more likely that Josh switched licenses at some point,
probably at the toll plaza while talking to the toll collector. He's
smart. She'll give him that.

She needs to be smarter.

"What are you going to have?" Josh says.

Charlie scans the menu, her stomach roiling at the thought of
eating anything. But she needs to order something to keep Josh
from getting suspicious. She settles on a plate of fries, thinking that
maybe she can manage to force one down if she needs to.

Marge returns with their drinks, setting a cup in front of Charlie, the water inside it still unsettled, as if it's just stopped boiling.
It's followed by a Lipton tea bag, a lemon slice in a tiny bowl, and
two plastic containers of creamer.

"Sugar's by the condiments," she says. "And be careful, hon. Don't burn yourself."

Charlie rips open the tea bag and drops it into the water. The cup's so scorching that even the handle is hot. She curls her fingers around it anyway, the heat on her skin the only thing preventing her from lifting the cup and tossing the contents at Josh.

She pictures it. More fantasy than a movie in her mind. The tea flying. Josh screaming, then recoiling, then falling out of the booth as Charlie runs. The fantasy ends when Marge comes back with Josh's drinks and says, "What'll it be?"

"Just an order of fries, please," Charlie says.

Marge grabs the pencil tucked behind her ear and pulls a small order pad from her deep apron pocket. "Gravy on the side?"

"Just plain."

Marge looks to Josh. "Your turn, handsome."

"What's your blue-plate special?" he asks, still studying the menu.

"Salisbury steak," Marge says.

Josh hands her the menu. "Sounds good."

"Sure thing, sugar," Marge says before departing with a wink.

She disappears through a swinging door with a circular window located at the rear of the diner. Through the window, Charlie can see Marge's high hair bobbing as she gives their order to the invisible cook.

It's just her and Josh now, alone again.

"This place needs some music," Josh says as he slides from the booth and walks to the jukebox. It's old and bulky, like the one in *Happy Days*. Josh drops in a couple of quarters and makes his selections.

First up is Don McLean.

"American Pie."

When he returns to the booth, Charlie knows it's time to move.

She had a plan. She needs to make it happen. Grabbing her back-pack, she gestures to the pay phone outside the window.

"I'm going to call my boyfriend real quick," she says. "He asked me to check in from the road. Be right back."

She slides out of the booth and heads to the door, forcing herself to go slow and not appear too eager. Josh is watching her. She knows that. He's been doing it all night. Watching her even when it looks like he's not. It's how he's been able to predict her every move.

But that'll be ending very soon.

Now, she's about to get away.

EXT. DINER—NIGHT

Charlie corrects herself as soon as she gets outside.

She's not about to get away. She's already gone. Out the door and walking to the pay phone. All that's left to do is call the police, tell them to hurry, and then wait outside the few minutes it takes for them to arrive.

Charlie rounds the corner of the diner and stops in front of the pay phone. Josh sits just on the other side of the window, sipping his coffee, not even looking her way.

Good.

She lifts the receiver from its cradle, bringing the steady hum of a dial tone to her ears. Then she pauses, unsure what to do next. She's never called 911 on a pay phone before. Does she need to insert coins? Does she press 0 for the operator? Or does she just dial 911 and hope someone will answer?

With the dial tone still buzzing insistently, she opts for the latter.

She presses 9.

She presses 1.

She presses 1 a second time, shooting a nervous glance at the window.

The booth is empty.

Josh is no longer there.

Charlie's heart stops at the same time the receiver lets out a light click. A 911 dispatcher answering her call. But to Charlie, it's the sound of fear taking her in its grip.

"Nine-one-one. What's your emergency?" the dispatcher says.

Charlie stays silent. Partly because she's terrified and partly because she senses someone nearby, hovering by the corner of the diner, startlingly close.

Josh.

Charlie slams the phone back in its cradle as Josh emerges fully around the side of the building.

"Something wrong?" he says.

Charlie wills herself to speak. She has no choice. Trying with all her might to keep her tone even, she says, "I dialed the wrong number."

"You don't know your boyfriend's number?"

"My finger slipped," she says with a silly-me shrug.

"You're not going to try again?"

Charlie lifts her backpack. "I'm all out of change."

"Allow me." Josh reaches into his pocket and pulls out a handful of coins, which he holds out to her. Charlie takes them, even though the feel of Josh's skin on hers prompts an internal cringe she hopes doesn't make its presence known on the outside.

Stay smart.

Stay brave.

Stay careful.

"Thanks," she says, the coins hot in her palm. So hot they feel like coal, glowing orange. She resists the urge to drop them to the ground.

"Go on and call him." Josh jerks his head toward the phone. "Don't mind me. Just here for some fresh air."

Charlie has to call Robbie now. There's no other choice. If she dials 911, Josh will hear every word she says and could easily make sure she's no longer here when the police arrive. She knows how small she is, how weak. It would take Josh no effort at all to grab her and drag her back into the Grand Am. Or, worse, he could just stab her right here in the parking lot. End it all with a few quick jabs of a knife, yank a tooth out of her mouth, and be gone.

Charlie dials quickly, pressing the numbers through muscle memory. Because of course she knows Robbie's number by heart. Josh is right about that. She couldn't misdial if she tried.

Through the receiver, she hears a recorded voice instruct her to insert seventy-five cents into the phone. Charlie does, her fingers trembling so hard it's a struggle to get one quarter into the pay slot, let alone three. With the coins deposited, each one landing deep inside the phone with a metallic clang, the phone begins to ring.

One ring.

Charlie looks to Josh, who's backed away a few feet. Standing at the corner of the diner, he has his hands thrust deep in his pockets.

Two rings.

Josh glances her way, smiles, looks to the sky.

Three rings.

Josh begins to whistle. A light, impatient trill. Hearing it reminds her of Uncle Charlie in *Shadow of a Doubt*. He whistled, too. A tune different from Josh's, but just as unnerving.

Robbie answers on the fourth ring, croaking out a groggy hello.

"Hey, it's me." Charlie knows her voice sounds off. Tremulous. A tad too quiet. "Just checking in from the road."

"How's the drive? Smooth sailing, sweetheart?"

Charlie shoots a glance at Josh. Even though he doesn't appear to be listening, she knows he is. The whistling has stopped.

"Actually, things took a detour."

"Very funny," Robbie says.

"I'm serious," Charlie says, sounding the opposite of serious. Because she has to. Because she knows that Josh is paying attention to every word. "We're no longer on the highway."

"I don't understand," Robbie says. "Where are you? What's going on?"

"I can't talk long. Just wanted to say hi."

"Charlie, I need you to tell me what's happening." Robbie sounds panicked now. It streaks through every word. "Just give me a hint."

"Oh, you know, we were driving along, got hungry, and decided to get off the highway," Charlie says, faking a smile and hoping that, like Robbie, it comes through in her voice. Not for his sake. And certainly not for hers.

It's for Josh, who's back to staring up at the sky, his hands still in his pockets.

"Where?" Robbie says. "Can you tell me?"

"The Poconos. We're at the cutest diner. It's called the Skyline Grille."

She hopes Robbie's writing this all down. Or at least committing it to memory. And as soon as she hangs up, she hopes he calls the police.

"Can you get away?" he says.

"Not at the moment. Our food's almost ready."

"Shit." Robbie pauses, helpless. "How can I help? Tell me what to do."

Charlie doesn't know how to respond. She's all out of code words. They hadn't taken it further than this because, honestly, it was all a joke. Just something Robbie came up with to ease the pain of her departure. But now her life might literally depend on what she says next.

"You should watch a movie," she says. "*Shadow of a Doubt.*"

She hopes Robbie gets the hint. He's seen the movie, of course.

She made him watch it their first month of dating so he'd understand how she got her name. Now she hopes he understands that the film's plot is coming true. Life imitating art in the worst kind of way.

"I should be home in about four hours," she says, this time completely for Josh's benefit. A not-so-subtle reminder that her boyfriend expects her to be home by a certain hour and will be worried if she isn't. "I'll call you when I get there."

"Charlie, wait—"

She hangs up before Robbie can say anything else, unable to bear hearing him sound so frantic and helpless. She also wanted to avoid a maudlin goodbye. There'll be no last words from her tonight. Not if she can help it.

"You all done?" Josh says.

Charlie nods.

"Good. It's cold out here." Josh flashes her that perfect smile. "Don't want you to catch your death."

INT. ROBBIE'S APARTMENT—NIGHT

Robbie still grips the phone, even though a full minute has passed since Charlie hung up on him. A recent birthday gift from his parents, it's one of those new, expensive cordless phones he thought were pointless. But now Robbie sees its purpose. It lets him pace the bedroom unhindered by a tangled cord.

And pace he does.

Back and forth.

Back and forth.

Hard enough to wear down the carpet if he paced long enough, if he did nothing. But he knows that's not an option. He has to do *something.*

So he dials *69 to call back the last number that called him.

He keeps pacing as the phone rings.

Back and forth.

Back and forth.

Five minutes ago, he'd been sound asleep, lost in a dream he can no longer remember.

Then the phone on his nightstand rang, yanking him like a fishhook back to the present. He took his sweet time answering, resentful of the phone for waking him, even though he knew it was likely Charlie checking in like he asked her to do. He was tempted to ignore it and just let the phone keep ringing. Because Charlie was right. They were going from New Jersey to Ohio. As boring a drive as exists in this country.

But that's not the only reason Robbie was slow to answer. Charlie had left him, after all. Not officially. But Robbie knows that's what's happening. A long, slow, painful uncoupling as opposed to a clean break. And he spent the rest of the night feeling sad and self-pitying about that.

So when the phone rang and he assumed it was Charlie, a petty, wounded part of him didn't want to pick up. He thought that maybe if he let the call go unanswered, Charlie might think he wasn't home. That he was out at one of Olyphant's many off-campus bars, chatting up one of the many drunk co-eds all too willing to go home with him. And that if she thought that, it would make her jealous. And that if she was jealous, then she might also start to miss him. And that if she missed him enough, then maybe she'd decide to come back to him.

Robbie ended up answering—as he knew he would.

Charlie was too special to ignore.

So he grabbed the phone and said hello and prepared himself for a quick check-in and maybe some awkward small talk. He certainly didn't expect what came next. That dire code he had devised as a joke.

Things took a detour.

At first, he thought Charlie was kidding. A bit of movie-based humor to signify she still loved him and was still thinking about him. But then Charlie said, "I'm serious," and everything changed.

So now he's here, pacing.

Back and forth.

Back and forth.

Meanwhile the phone keeps ringing and he keeps hoping that Charlie will pick up and tell him it was all just a joke, that everything is fine, that it's smooth sailing, sweetheart.

When the fifth ring goes unanswered, Robbie ends the call, stops pacing, decides on another course of action.

He dials 411. Trusty, reliable information. This time, someone answers. Robbie gives them the name of the diner Charlie told him she was at, says it's somewhere in Pennsylvania, and asks where, exactly, it might be located. The operator, God bless her, comes through in a jiff.

Monroe County. Peak Township. Dead River Road.

"Do you also have the phone number for the Peak Township police department handy?" Robbie says.

The operator does. She connects them. Two rings later he's on the phone with a local dispatcher.

"I'm worried about my girlfriend," he says. "I think she's in trouble."

"What kind of trouble, sir?"

"I don't know."

"Is she there with you?"

"No," Robbie says. "She's in the Poconos. In your town. At a diner called the Skyline Grille."

"She contacted you from there?"

"Yes."

"Did she say she was in danger?"

"Not explicitly," Robbie says. "She had to be vague. There's a man with her. I think he was listening in. They were supposed to be driving to Ohio together and they got off the interstate and now they're at a diner."

The dispatcher's voice, so calm and efficient seconds earlier, sours into skepticism. "Sir, that's hardly an emergency."

"It *is*," Robbie says.

Charlie told him to watch *Shadow of a Doubt*, which he assumed was another code. The main character's name was Charlie, for God's sake. And since *that* Charlie had figured out her uncle was a killer, Robbie took it to mean that *his* Charlie learned the same thing about the man she was riding with.

"Please believe me," he says. "This guy she's with, she doesn't know him. And I think she's afraid of him. I think she could be in real danger. Could you please just send a cop over there to see if she's okay?"

"What's your girlfriend's name?" the dispatcher says, her voice softening again.

"Charlie."

"Charlie?"

"Yes," Robbie says. "It's a long story."

"Sir, this whole call has been a long story." The dispatcher sighs. "I'll try to send an officer there to check things out."

Robbie hangs up without thanking her, a bit of rudeness that he assumes can be excused, considering the circumstances. Besides, she merely said she'd *try* to send a cop to the diner, which means it might not happen soon. Or at all. And Charlie could be in danger right now.

He gets dressed, throwing on a T-shirt, socks, and shoes, opting not to switch out his sweatpants for jeans. On his way out the door, he grabs his coat, his wallet, and his cars keys.

He needs to do more than stay here, pacing back and forth, back and forth, hoping Charlie will call him again.

He needs to act.

And with a lot of miles between the two of them, there's no time to waste.

INT. DINER—NIGHT

The jukebox is still playing when they return indoors, although Don McLean's no longer saying bye, bye to Miss American Pie and the Beatles are instead saying hey to Jude. At Josh's overly polite insistence, Charlie enters first, marching inside feeling both defeated and frightened.

That didn't go at all like she planned. Now she has no idea what to do next. The only other option, short of running out of the diner and hoping Josh doesn't catch up to her, is to tell Marge.

Which isn't much of an option at all.

Marge, despite a formidable combo of tip-garnering sass and grandmotherly concern, is no match for Josh. He'd hurt her, if he needed to. And then he'd hurt Charlie. And then it would be over.

As for the cook, Charlie hasn't even seen him. Unless he's a former professional wrestler, she doubts he's going to be much help.

She returns to the table because, for now, it's all she can do. She'll tuck herself into the booth, pretend to not be terrified out of her mind, and try to come up with a new plan. Meanwhile, she'll continue to hope that Robbie got the hint and called the police and that in five minutes this place will be swarming with cops.

Outside, the pay phone begins to ring. Charlie hears it, sounding tinny through the window's glass. Josh hears it, too, and gives her a questioning look.

"You expecting a call?"

The phone rings a second time.

"No," Charlie says.

Third ring.

"You sure?" Josh says. "Maybe you should go answer it."

Fourth ring.

Charlie stares at it, knowing it's Robbie using *69 to call her back. She's certain because it's exactly what she would do if their roles were reversed.

Fifth ring.

Josh starts to slide out of the booth. "Fine. I guess I'll do it."

"No," Charlie says, reaching across the table to grab Josh's forearm. It's thick, the muscles taut. She assumes the rest of him is the same way. Strong. Stronger than her. She lets go, her hand slithering back across the table and into her lap.

Outside, the phone has gone silent.

"Too late," Josh says. "We missed him."

"It wasn't my boyfriend," Charlie says.

"Sure," Josh says, unconvinced. "Whatever you say."

They sit in silence, Charlie eyeing her scalding hot cup of tea while Josh alternates sips of Coke and coffee. Eventually, Marge emerges from the back of the diner with their food.

"Soup's on," she says cheerily, placing their plates in front of them. "Eat up before it gets cold."

Charlie stares at the plate of French fries, which glisten with grease. The sight of them makes her stomach do a sickly flip. Across from her, Josh tucks his napkin into his shirt collar like he's a farmer at a picnic. He grabs his utensils—a fork and a surprisingly sharp steak knife—and looks at the food on his plate. A circle of meat smothered with gravy, creamed corn, and a clump of gray stuff that Charlie assumes is supposed to be mashed potatoes. Josh lowers the fork but keeps the knife in hand.

"Something's been bugging me," he says. "Outside, when you were on the phone, talking to your friend."

"Boyfriend," Charlie says, hoping those three extra letters make a difference. She thinks they might. They mean there's someone out there who seriously cares about her. Someone who'll be angry if something should happen to her.

Josh nods. "Boyfriend. Right. When you were talking to him, were you using some sort of code?"

Charlie picks up a French fry and takes a nervous bite. She washes it down with still-too-hot tea. "What do you mean?"

"You know exactly what I mean. 'Things took a detour'? No one talks that way. In the movies, maybe, but not in real life."

Charlie should have known how ridiculous she sounded on the phone. Because he's right. No one talks that way and Josh saw right through it, which is why he now stares at her across the table, a steak knife still gripped in his fist. He holds it with the blade aimed her way, the light glinting off its tip, letting her see how sharp it is, how easy it would be to sink into her flesh.

"I don't know what you want me to say," she says, which is the truth. She's not sure if Josh wants an explanation, an apology, or simply a reason to shove that knife into her heart.

"You don't need to say anything. I just think it would be nice to admit it."

"Admit what?"

Josh reaches across the table, grabs one of her fries, and pops it into his mouth. "That you're still scared of me."

Charlie scans the diner, hoping to see Marge or the cook or even a couple of other patrons come inside. But it's still just her and Josh.

And the knife.

That sharp, glinting extension of his hand.

Josh catches her looking at it and says, "You shouldn't be scared, is what I'm trying to tell you. I'm not going to hurt you, Charlie. We're friends, right? Or at least friendly."

He lowers the knife, as if to prove his friendliness. It doesn't make Charlie feel any better. Nothing about the situation has changed. They're still alone, and Josh is still the Campus Killer.

"Listen," he says. "I think it's best if we don't do this anymore. I think that maybe, once I'm done eating, you should stay here."

Charlie does a little headshake, thinking she misheard him. "What?"

"You should stay here. I get back in the car, drive off, and you find another way to get home."

"Seriously?"

"Yes, seriously." Josh leans back in the booth, his hands up and palms open, like a magician showing there are no more tricks up his sleeve. "I mean, I don't like the thought of just ditching you here. But you clearly don't trust me. And while I'm hurt by that, I also understand that you've been through some hard times. Your friend being killed and all that. It would make anyone suspicious. I'm happy to have taken you this far. Now it's time for us to part ways."

Charlie sits in utter silence, not moving, not even blinking.

He's lying.

She can't help but think that.

He isn't really offering to simply go away and leave her alone, no questions asked. That doesn't make any sense, therefore it must be false.

On the flip side, she wonders if maybe he's being serious. That, through some small miracle she'll never understand, Josh really is letting her go. Maybe he's decided she's not worth the risk or the effort. Or that he's bored with toying with her. Or that he's taking pity on her.

"So you're letting me go? Just like that?"

"Letting you go makes it sound like I've been holding you hostage," Josh says. "That's never been the case. I didn't force you into my car. You got in all on your own."

Charlie doesn't see it that way. Yes, she eagerly accepted a ride from Josh, but only because she was desperate to get away and he told all the right lies. And he continued to lie so she'd stay in the car long after she suspected who he was and what he'd done. So even though she was far from forced into his Grand Am, she was definitely deceived into it.

Part of her thinks she's *still* being deceived. That, instead of a movie in her mind, this is Josh toying with her some more. Getting her hopes up and then enjoying her crushed reaction when he snatches it all away.

A patch of heat forms on the back of her neck. An angry prickle. It matches her mood. Having been gaslit all night, she's nothing if not prickly. As for anger, Charlie can feel it spreading just as quickly as the warm spot on her neck.

She's tired of being lied to.

Tired of being deceived.

Tired of being so fucking sad all the time.

Tired of feeling guilty and confused and living a life so pathetic that she has to make imaginary movies in her head just to be able to cope.

Charlie's so tired that she's tempted to tell Josh she knows everything. She's struck with an overwhelming urge to shatter the good-guy facade he's created and watch the pieces fall away, revealing the monster behind the mask. She almost does it, too. Her jaw unclenches and her tongue loosens, ready to unleash the truth.

But then Marge appears, coming through the swinging door with a pot of coffee. "Let me top that off for you, handsome," she says, even though Josh hasn't taken more than a few sips.

She fills the cup to the brim and pulls back, her elbow moving across the table. Charlie watches its progress, the elbow as sharp and spindly as the knife discarded next to Josh's plate. It keeps moving, even after it hits Charlie's teacup.

The rest is as quick as it is inevitable.

Elbow moving.

Teacup sliding.

Both not stopping until the cup is knocked off the table and the tea spills over Charlie's red coat.

Charlie leaps from her seat, dripping tea that, while no longer scalding, is still hot enough to sting through her wet clothes. Marge backs away, aghast, one age-spotted hand to her mouth while the other continues to grip the coffeepot.

"Aw, shit," she says. "I'm so sorry, sweetheart."

Charlie slides out of the booth, pressing her napkin to the front of the coat.

"It's fine," she says, more relieved than angry. Marge's accident gives her a chance to get up, to get away from Josh, to regroup. "Where's the bathroom?"

Marge points to a small alcove next to the swinging door. "Right there, hon."

Charlie makes a beeline toward it, the napkin still pressed to her coat even though it's now so soaked that tea squishes between her fingers. Inside the alcove, she sees two doors, one marked GUYS and the other, disconcertingly, DOLLS. She pushes the door open and rushes inside, not bothering to take one last look at Josh.

Even though this is the perfect time for him to, as he put it, part ways, Charlie has a feeling he's not going anywhere.

When she returns from the bathroom, he'll still be waiting for her.

INT. DINER—NIGHT

Marge swore she wasn't going to intervene, even though she sensed trouble the moment they entered the diner. It was clear from their body language that something wasn't right with the two of them. The girl in the red coat looked scared and the man she was with looked surly. Never a good combo in Marge's experience.

Yet she held her tongue, which has gotten her in trouble more often than not. She only speaks up when she's truly concerned, like when that other couple left still three sheets to the wind. They didn't listen to her—people their age never do—but she had to say *something*, even if it was just to keep her conscience clean. She offered advice. They ignored her. Whatever happens after that isn't her concern.

And these two were none of her business. They looked to Marge like a couple that just had a fight in the car and needed to stop somewhere to decompress. She sees it all the time.

Concern didn't truly set in until she took the surly-looking man's order.

"What's your blue-plate special?"

Marge was watching the girl when he said it, thinking about how she looked like a hostage and how much that fact worried her. Then the girl went to the pay phone and he followed her out, like some kind of stalker, afraid that his prey was going to run away. Yet another reason for concern.

After that, Marge knew she absolutely had to do something, even though she knew she shouldn't. She couldn't help herself. Standing back and doing nothing just isn't in her nature.

So she grabbed a fresh pot of coffee, flexing her elbow in the process. They were pointy, her elbows. Marge knew it because she'd been told so her entire marriage. Howard, bless his dearly departed heart, always complained that she elbowed him in her sleep. "Damn, Marge," he used to say, "do you use a pencil sharpener on those things before you go to bed?"

She can only imagine what he'd say now that the cancer has whittled her down to nothing but skin and bones.

Pot in hand, Marge went back to that corner booth and put one of those pointy elbows to use. She hated to do it, knocking over the cup of tea like that. Especially on that pretty red coat. But the way Marge sees it, she didn't have a choice. She needed to get the girl alone. And so she did.

Now the girl is in the bathroom and Marge is grabbing a clean washcloth from the kitchen, which is stacked with dirty plates because she told the high school boy who usually washes the dishes not to come in. It's a Tuesday night in November. There's no crowd beating down the door. Which is a good thing, Marge thinks as she grabs a bottle of club soda from the mini fridge under the fountain drinks.

It means she won't be bothered by other customers.

She and the girl in the red coat will have plenty of time for a long talk.

INT. DINER BATHROOM—NIGHT

The bathroom is small and windowless. A prison cell with pink walls that make Charlie think of Pepto Bismol. There's a single stall, also pink, and a sink that's white but stained with rust around the drain. On the wall next to the soap dispenser is a sign.

EMPLOYEES MUST WASH HANDS.

Charlie yanks off her coat and holds it up to examine the damage in the wan light coming from a UFO-shaped fixture in the ceiling.

The stain is both big and noticeable. A dark splotch roughly the same shape as the state of Texas. Tears burn in Charlie's eyes as she sees how deeply the tea has seeped into the fabric. And even though she sees the irony that this, of all things, is what's going to make her lose it tonight, she also understands why.

This coat, so not her style in any way, is the only reminder of Maddy she has left. Now it's, if not completely ruined, at least damaged. She can wear it again—and there's no doubt she will—but it will be just like her memories of Maddy.

Irrevocably marred.

There's a knock on the bathroom door, followed quickly by the smoke-scarred voice of Marge the waitress.

"You okay in there, hon?"

"I'm fine," Charlie says, not knowing why, because no, everything isn't fine. Everything is about as far from fine as it can get.

"I brought you a washcloth and some club soda," Marge says. "In case you need it."

Charlie opens the bathroom door, and Marge slinks in with an apologetic look on her face. She takes the coat from Charlie, goes to the sink, and, tut-tutting at her own handiwork, pours club soda over the stain and starts to dab.

"I feel awful," she says. "Just awful. Give me your address before you go. I'll mail you a check and you can buy yourself a nice new coat."

Charlie doesn't have the heart to tell Marge that the coat is almost as old as she is and therefore can't be easily replaced. Nor does she tell the waitress that she doesn't even particularly like the coat, that she only wears it because it reminds her of Maddy.

"That's very kind of you to offer," she says. "But it's not necessary. Accidents happen."

"Not on my watch. Been doing this for decades and I can count on one hand the number of times I spilled something on a customer. Such a pretty coat, too." Marge flips it open and checks the label. "Pierre Balmain. Fancy."

"It was given to me by a friend," Charlie says.

"That's some generous friend."

"She was," Charlie says. "I just didn't appreciate it enough at the time."

Charlie wills herself not to cry. Not here. Not in a crappy diner bathroom in front of a stranger. But she can't stop thinking about how much Maddy would have loved this place. So unironically retro. She would have gabbed with Marge and played Peggy Lee on the jukebox and laughed like mad when she saw the DOLLS sign on the ladies' room door. Imagining herself here with Maddy instead of with Josh makes the tears pooling in Charlie's eyes keep coming. When one escapes down her cheek, she quickly wipes it away.

At the sink, Marge dribbles some more seltzer on the coat and resumes dabbing at it. "What's your name, sweetie?"

"Charlie."

"Charlie?" Marge says, not even trying to hide her surprise. "I've met a lot of Charlies in my day, but none of them looked like you. Family name?"

"Kind of," Charlie says.

"That's nice. Family's important. It's everything, if you ask me."

Marge pauses, seemingly reluctant to say what else is on her mind, which Charlie assumes to be a first. The waitress doesn't strike her as someone who holds back or minces words.

"Listen, Charlie, I know I should mind my own damn business, but is everything okay? I saw you out there with your friend, and you seemed, well, a little distressed."

"Little" is the only part of the sentence that surprises Charlie. She's a *lot* distressed, especially in her current state of being perched on the razor's edge between fear and anger. That's another surprise—how mad she got at the table. It was a new feeling for her. Since Maddy died, she'd only been mad at herself.

But Josh has certainly earned her ire, even though she's also scared shitless in his presence, terrified by what he's done and what he still might do. Charlie never knew one could be both furious and frightened at the same time. Now she does, and the result is what Marge saw back at the table.

Distress.

"Like I said, it's none of my business, but is he—" Marge pauses, trying to be delicate. "Is he treating you okay?"

Charlie knows she could—and should—tell her about Josh.

Marge would believe her. Watching the waitress furiously dab at her coat, worry wrinkles joining her regular ones, Charlie begins to doubt the spill at the table was an accident. Marge is a pro, and that was a rookie mistake. It's more likely she saw Charlie looking distressed, got worried for her, and devised a way to get them alone. Now that they are, all Charlie needs to do is tell her what's going on, ask to use the diner's phone, and call the police without Josh ever knowing a thing. Then this long, horrible night will be over.

But it might already be over. It all depends on if Josh is serious about leaving her behind. Charlie doubts he is. Josh has been dishonest all night. Why stop now? Either way, it doesn't mean she should get Marge involved. Doing so might make things worse. If Josh isn't planning on leaving her behind and does get wind that Charlie told Marge about her suspicions, it could put both of them in danger.

Charlie doesn't want that. Marge is a good person. A *nice* person. And nice people shouldn't be mixed up in what she's going through.

"I'm just tired," she says. "It's been a long drive."

"I understand," Marge says. "Especially this time of night. All I'm saying is, you're welcome to stay here awhile. If you don't feel safe with him."

"I'm fine," Charlie says. "Really."

Marge gives the coat two more dabs before studying the result. "Well, I'll be damned. Looks like the club soda worked."

She holds up the coat, revealing only a wet patch where the tea stain had been. Handing it back to Charlie, she says, "Give it a little while to dry and it should look like new."

Charlie examines the wet spot. The wool there is now pilled slightly and specked with bits of lint from the washcloth, but she's okay with that. Maddy would have said it added character.

Marge pauses by the door. "I didn't mean to make you uncomfortable with all those questions."

"I know. And you didn't. Everything's fine."

"I was just looking out for you," Marge says. "Women need to do that, you know. Look out for each other. There's a special place in hell for those who don't."

"I appreciate it," Charlie says. "I really do. But I'm doing great. Thank you for cleaning my coat."

Marge nods and slips out of the bathroom. "Anytime, sweetie."

Left alone, Charlie slips into the coat and stares at her reflection in the bathroom mirror, shocked by how pale she looks. Like Greta Garbo. That's another one of Nana Norma's sayings. *You're as pale as Garbo.*

In this case, it's true, although it looked good on an icy beauty like Greta Garbo. Charlie just looks sickly, as if she's going to pass out. She assumes that's because she is. Her legs are weak and wobbly, and her vision comes in and out of focus, thanks to the tears. Charlie wouldn't be surprised if, at any second, she crumpled to the floor. Considering the night she's having, who could blame her?

Staring at the ghost of who she had once been, Charlie assures herself she did the right thing by not telling Marge the truth about Josh. It's better this way. Now only one of them is in danger.

She also knows it's a lie. Just like thinking that no one will believe her if she tried to get help. Or that Josh will charm and fib his way out of it. Or that he has no intention of leaving without her, despite flat-out stating he does.

They're all lies.

Ones different from what Josh has been feeding her all night, but lies nonetheless. Meager excuses to hide the truth: that part of her doesn't *want* to get away from Josh.

Not just yet.

Charlie had left home with only a vague understanding about all the dangers young women face. Youngstown wasn't Mayberry. Bad things happened there all the time. Date rape and abuse and a hundred tiny threats directed at women. But Charlie hadn't given them much thought. Not even after her high school health teacher did a lesson on sexual assault. Or on the day she left for Olyphant and Nana Norma gave her that tiny pink bottle of pepper spray. Or during the self-defense class every female Olyphant student had to take the week of orientation.

It took Maddy being killed for her to understand the brutal truth that there are men out there who won't hesitate to hurt women.

Men like Josh.

After Maddy's murder, Charlie had assumed there was nothing she could do about it. She loved Maddy and Maddy loved her and they would have been friends forever, no matter what Robbie thought. But then she was gone and all that remained was a burning rage. So Charlie internalized it and blamed herself.

For leaving Maddy behind.

For telling her to fuck off as she departed.

For not being able to identify Josh after she saw him outside the bar.

She blamed herself and hated herself and punished herself because that's what women are taught to do. Blame themselves. Blame the victims. Tell themselves that since the Angela Dunleavys and Taylor Morrisons and Madeline Forresters of the world had sat through the same lessons on assault, received the same tiny bottles of pepper spray, and endured the same self-defense classes, it must have been their fault they were attacked. Or raped. Or killed.

No one tells women that none of it is their fault. That the blame falls squarely on the awful men who do terrible things and the fucked-up society that raises them, molds them, makes excuses for them. People don't want to admit that there are monsters in their midst, so the monsters continue to roam free and the cycle of violence and blame continues.

A thought pops into Charlie's brain, so sudden and jolting she can actually hear it. A light click at the back of her head as her synapses explode like fireworks.

If Josh leaves, she'll be safe. But nothing will stop him from hurting someone else. Someone like Maddy. The world is full of them. And none of them are safe while Josh roams free.

Marge was right. There *is* a special place in hell for women who don't help other women. Charlie knows it well, having spent the past two months dwelling there. Now it's time to get the fuck out.

Something in Charlie's chest begins to harden.

Her heart.

Shattered after Maddy died, it's now being put back together, its jagged pieces fitting into place, bound together by anger.

Another look in the mirror confirms it. She *is* changing. Her face has gained some color. A pink flush—brighter than the bathroom walls—spreads across her cheeks, her forehead, the bridge of her nose.

Like her heart, her eyes have also hardened. Where once she had seen only despair, Charlie now sees a flicker of fire.

She feels bold.

Fearless.

Dangerous.

Wrapped in Maddy's red coat, she feels almost possessed by all the tough women she's admired in movies. Stanwyck in *Double Indemnity.* Hayworth in *The Lady from Shanghai.* Crawford in, well, everything. The kind of women men don't know if they want to kiss or kill. Women who claw and scrape through life because they have to.

Now it's Charlie's turn.

She's no longer the scared, self-loathing girl she was when she left campus. She's something else.

A fucking femme fatale.

She's going to leave this bathroom, then the diner, and get back into the car with Josh.

She doesn't know how and doesn't know when, but she's going to make him pay for what he's done.

And she intends to enjoy it.

"Charlie?"

INT. DINER BATHROOM—NIGHT

Charlie shudders back to the present at the sound of her name. It's Marge, who punctuates it with a rap on the door.

"Everything still okay in there?"

"Yes, I'm fine," Charlie says. "Just freshening up."

She checks her reflection in the mirror. She's still the pale, fragile wraith she was when she walked in. All the tough personas she wore in the movie in her mind have peeled off like snakeskin. The only similarity between that Charlie and the one she sees before her now is the understanding that she can't let Josh leave.

Not alone.

She's not sure if she actually thought that or if it was part of the mental movie. She assumes it doesn't really matter, seeing how it came from her brain either way. A realization is still a realization, even if its delivery is unorthodox.

And the realization consuming Charlie is that Josh needs to be stopped. And she's the one who must do it. She can't rely on the hopeful notion that Robbie called the police and that any second now a cop will show up and arrest Josh.

Nor can she enlist kindhearted Marge for help. The waitress might be quick with a cup of scalding-hot tea, but that means nothing when Josh has a knife within reach.

Earlier, Charlie had toyed with the idea that fate is what led her into Josh's car. She assumed it was punishment for how she'd treated Maddy. But now Charlie suspects that if fate did have a hand in creating the situation, it's for an entirely different purpose.

Not punishment.

Redemption.

Right now, Charlie has a chance to clear her conscience. The guilt that's consumed her for two months could be gone in an instant. Her slate thoroughly wiped clean. All she needs to do is make sure Josh doesn't ride off alone.

She owes it to herself.

And to Maddy.

And to Maddy's family. And to the other women Josh has killed. And to those he might kill in the future if she lets him get away.

But she's not going to let that happen.

She's going to leave this bathroom, then the diner, and get back into the car with Josh.

It's not smart. It's not careful. It's probably not even brave. Right now, it doesn't really matter. It's what Charlie feels she must do. And at this point, she has nothing left to lose.

She takes one last look in the mirror, hoping to see that her eyes have hardened just like they did in the movie in her mind. On the contrary, they're moist and red at the edges. No hardness there. Her whole body, in fact, feels soft and vulnerable. But that doesn't keep Charlie from flinging open the bathroom door and stepping back out into the main part of the diner.

Josh is still at the table. He leans over his coffee cup, staring into it, waiting for her return as the jukebox plays the last notes of a Rolling Stones song.

"Sympathy for the Devil."

Ironic, seeing how a devil currently occupies the corner booth. And he's anything but sympathetic.

Charlie pauses at the jukebox and flips through the selections. Classic rock, mostly, but a few current songs by Bryan Adams, Mariah Carey, and, to Josh at least, the twin scourges of Amy Grant and Paula Abdul. Charlie considers playing the two of them back to back, just to irritate him. A different idea forms when she sees another song. One she absolutely has to play.

She drops one of the quarters Josh gave her for the pay phone into the jukebox and enters the record number. A second later, music fills the diner.

A guitar riff she's heard twice before that night.

"Come as You Are."

Josh lifts his head when he hears it. Slowly. Like a movie villain who knows he's just been found out. Raymond Burr in *Rear Window* when he realizes he's caught in Jimmy Stewart's telephoto lens.

He turns his head a little bit, listening, making sure his ears aren't deceiving him.

"Great song, isn't it?" Charlie says as she slides back into the booth. "Do you want to wait until it's over? Or should we leave now?"

"We?"

Charlie swallows, knowing she's about to cross some invisible threshold that might forever change the course of her life. It might even end up getting her killed. But there's no avoiding it.

She can't wait for others to stop Josh.

She needs to do it herself.

Even though she has no idea how.

"Yeah," she says. "As in you and me getting into your car and driving to Ohio like you agreed to do."

"That's not happening," Josh says. "And I already explained why, Charlie."

"And I'm explaining that you're not going to get rid of me so easily." Charlie's body hums with fear as she talks. She's doing this.

She's actually going ahead with it. "Here's the way I see it. The situation hasn't changed. I need to get home. You can get me there. Now, we can stop wasting time and leave or we can wait until the police get here."

"What police?"

"The ones that my boyfriend called after I used that code you were so smart to pick up on," Charlie says, even though she has no clue if Robbie did any such thing. She assumes that if he had, a cop would have shown up by now.

Josh goes quiet, no doubt replaying the conversation at the pay phone in his head. Charlie knows he was listening. It's why she chose her words so carefully. Now Josh is wondering what, exactly, those words could have meant.

"You're bluffing," he says. "Besides, why would I need to be worried about the police?"

"You tell me, *Jake.*"

For the first time since they met, Josh looks worried. He tries to hide it by taking a swallow of coffee and leaning back in the booth, his arms crossed, but Charlie knows he's concerned. She can see it in his eyes.

"You don't know what you're talking about," he says. "You're confused, Charlie. And kind of sad."

Charlie shrugs. She's been called worse.

"Then we'll wait."

They stay that way, staring each other down, until the song ends. Only then, when the diner is plunged into silence, does Josh decide that maybe Charlie's tougher than she looks and that maybe—just maybe—she's not bluffing. He waves to Marge, who's been watching them from behind the counter.

"Could we get the check, please?"

"Sure thing," Marge says, seeming surprised, probably because they barely touched their food. Charlie feels bad about that. All that work for nothing. Marge brings the check and places it on the table.

To Charlie, she says, "I took your order off the bill. After what I did to your coat, it's the least I can do."

"You've done so much already," Charlie says, meaning every word. Without Marge, she might not have realized what she needed to do. As far as she's concerned, the waitress helped her realize this situation could be more blessing than curse.

"It was nothing," Marge says, locking eyes with Charlie. "I help when I can."

On the other side of the table, Josh reads the check and pulls out his wallet. Watching him count out bills, Charlie says, "Be sure to leave a big tip."

Josh slaps twenty dollars onto the table. Satisfied that the tip is indeed big, Charlie says, "Shall we go?"

Josh doesn't move. He's preoccupied—looking past her, over her shoulder, out the front window. Charlie swivels in the booth until she sees what he's looking at.

A cop car.

Local.

Pulling up to a stop in front of the diner.

Charlie can't believe her eyes. Turns out she *wasn't* bluffing, even though she certainly thought she was. But Robbie understood her message loud and clear and had indeed called the police, a fact that leaves her feeling proud and relieved and grateful.

Josh waves to Marge, who's now behind the counter, dutifully cleaning the Formica even though no one's probably sat there for hours.

"You're working too hard, Marge," he says, patting the space next to him. "Join us. Take a load off."

"I don't think the boss would like that very much," she says.

"Is he here?"

"No."

"Then you're the boss."

Charlie's attention is split between the cop car outside and the waitress tittering behind the counter. Her head moves back and forth, like she's at a tennis match, trying to take it all in.

The cop getting out of his patrol car.

Then Marge dropping her rag on the counter.

Then the cop ambling toward the front door, in no hurry at all.

Then Marge coming to their table, taking a seat next to Josh, and saying, "I suppose it won't hurt to get off my feet for a second."

By the time the cop enters the diner, Charlie's hit with a third distraction.

The steak knife.

It's no longer on the table.

Josh holds it again, gripping it the way a movie thug wields a switchblade, the tip vaguely aimed in Marge's direction.

Charlie's gaze hopscotches around the diner, going from the knife to Marge to the cop now standing at the counter. He's tall and lanky and young. Face like a choirboy.

"Evening, Tom," Marge says. "Didn't think you'd be coming in tonight. I thought you hit the pizza place on Tuesdays."

At first, Charlie wonders if the cop can see the steak knife in Josh's hand and how in the past few seconds it seems to have moved a little closer in Marge's direction. It's not until she follows the cop's gaze from the counter to their table that she realizes everything below Josh's shoulders is blocked by the back of the booth.

"I'm here on business," Officer Tom says, looking not at Marge but to Josh seated beside her. "We got a call about a possibly dangerous situation."

"*Here?*" Marge says, incredulous. "Nothing happening here. Slow night as usual."

"We're just passing through, Officer," Josh adds.

Officer Tom turns to Charlie. "Is that true, miss?"

"Me?"

Charlie turns her head in a way that lets her see both the cop and, in the edge of her vision, the knife in Josh's hand, which seems to have gotten even closer to Marge. Then again, it might just be Charlie's imagination. It's steered her wrong before.

"Yes," she says. "That's the truth."

Charlie eyes the holster on Officer Tom's hip and the police-issued pistol strapped inside of it. She wonders how much experience a cop so young has had. If he's ever had to face a man with a knife. Or defuse a hostage situation. Or shoot someone in the line of duty.

She gives the scene another all-encompassing glance, skipping from Officer Tom's gun to Josh's knife to Marge and then back to the cop, trying to gauge the distance between all of them.

She wonders if she should yell to Officer Tom that Josh is a killer.

She wonders if he'd be able to draw his weapon before Josh jammed the steak knife into Marge's stomach.

She wonders if Officer Tom would then open fire on Josh.

Charlie pictures the immediate aftermath. Her cowering in the booth, her hands over her ears as Josh lies dead on the table and Marge bleeds on the floor and smoke still trickles from the barrel of Officer Tom's gun.

She wonders if this, right now, is all just a movie in her mind. It doesn't matter that Josh can see the cop and Marge can see him and that both spoke to him. All of that could also be part of the movie. A fever dream built out of hope and denial and wishful thinking.

It wouldn't surprise her if it was. She's experienced them enough to know the drill. They emerge when she's stressed and scared and needs to be shielded from the harshness of reality, which describes her current mood in a nutshell.

Sitting in that booth, looking at a cop who may or may not exist, Charlie thirsts for a reality check the same way an alcoholic craves booze. An intense yearning that threatens to overwhelm her. But asking Officer Tom if he's real isn't a good idea. Charlie learned her lesson in the rest stop bathroom. She knows that saying what she's thinking will only make her look crazy and, ultimately, untrustworthy.

Plus, there's Marge to consider. Poor, innocent Marge, who has yet to realize that inches from her midriff is a knife sharp enough to take out her spleen. If Charlie says or does anything suspicious, Josh might hurt her. He might even kill her. Charlie can't let that happen. Her conscience, already so burdened, wouldn't be able to take it.

"So there's no trouble here?" Officer Tom says.

Charlie forces a smile. "None at all."

"You sure about that?" His gaze darts to Josh for a moment. "You feel safe in this man's presence?"

"Of course she does," Josh says.

"I was asking the lady," Officer Tom says.

Across the table, Josh gives her an unnerving look. Cold smile, dark eyes, weighted stare. The knife in his hand continues to glisten.

"I feel absolutely safe," Charlie says. "But thank you for your concern."

Officer Tom studies her, his gaze surprisingly piercing as he decides whether to believe her.

"I'm sure it was a crank call," Marge says, deciding for him. "Some bored kid trying to stir up trouble. Now if you stop bothering my customers, I'll fix you a coffee for the road. On the house."

She stands.

Josh sets the steak knife back on the table.

Charlie lets slip a tiny huff of relief.

Marge joins Officer Tom at the counter and pours coffee into a to-go cup. "Thanks for checking in on us, Tom. But we're fine. Isn't that right, folks?" She turns to Charlie and Josh, giving them an exaggerated wink.

"We're fine," Josh says.

"Yes, fine," Charlie says, a weak echo. She looks to Josh. "In fact, we were just leaving. Weren't we?"

Josh, surprised, takes a beat before replying. "Yes. We were."

He slides out of the booth. Charlie does the same and follows him to the door, knowing that she's about to lose her last chance at rescue.

It's a risk she needs to take.

A couple of years ago, in one of her elective psych classes, she'd read about kidnap victims who stayed with their captors long after they could have escaped. Stockholm syndrome. The mind warping over time until the abducted came to sympathize with those who took them. At the time, Charlie judged those young women. And they were all young women. Weak, vulnerable, victimized women who didn't have the good sense to flee at the first opportunity.

"I'd never let that happen to me," she told Maddy.

But now she understands.

Those women didn't stay because they were weak.

They stayed because they were scared.

Because they feared what would happen to them if their escape plan failed. That it would be worse than their current situation. And it could always get worse.

In this case, "worse" means Josh doing something rash and hurting not just her but also Marge and Officer Tom in the process. And this has nothing to do with them.

This is between her and Josh.

Because of that, it's best to get out of the diner and back in the car, where she's the only one in danger. Sometimes you can't simultaneously be smart, brave, and careful. Sometimes you need to choose one.

By following Josh to the door, Charlie's choosing bravery.

When she reaches the dessert case, still lit and lazily spinning, Officer Tom calls out to her from his spot at the counter.

"You forgot your backpack, miss."

"Oh, my goodness," Charlie says, hoping it sounds authentic. "Thank you."

She returns to the booth and grabs the backpack she'd left there on purpose. Then, after an over-the-shoulder glance to make sure Marge and Officer Tom aren't looking, she snatches the steak knife from the table and stuffs it into a pocket of her coat.

MIDNIGHT

INT. GRAND AM—NIGHT

Charlie watches the diner recede in the Grand Am's side mirror—a blur of chrome and neon that's soon replaced by night sky, moonlight, and the ghost-gray trees crowding the edge of the road. They've reentered the middle of nowhere. Just the two of them.

They ride in silence, both of them facing forward, their eyes fixed on the sweep of headlights brightening the road ahead. Charlie has no idea if they're heading toward the interstate or away from it. Not that it matters. She already assumes that wherever they're going, it's definitely not Ohio. And that there'll be no coming back from this.

"How much do you know?" Josh says after they've traveled a mile without another car or building in sight.

"Everything," Charlie says.

Josh nods, unsurprised. "I figured as much. Why'd you get back in the car?"

"Because I had to."

It really is that simple. Charlie couldn't risk letting Josh do something to Marge or Officer Tom. And she certainly couldn't let him leave on his own, where he could do the same things he did to Maddy to someone else. So now she's here, sitting next to a killer.

Call it fate.

Call it karma.

Whatever it is, she understands she needs to be the one to stop Josh. It's her duty and hers alone.

That doesn't make her any less frightened. She's more scared now than she's been the entire car ride. Because now she knows the stakes.

Stop Josh from getting away, or die trying.

The problem is that Charlie doesn't know how, exactly, she should try to stop him. She sits with her hand thrust deep in her coat pocket, her fingers curling and uncurling around the handle of the steak knife. Part of her is tempted to attack Josh now and just get it over with. She doesn't because the idea of stabbing someone— literally thrusting a knife into another human body—frightens her as much as thinking about what Josh might try to do to her.

"Most people wouldn't have done that," he says.

"I guess that makes me plucky."

Josh chuckles at that. When he looks Charlie's way, it's with what she can only discern as admiration.

"Yes, you are certainly that." He pauses, as if debating whether he should say what's on his mind, ultimately deciding to just go for it. "I like you, Charlie. That's what's so fucked-up about all this. I like talking to you."

"You like lying to me," Charlie says. "There's a big difference."

"You got me there. I told you a lot of things that weren't true. I won't deny that."

"Like your name being Josh."

"That's one of them, yes. My real name is Jake Collins. But you already knew that."

Charlie nods. She did. Even at the height of Josh's mind games, a small part of her knew she was right about that.

"Your real name. Your real driver's license. That game of Twenty Questions. Why did you let me think I'd imagined all of that?"

"Because I needed to keep you in the car," Josh says. "You looked like you were about to bolt, so I came up with something on the fly. I guess it worked."

That it did. And Charlie feels stupid and angry with herself for believing it, even though she shouldn't. It's not stupid to want to believe the best in people. You shouldn't get mad at yourself for thinking someone is good and not inherently evil.

"Is there anything you told me tonight that *is* true?" she says.

"That story about my mom. That's all true. She left on Halloween just like I said. I haven't told too many people about that."

"Why did you tell me?"

"Because I like talking to you," Josh says. "That wasn't a lie, either."

Inside her coat pocket, Charlie's fingers continue to clench and unclench around the knife handle. Earlier, they did the same thing around the handle of the passenger-side door. Once eager for escape, now eager for a fight.

But Josh shows no sign of giving it to her. He simply drives, unhurried, ready to say something else he's unsure about.

"My dad always blamed me for my mom leaving," he says. "He said it was my fault. Right up until the day he died."

"Another thing you lied about."

"Not really," Josh says. "He did have a stroke. It's what killed him. And I would have dropped everything to take care of him, if I'd needed to. Even though he hated me and, well, I guess I hated him."

"Because he blamed you for what your mom did?" Charlie says.

Josh shakes his head. "No. Because he convinced me to blame myself. It didn't matter that my mother chose to leave all on her own. I thought it was because of me. I still do."

Charlie knows that feeling all too well. So heavy and cumbersome and exhausting that she would do anything to rid herself of it.

Even die.

She knows because she almost did. Not tonight. Before that. Four days before.

"I almost killed myself," she says.

The words surprise Josh. They surprise Charlie even more. She's never admitted it before. Not even to herself.

"Why?" Josh says, shock still potent in his voice. Charlie notices something else there, too—a note of concern.

"Because I wanted the guilt to go away."

"So that's why you accepted a ride from a stranger."

"Yes," Charlie says. "That's exactly why."

Josh stays silent a moment, thinking. "How did it happen?"

"Accidental overdose," Charlie says. "Sleeping pills."

They were the little white pills, prescribed to offset the restlessness brought on by the little orange ones. Charlie hadn't taken many, preferring to spend her nights indulging in revenge fantasies that bore zero resemblance to the real-life one she's now experiencing.

But then came the night in which the human-shaped blank she normally fought was replaced by a mirror image of herself. It startled her so much that she put a movie into the VCR, crawled into bed, and downed a handful of little white pills.

She told herself that she just needed to sleep.

That it was just a coincidence the VHS tape she picked was *Singin' in the Rain*, which she once told Maddy was the last movie she wanted to see before she died because it was as close to heaven as any film could get.

Charlie continued to lie to herself even after her body rebelled and she threw up the pills and then flushed the meager few that remained down the toilet. She let herself think every excuse in the book. She was too tired to know what she was doing. She wasn't thinking straight. It was all an unfortunate accident.

That's the real reason she needed to leave Olyphant immediately. Why she couldn't wait until Thanksgiving or when Robbie was free. Why she went to the ride board and put up that flyer and jumped at the chance to share a ride with Josh.

Charlie was afraid that if nothing changed, she'd experience another unfortunate accident, this time with a different result.

But as the shame and sadness of that morning come back to her, she knows the truth.

None of it was accidental.

For a brief, soul-shaking moment, she would have preferred to die than spend one more minute weighed down by her guilt.

Now, though, she wants to live. More than anything.

"I'm glad that didn't happen," Josh says. "And I'm sorry we didn't get to meet under different circumstances. I think I would have liked that."

Charlie stays silent. It's better to do that than admit she feels the same way. There were points in this drive when she actually *liked* Josh, before suspicion and fear kicked in. She felt a kinship with him, probably because he's as much of an outcast as she is. Lonely, too. She can tell that even now. Like recognizes like. In a weird, twisted way, Josh seems to understand her better than even Maddy sometimes did.

Or maybe it's simply Maddy who makes her feel tied to Josh. There's a reason Josh chose her to be one of his victims. Perhaps he was drawn to Maddy for the same reasons Charlie was. And it's possible that's another reason she got back into the car with him at the diner, even though it defied logic and reason.

She wants to know why.

Why Josh picked Maddy.

Why he approached her outside the bar.

Why he decided to kill her.

But instead of trying to articulate all that, Charlie lets the silence grow. It fills the car, uneasy, the two of them never taking their eyes off the road, which seems to have narrowed. On both sides, the forest presses in close. Bare branches arc overhead, connecting like elderly couples holding hands. Bits of snow still sit in the evergreens. Occasional clumps of it drop from the branches and hit the roof of the car with a muffled thump.

"So what now?" Charlie eventually says.

"We drive."

"But not to Ohio."

"No, Charlie. I'm afraid not."

"What's going to happen when the driving stops?"

"I think you already know the answer."

Charlie's fingers again curl around the knife in her pocket. This time, they stay that way. Gripping it tight. As ready as she'll ever be.

"Maybe you should stop driving now," she says.

Josh gives her a look. "You sure you want that?"

"No," Charlie says. "But I've gone through a lot of things I didn't want."

"Like what happened to your parents."

"Yes. And Maddy."

Charlie finally senses it—the hardening of her heart she's been waiting for. All it took was saying Maddy's name out loud to the man who killed her. Yet it feels nothing like what she experienced in the movies in her mind. She's angry, yes, but also sad. So exhaustingly sad.

"Yes," Josh says. "And your—"

A deer suddenly leaps into the road, right in front of the car, the headlights making its eyes glow.

Josh pounds the brakes, and Charlie's jerked forward a sliver of a second before the seat belt locks and yanks her back. Her head snaps against the back of the seat. Beside her, Josh cuts the wheel to the right, trying to avoid the deer. The animal springs across the road and into the woods, but the car keeps moving. Fishtailing at first, then rotating, the back of the Grand Am whipping in an arc across the road.

When the car stops, it's still on the road but facing the wrong direction.

They sit there a moment, the car idling, the engine pinging, the headlights pointing in the direction from which they'd just come.

"Are you okay?" Josh says.

"I think so," Charlie says before having two thoughts, right on top of each other.

The first is: If Josh plans on killing her, why does he care if she's okay?

The second is: The driving has stopped.

Josh unhooks his seat belt. "We might have clipped that deer. I'm going to check the front of the car."

He pauses, waiting for Charlie to say something. But she can't say anything because that second thought she had repeats through her head like a siren.

We've stopped driving. We've stopped driving. We've stopped driving.

A third thought joins it.

I don't know what's going to happen next.

But Charlie does.

She's known the moment they left the diner.

Josh is going to try to kill her and she's going to try to kill him and only one of them is going to succeed.

With her hand in her coat pocket, her fingers in a death grip around the knife, Charlie watches as Josh gives up waiting for a response and gets out of the car. He crosses in front of it, his sweatshirt bright in the glow of the headlights. When he bends down to examine the front bumper, Charlie notices wisps of steam rising from the Grand Am's hood. It takes her a second to realize the cause of it.

The engine.

It's still running.

Ready to drive.

To end this, right now, all she needs to do is slip behind the wheel, shift into first gear, and stomp on the gas pedal.

Charlie moves quickly.

Snapping off the seat belt.

Sliding over the center console.

Grabbing the steering wheel for leverage.

She's halfway behind the wheel when Josh catches sight of her. In a flash, he's beside the car, flinging open the driver's-side door before Charlie can hit the lock. As Josh pushes his way into the car, Charlie scrambles back into the passenger seat.

Josh gazes at her with regret in his eyes.

"Listen, Charlie," he says, "I don't want to hurt you, okay? But I can. Hurt you, that is. I'm quite capable of it. So we can do this two ways. You can be calm about it, which is my recommendation. Or you can try to fight it and I'll be forced to get rough, which—I reiterate—I really, *really* don't want to do."

Shrinking against the passenger-side door, Charlie tries to put her hand back in her pocket.

"Keep those hands where I can see them," Josh says. "Don't make this hard on yourself."

He plunges a hand into the front pocket of his jeans. He pulls something out and tosses it to Charlie. Unwilling to catch it, Charlie recoils and lets it drop to the floor with a rattle.

She looks down and sees it's a pair of handcuffs.

"Pick them up and put them on," Josh says.

Charlie shakes her head, and a tear flings from her eyes. A surprise. She didn't know she'd started crying.

"You need to be smart now," Josh says, his tone a warning. "Pick them up."

"I—" Charlie's voice cracks, cut short by fear and anger and sadness. "I don't want to."

"Please don't make me get rough," Josh says. "You don't want that. *I* don't want that. So I'm going to count to three. And when I'm done, those cuffs need to be around your wrists."

He pauses.

Then he starts to count.

"One."

Still shaking her head and still crying, Charlie reaches for the handcuffs at her feet.

"Two."

She scrunches down, one hand scooping up the handcuffs, the other burrowing back into her coat pocket.

"Three."

Charlie sits up, the cuffs cold in her left hand, the knife handle hot in her right.

She doesn't move.

"Damn it, Charlie. Just use the fucking cuffs."

Josh lunges over the center console, moving in an instant from driver's side to passenger side.

Charlie pulls the knife from her coat.

She closes her eyes.

Then, with a scream so loud it shakes the car windows, she thrusts the knife forward and plunges it into Josh's stomach.

She thought it would go in easier than it does. In the movies, knives slide in smoothly, like a blade through butter. The truth is that it takes force. Teeth-gritting, grunting force to push it through Josh's sweatshirt, then his flesh, then deeper still, into places Charlie doesn't want to think about. She stops only when she feels blood on her hands and hears Josh moan her name.

"Charlie."

INT. GRAND AM—NIGHT

Charlie opens her eyes.

She turns her head.

Slowly.

So slowly.

Her gaze inches to the left, stopping when the tree-shaped air freshener dangling from the rearview mirror hits the edge of her vision.

Charlie sucks in a breath, taking in the too-strong scent of pine.

"Whoa. You there, Charlie?" a voice next to her says.

Her head resumes turning. Fast now. A neck-snapping swivel that brings her face-to-face with Josh. He sits behind the wheel, looking both amused and expectant. Like he's been waiting a long time for this moment, and now that it's here, it pleases him.

"Is this real?" she says.

Josh studies the back of his hand, humoring her. "Looks pretty real to me. Were you, uh—"

"At the movies?"

"Yeah."

"I don't know."

But she desperately hopes so. She wants to think she's not capable of doing in real life what she'd just done in her imagination.

"How can you not know?" Josh says.

"It was—"

Scary.

So scary and detailed and confusing. Enough that Charlie feels dizzy. Gray clouds float in and out of her vision. Riding with them is a skull-filling headache. She feels like Dorothy waking at the end of *The Wizard of Oz*, suddenly in a sepia-tinted world that had minutes earlier been dazzling color.

"I don't know what's going on," she says.

And she truly doesn't. She has no idea if she's in reality or a movie or a memory. Maybe it's all three, which is a perfect description of movies themselves. They're a combination of life and fantasy and illusion that becomes a kind of shared dream. Charlie imagines this moment being projected onto a big screen, watched by all those beautiful people out there in the dark.

At this point, nothing would surprise her anymore.

The car is still stopped in the middle of the road. Through the windshield, Charlie sees trees on both sides of the car, their bare limbs skeleton-gray against the sky.

"We don't need to stop driving," Josh says, a tinge of hope in his voice. "We can keep going."

"All the way to Ohio?"

"If that's what you want, yeah."

"Or," Charlie says, "we could go to a movie."

The suggestion makes Josh chuckle. "I wouldn't mind that. Not one bit."

"So you're not going to try to kill me?"

"I can't," Josh says. "You already killed me."

Charlie looks down at her hands. One grips a pair of handcuffs. The other is smeared with blood. On the other side of the car, Josh chokes out her name.

"Charlie."

INT. GRAND AM—NIGHT

Charlie's eyes open on their own. A willful snap.

In front of her, sprawled sideways in the driver's seat, is Josh. His head is propped against the window, which has become fogged by his pained grunts. When he spasms, his hair makes a jellyfish pattern in the glass.

The knife remains in his side, poking out like a meat thermometer. Josh stares at it, wild-eyed and sweaty, the fingers of his left hand reaching for it.

"Charlie," he grunts. "Help me."

She stays frozen, save for her eyelids, which she rapidly blinks, hoping that doing so will jolt her out of this nightmarish movie in her mind. Because that's all it is.

A movie.

It has to be.

This can't be real.

Even though it looks that way. Blood has started to seep into Josh's sweatshirt. A wet bloom around the knife that's darker than the fake blood used in movies. Almost black. Like it's not really blood at all but some kind of primordial ooze.

Seeing it makes Charlie back against the passenger door. She fumbles for the handle, finds it, pulls. The door swings open, and the Grand Am's dome light flicks on, casting a brutal glow over the inside of the car. No longer dark, the blood now looks Technicolor bright in the dome light's glare.

Charlie resumes blinking. Faster now. Her eyelids working in a way that makes everything flicker like a projector not running at full speed. She slides out of the car backward, dropping through the door, landing on the road with a burst of pain in her lower back.

She crawls away from the car, scuttling backward like a crab. She doesn't want to be here. She wants to be anywhere else. Any *time* else. She wants to wake and find herself in a whole other existence. One without Josh and that car and that blood.

When thinking about stabbing Josh, she didn't know how she'd feel if she actually went through with it. Victorious, maybe. Or sated. Or proud.

Instead, she just feels scared.

But it's a strange kind of fear.

She's no longer scared about what might happen to her. She's scared about what she's done.

Charlie climbs to her feet.

She takes one last look at the Grand Am.

Then she begins to run.

INT. GRAND AM—NIGHT

He removes the knife from his gut in one quick yank. Better that than trying to pull it out little by little, which hurts more than helps. And there's plenty of pain already. The moment air hits the stab wound, a fresh bolt of agony pulses through him and there's nothing to do but yell.

When it's over and the boiling pain lowers to a more manageable simmer, he takes a few deep breaths and checks the damage. The first thing he notices—because it's impossible to miss—is the blood. The side where Charlie stabbed him is crimson from hip to armpit. He doesn't know if it's because his sweatshirt is extra absorbent or if he's really lost that much blood. Either way, the sight of it makes him dizzy.

It takes some effort to lift the sweatshirt to see the actual knife wound. The blood-soaked fabric sticks to his skin like glue. He considers leaving it like that. A makeshift bandage. But he's been stabbed before, and he knows that doing nothing will lead to more blood loss, then infection, then death.

Like it or not, this bitch needs to be stitched.

So he pulls up the sweatshirt the same way he pulled out the knife—in one swift motion. Riding out another blast of pain, he looks down and sees an inch-long slice on the left side of his abdomen.

It's good that the knife was small.

It's bad that it was long.

The wound it left behind is deep enough to make him worry that the knife could have hit a major organ or severed some nerves, although if that were the case, he thinks he'd be in more pain. Or dead. And since he's alive and not paralyzed in agony, he assumes he got lucky.

He reaches under the driver's seat, his left hand fumbling for the first-aid kit he keeps there in case of emergencies. Each movement prompts a fresh wave of pain that makes him curse everything about this night.

It was supposed to be easy. Now it's just a shitshow. And he knows exactly who to blame.

Charlie.

He wasn't lying when he said he liked talking to her. He can't remember the last time he enjoyed being in someone's company. People, generally speaking, suck. It's why he does what he does. Most human beings can't stop being selfish, greedy, piggish assholes. And it's his job to make sure they pay for that.

But Charlie's different. So weird and wounded and, as he now knows, secretly fierce. It made him lower his guard. He told her things he'd never told anyone else, ever. All it got him in return was a knife to the gut.

Beneath the seat, his fingers brush smooth plastic. The first-aid kit. Finally. He picks it up, drops it on the side of his stomach that doesn't have a stab wound, and clicks it open. He rifles through it, finding a small bottle of rubbing alcohol, a gauze pad, some medical tape, a needle, and a tiny spool of thread. Everything he needs for a little amateur surgery.

Now comes the hard part. The thing he doesn't want to do but knows he has to do if he's going to catch up to Charlie. And he needs that to happen.

He's not done with her just yet.

Steeling himself with a ragged breath, he pours the alcohol onto the wound and screams through the pain. His hands tremble so much it takes four tries before he's able to thread the needle. And when that's done, he grunts, grits his teeth, and begins to stitch.

EXT. DINER PARKING LOT—NIGHT

The diner is dark by the time Charlie reaches it. So dark that she almost misses it in her mad sprint down the road. She'd been looking for its light, not its shape. The neon and pink and blue around the entrance. The gaudy brightness of its sign. The warm glow spilling through the wide windows. All of it is now gone, replaced by an unnerving blackness.

It's closed.

There's no one here.

But then she spots a lone car still in the parking lot. The powder-blue Cadillac she'd noticed when they first arrived. She hopes it means someone's still there.

Charlie moves to the door, her legs heavy and her chest tight. She ran for at least half an hour. The longest she's ever run in her life.

Despite the cold, her body is soaked with sweat. Charlie feels it underneath the coat. A damp stickiness that makes her shirt cling to her skin. She places a hand on her heart and realizes that she's still holding the handcuffs. Her grip is so tight around them that she has to force her fingers loose.

Not knowing what else to do, she shoves the cuffs into the front pocket of her jeans. A good idea. They'll serve as evidence. Proof that Josh had tried to use them on her and that she had killed him in self-defense.

The thought knocks the air out of her.

She just killed someone.

No, she didn't see Josh die. She couldn't bring herself to stick around for that. But she knows he's dead. A fact that makes her look down at her blood-caked hands. She uses the coat to wipe them clean, knowing deep down that it's pointless. It doesn't matter that she killed a killer. Her hands will be forever stained.

Charlie tries the diner's front door. Although the blinds have been lowered over the windows and the sign on the door has been turned to read CLOSED, the handle still gives when she pushes on it.

Opening the door a crack, she looks inside. The only lights she sees come from the dessert case, the pies within still aglow, still spinning, and the jukebox. All the booths are empty. Chairs have been placed upside down on the counter. Under her feet, the floor glistens with moisture. It's just been mopped.

"Hello?"

Charlie pauses, hoping for a response. When none comes, she steps inside and says, "Please. I need help."

She turns to the booth she and Josh occupied a mere hour ago, shocked by how much can change in that short span of time. Sixty minutes ago, she was just a scared college student. Now she's a killer.

Charlie hears a noise from the rear of the diner, just behind the door to the kitchen. She whirls around to see the door swinging open as Marge pushes through it, still in her uniform. In her hand is a wet rag. She sees Charlie and stops just beyond the door, surprised.

"Charlie?" she says. "Sweetie, what happened?"

Charlie can only imagine how she looks to the waitress.

Panting.

Sweaty.

Bloody.

"Josh," she says. "He attacked me. And I—I stabbed him."

A bony hand flies to Marge's mouth. "Are you okay?"

Charlie's body answers for her. Her legs, numb from shock and fear and all that running, buckle. The rest of her sways. At first a little, then a lot. A sudden, shocking tilt during which she manages to blurt out a complete sentence.

"I think we should call the police."

"Of course," Marge says, rushing toward her. "Of course, of course."

Charlie's still tilting when Marge reaches her and shuffles behind her, out of view. At first, she thinks the waitress is trying to keep her upright. But then one of Marge's hands clamps over her nose and mouth.

In that hand is the rag she was holding, now wet against Charlie's skin, stinking of mildew and something else. Something strong that makes Charlie twitch and grow dizzy.

The tilting continues. The diner doesn't spin so much as fade, the walls, the floor, the ceiling all turning to mist. The jukebox is the last to go. Its colored lights flare like a match just before it's blown out.

Then it, too, is gone.

ONE A.M.

INT. DORM ROOM—DAY

Charlie wakes up in bed.

Her bed.

The one in her dorm room at Olyphant. She knows this without even opening her eyes because of the way it sags in the center like a hammock, which always helped her sleep better even though it meant she'd wake with her lower back throbbing.

There's no throb now, though. She feels like she's floating. Not in the bed but slightly above it, hovering like Linda Blair in *The Exorcist.*

Someone else is there. Standing by the bed. Smelling like cigarette smoke and Chanel No. 5.

Maddy.

"Wakey wakey," she says.

Charlie's eyes flutter open as she takes in the welcome sight of her friend. Maddy's wearing a Chanel suit. A classic. The kind Jackie Kennedy wore in Dallas, only hers is lime green and the fabric on the sleeve is pilled. In one white-gloved hand is a glass of champagne. The other holds a plate topped with a slice of cake.

"Happy birthday, Charlie."

Maddy smiles.

Wide.

Her red lips curdle into a grimace that reveals a dark space where one of her canine teeth should be. It's still bleeding—a steady trickle that overflows Maddy's bottom lip and spills down her chin before dripping onto the cake in crimson dollops.

INT. DINER—NIGHT

Charlie wakes with a start.

Not in bed. Not in her dorm room.

She's in a wooden chair. Creaky. Uncomfortable. Its ramrod-straight back forces her to sit unnaturally upright, her spine pinched from the effort. She tries to slouch but can't. It's as if she's been glued to the chair.

It isn't until she tries to move her arms that she notices they've been strapped down with ropes. They wind around her wrists and the chair's arms, binding them together, the ropes so tight they dig into her skin and cut off the circulation in her hands. Her fingers have turned white. She wiggles them but feels nothing.

It's the same with her toes, thanks to rope around her ankles, lashing her legs to the chair.

More rope winds around her upper body in two spots—just under her rib cage and again at the base of her neck. It's so tight that she struggles to breath. Panic fills her like water, threatening to drown her.

"Help!" she yells, her voice gurgling, like there really is water in her lungs. "Someone please help me!"

Marge speaks in the darkness, her voice husky, hushed.

"No one can hear you, sweetie. No one but me."

A light is switched on. A single bare bulb hanging from the ceiling that casts a bright, unsparing light on her surroundings.

A small room.

Perfectly square.

Along the walls, shelves stretch from floor to ceiling. Filling them are cans and boxes and cartons and bins. Marge leans against one of the shelves, watching her.

"Welcome back," she says.

Through the doorway behind her, Charlie can see a walk-in refrigerator on the other side of a narrow hallway. Its door is shut tight, a steady hum muffled behind it. To the right of the fridge is a stack of wooden crates, beyond which Charlie can see a sliver of kitchen.

She's still in the diner.

She has no idea why.

Charlie struggles beneath her restraints, the chair bucking. "What's going on?" she says.

"It's best if you stay quiet," Marge says.

That's not going to happen. Not while Charlie's tied to a chair in what looks to be a storeroom.

"I don't know why you're doing this, but it's not too late to stop. You can just let me go and I'll leave and never tell anyone."

That idea doesn't go over well with Marge. The waitress scowls and thrusts a hand into her apron pocket.

"Are you going to hurt me?" Charlie says.

"I don't know yet," Marge replies. "Maybe. That depends on you."

Charlie doesn't know what to do with that information. It sits in her brain like a rock in a stream—heavy and immobile, even though the current swirls all around it.

"What do you want from me?"

A circle of light forms on the refrigerator behind Marge, growing larger. Charlie assumes it's from a car pulling into the parking lot, its high beams shining through the round window in the door leading to the main dining room. That would put the door and dining room to their left. Good to know for when Charlie tries to escape. If she gets the chance. The ropes around her remain tight no matter how much she strains against them.

The light on the fridge vanishes.

Charlie hears—or thinks she hears—a car door slowly opening. She's only certain when she hears a telltale slam two seconds later.

Definitely a car door.

Someone's out there.

And from the look of concern that crosses Marge's face, she's not expecting whoever it is.

Charlie's heart pounds in her ears. This could be help. It could mean rescue. She opens her mouth to scream, but Marge is upon her before she can let it out, stuffing a dish towel into her mouth. It tastes faintly like dish soap. Enough to make Charlie gag as Marge connects the ends of the towel in a tight knot at the back of her head.

Out front, someone tries the diner's front door, finding it locked. Undeterred, whoever it is raps on the glass.

"Hello? Is anyone there?"

Charlie gasps beneath the dish towel, sending more soap taste against the back of her throat.

She'd recognize that voice from a mile away.

Robbie.

"Hello?" he calls again, punctuating it with another knock on the door.

Charlie goes completely silent and still, wondering if she's mistaken. There's no way it could be Robbie. It must be someone else. The police. A hungry motorist. Anyone but her boyfriend, who would have needed to drive more than an hour to get here. She's proven wrong when the person outside calls, "Charlie? Are you in there?"

It *is* Robbie.

Charlie thinks: He's here to rescue her.

She thinks: He can easily overpower Marge.

She thinks: In a few seconds, this will all be over.

But then another thought emerges, one less hopeful than the others.

She thinks: Right now—this very moment—could be another movie in her mind. It doesn't matter that Marge also hears him, her lips forming an irritated scowl. That might also just be part of the movie. Irrational hope projected onto the backs of her eyelids.

Robbie calls her name again, prompting Marge to reach into her apron pocket and remove what she's been hiding there.

A pistol.

It's small. Almost dainty. There's ivory at the handle and a polished shine to the slate-gray barrel.

"Make one sound," Marge whispers, "and I'll shoot him."

She leaves the storeroom and pushes into the dining room. Left alone, Charlie feels hope and fear collide in her chest as, silent behind the makeshift gag, she listens to Marge unlock the front door and open it just a crack.

"Sorry," Marge says, using her sassy-yet-weary waitress voice. "We're closed."

Charlie pictures her standing by the dessert case, the gun hidden in her apron as Robbie tries to peer around her, deeper into the diner.

"Was there a girl here earlier?" Robbie says.

"Lots of girls come here, hon."

"How many were here tonight?"

"Can't say I was keeping count."

Charlie's tempted to make noise, whether it's screaming into her gag or toppling the chair or trying to throw herself against one of the shelves. She knows Robbie could easily overpower Marge. He's got her beat by several inches and probably fifty pounds of muscle. The only thing keeping her silent is the gun.

Before tonight, Charlie wouldn't have believed that someone like Marge was capable of doing harm. But in the span of a few hours she now knows better. Now she knows that ordinary people are capable of violent, vicious deeds. Look at her, for example. She just plunged a knife into a man's stomach and left him to die.

So, no, she's not going to test Marge. She's going to stay silent and still because she refuses to let Robbie get hurt. Charlie has enough regret for one lifetime. She can't take any more.

"My girlfriend called me from here earlier tonight," Robbie says. "About two hours ago."

"Are you sure she was calling from here, hon? There's lots of places like this around here."

"Yes," Robbie says. "She referred to it by name. The Skyline Grille. She told me she was in danger."

"What kind of danger?"

"She didn't say. But I know she was here and in trouble and I—" Robbie, flirting with sounding hysterical, stops to collect himself. "I haven't heard from her since, and I'm very worried about her."

"What does she look like?" Marge asks, as if she doesn't already know.

"She's young. Twenty. Brown hair. Pale complexion. Her name is Charlie, and she would have been wearing a red coat."

"Now I remember her," Marge says. "Pretty girl. Friendly. Told me goodbye on her way out the door. She was here with another fella. Big guy. Good-looking."

"But they're gone now?"

"There's no one here but me, sweetie."

Robbie pauses, thinking. Even without being able to see him, Charlie knows he's got his head lowered and the thumb of his right hand running along his bottom lip. His usual lost-in-thought pose.

"Did she look scared in any way?" he says. "Or like she appeared to be in danger?"

"Not from what I can recall," Marge says. "They weren't here long. Just ordered some food and some drinks, scarfed it down, and left."

"Did you see what kind of car they were in?" Robbie asks. "Or what direction they went?"

"I didn't. I was in the kitchen when they left. Came back to an empty table. They paid the check and left."

A shout forms in the back of Charlie's throat, rising upward, threatening to slip free. *She's lying!* it wants to yell. *I'm here! I'm right here!*

She forces the words back down, even though Robbie's now preparing to leave.

"If she comes back, could you tell her Robbie is looking for her?" he says.

"I will," Marge says. "But I won't be here for much longer. I'm fixing to leave myself in a few minutes. Sorry I couldn't be more of a help."

"It's fine," Robbie says. "Thank you for your time."

"No problem, hon. Hope you get in touch with her real soon."

Charlie hears the door close, the lock being snapped into place, the start of a car engine. The circle of light appears on the fridge door again before sliding away. A moment later, Marge returns to the storeroom, the pistol back in her apron and a dark-brown bottle and handkerchief now in hand.

"Your boyfriend says hi," she says. "Devoted fella you've got there. I hope you appreciate him."

Charlie nods, unable to speak and too overwhelmed to do anything else.

She does appreciate Robbie. More than he could possibly know. He came for her. Even though she was leaving him—and breaking his heart in the process—he drove all this way to help her. A tear slips down her cheek, making it all the way to the side of her mouth before being sucked up by the gag.

"There's nothing to cry about," Marge says, more judgmental than consoling. "You stayed quiet and I didn't hurt him. I kept my part of the deal."

Yet another tear falls. Charlie can't help it. She had been so ready to abandon what she and Robbie had. Because she felt guilty. And that she didn't deserve him. And that he would leave her soon enough. But then he showed up here, and now she understands that she was wrong. Yes, she still feels guilty, and, no, she doesn't deserve him. But he never intended to leave her. He came to get her back. And now it might be too late.

"We're leaving," Marge says. "In order to do that, I need to use this again."

She holds up the bottle and handkerchief, making sure Charlie can see them.

"I'm going to remove the gag now. If you scream, I will shoot you. If you fight me, I will shoot you. Do I make myself clear?"

Charlie nods.

"Good," Marge says. "I hope you really mean that. Because I'm warning you, hon, you don't want to fuck with me."

She opens the bottle, letting out a noxious vapor that hits Charlie all the way on the other side of the storeroom. Marge places the handkerchief over the bottle before tipping it, dousing the cloth. Then she steps toward Charlie.

"Please," Charlie says, struggling to form the word behind the gag. "Don't."

Marge yanks the gag from Charlie's mouth. Now free to speak clearly, she says, "Please just let me go."

"Now why in the world would I do that, sweetie?" Marge says. "You were never supposed to leave. I knew you'd be back, but I didn't think it would be on your own."

It takes Charlie a moment to understand what she means. Her

brain's still reeling from a night full of movies in her mind, stress, shock, and whatever liquid Marge has been dousing onto the handkerchief. Chloroform, most likely. Something not carried by an ordinary waitress in an average greasy spoon.

Marge had been waiting for her. This wasn't a spur-of-the-moment detour. Josh had brought her here on purpose.

The entire night had been planned in advance.

"Are you working with Josh?"

"Who?"

"Jake," Charlie says, correcting herself. "Jake Collins. Are you working with him?"

"It's more like he's working with me."

Marge is upon her now, swooping in with the handkerchief and slapping it over Charlie's nose and mouth. Charlie tries to hold her breath, but it's not possible for very long. The pressure from Marge's hand makes her body thirst for air. Charlie cries out from beneath the handkerchief as the fumes fill her nose, her mouth, her lungs.

Everything begins to fade. Marge's face and the storeroom and even her thoughts. As her surroundings once again evaporate, Charlie manages one single thought, spurred by what Marge just said.

He's working for me.

Charlie thinks it means that Josh isn't the Campus Killer.

Or, at least, he's not the only one.

EXT. DINER PARKING LOT—NIGHT

Fifteen minutes later, Charlie shuffles out of the diner still woozy from the chloroform, which lingers far longer than a movie in her mind. Those she snaps out of almost instantly. But the chloroform takes it sweet time to go away. Right now, only half of her world has returned. Just what's directly in front of her. Everything on her periphery is still out of focus. Nothing but shifting blurs.

But she's aware of Marge directly behind her, holding the pistol at the small of her back. The end of the barrel knocks against Charlie's spine as they move, awkwardly, toward Marge's Cadillac.

When she came to in the storeroom, Charlie found herself in a standing position, propped against a shelf like a mummy on display. An apt description, seeing how she has again been wrapped with rope. This time it's around her ankles, binding them closely together, hence the shuffle.

Her wrists are also tied, forcing her to hold her forearms awkwardly together in front of her. Marge clearly hadn't searched her, otherwise she would have found Josh's handcuffs still in the front pocket of Charlie's jeans and used those instead. It would have been more comfortable for Charlie—even though she suspects making her comfortable isn't something on Marge's agenda.

In addition to the gun, Marge also sports a black parka thrown on over her uniform. Hanging from her shoulder is a bulky satchel. Whatever's inside clangs together as they walk around the rear of the car. Charlie also hears a crunching sound beneath her feet. When she looks down, she spots bits of red glass scattered across the parking lot surface.

"Get in," Marge says as she opens the rear door on the passenger side.

Charlie stares at the inside of the car and thinks about running. She knows it's not possible. Not with her legs and arms tied like they are. Even if it were, Marge could easily put a bullet in her back.

Yet Charlie considers it all the same.

Just springing away from Marge, hoping the old woman is a lousy shot and somehow misses her as she hops out of the parking lot and into the road, not stopping until she reaches the highway. Surely someone would stop for her. A truck driver or a cop like Officer Tom or someone coming home from the late shift. Some Good Samaritan who'd slam on the brakes as soon as they spotted her hobbling along the road's shoulder, panic writ large in her eyes.

Charlie pauses beside the car, doing the math, gauging to see how quickly she might be able to do it.

It doesn't take her long to deduce that it's impossible.

Even if it takes her only ten seconds to get out of the parking lot, she knows Marge can use those same ten precious ticks of time to jump into the car, start the engine, and make chase. Even if it took Marge minutes—one, five, ten—Charlie would still be shuffling down Dead River Road, with no guarantee of stumbling upon a kindly motorist. Especially at this hour.

"Get *in*," Marge says again, this time nudging her with the gun barrel.

Charlie does, with much reluctance and even more struggle.

With her arms tied, she's forced to turn around, bend at the waist, and slide inside. She then twists her legs until she's completely in the car, leaning awkwardly against the back seat.

Marge shuts the door, rounds the front of the car, and slides behind the wheel. Before turning the key, she hits the button that locks all the doors.

Charlie is trapped. Again.

They leave the parking lot quickly, tires kicking up gravel as Marge swerves onto the road, heading toward the highway.

Charlie looks out the window, spotting the same scenery the Grand Am passed when she and Josh traveled to the diner from the opposite direction. That was two hours ago, and she's now in a different car with a different captor.

The only thing that remains the same is her fear.

INT. VOLVO—NIGHT

Robbie watches the dented Cadillac leave the parking lot. Since he doesn't want the waitress to know he's following her, his plan is to let her gain a little bit of distance before going after her.

It shouldn't be hard to keep up. There aren't any other cars on the road, for one thing. Then there's the fact that he knocked out one of her taillights in the parking lot, a trick he learned thanks to Charlie. It was in a movie she'd made him watch. A black-and-white one from the forties that mostly bored him. But he remembered the taillight trick, and the broken one now winks at him as the Caddy glides down the road.

It wasn't easy getting to the diner as fast as he did. After sprinting out of his apartment, Robbie got in his Volvo and hightailed it to I-80. On the interstate, he drove like a bat out of hell, not caring if he got pulled over. In fact, he hoped that he would, thinking he might get a police escort out of it.

He didn't know what to expect once he got to the Skyline Grille. He'd hoped to find the place open and bustling and Charlie enjoying a milkshake, the whole thing a complete misunderstanding. Instead, the diner was closed and the only person around seemed to be that waitress, who clearly had been lying. In the span of a few sentences, she told him that Charlie had said goodbye when she left *and* that she hadn't seen her depart.

So after breaking her taillight, he decided to drive a few hundred yards up the road and wait, the front of the diner still within view. He wanted to see the waitress leave. He thought he'd follow her, ask her a few more questions, get the police involved if necessary. Not that the police had been useful the first time he called them. Considering the way that dispatcher brushed him off, he doubted a cop ever stopped by the diner.

Which is why he sat in his car, the engine off but the keys still in the ignition, watching for the waitress. What Robbie didn't expect was to see Charlie with her, being led out of the diner like a death row inmate heading to the gas chamber. It was such an awful sight that he almost jumped out of the car and ran to rescue her.

But then he saw the gun the waitress was pointing at her back and decided that running was the worst thing he could do at the moment. As Charlie got into the back of the car, Robbie tried to get a good look at her. Although it was hard to tell from such a distance and in the middle of the night, she didn't appear to have been physically harmed.

He hopes it stays that way.

What he doesn't understand—and hasn't since the moment Charlie called him—is what the hell happened between the university and here. What little she told him on the phone suggested it had something to do with the guy Charlie had gotten a ride with.

Josh.

Robbie thinks that was the name she had mentioned.

But he saw no sign of any guy when he peeked into the diner as the waitress was lying to him. Nor did it look like there was anyone else inside the Cadillac as it sped out of the parking lot.

He can only assume that this Josh—whoever he is and wherever he might be now—is working with the waitress.

What they want with Charlie, however, is impossible to know.

Not until Robbie gets to wherever it is the Cadillac is heading.

Up ahead, the broken taillight disappears below the horizon. Time to move. Robbie quickly starts the car, puts it in gear, and begins to follow.

INT. GRAND AM—NIGHT

He drives toward the diner, even though what he's doing doesn't really qualify as driving at all. It's merely rolling and steering at the same time. And he's doing a shit job of it. Moving down Dead River Road at a snail's pace, he can barely manage to keep the Grand Am inside the lane.

The stab wound is to blame. Each time he presses a pedal or shifts gears, pain flares along his side, making it feel like everything from shoulder to knee is on fire.

At least the bleeding's stopped, thanks to his stitch job, the gauze pad, and an abundance of medical tape. Crisscrossing the gauze multiple times, the tape has seared to his skin, pulling it whenever he moves and creating another, more pinching layer of pain.

It's still better than what he felt while sewing himself back up. He's been stitched up plenty of times. That's nothing new. And back when he was still on active duty and serving in Beirut, circumstances forced him to give stitches to others. But he's never had to do both at the same time before.

It wasn't pretty.

When you're about to hurt yourself, your nerves send a signal to the brain that tells you to stop doing whatever it is that's causing the pain.

Simple.

Not so simple is forcing yourself to do it anyway, no matter what your brain tells you, knowing you're about to cause yourself a world of hurt. He paused as the needle went in and paused as it went out, repeating the process five times before the cut in his side was fully closed.

Now he's driving.

Or trying to.

Heading to the Skyline Grille instead of a hospital, which is where he really should be going. But he doesn't like hospitals. He's not a fan of all the questions they ask in the ER. And the first one he'll get when they take one look at his amateurishly stitched, overly taped wound is "Who stabbed you?"

Because of that, he'd rather skip the hospital for now.

There may come a time tomorrow when he can't avoid it. If that moment comes, he'll be sure to make up some excuse as to how he took a steak knife to the gut. He has no plans to mention Charlie. That wouldn't be wise.

So it's off to the diner, drifting out of the lane with each line of pain that burns up his side. He needs to get to the diner because that's where Marge is. It's also likely Charlie's location, considering how there's really nowhere else to go around these parts.

Just the Skyline Grille.

The place where Charlie was supposed to have stayed.

That was the plan, at least. Find her, get her into the car by any means possible, and take her to the diner. Done, done, and done.

Once at the diner, when Marge came to take their order, he gave the signal that Charlie, no stranger to code words herself, didn't notice.

What's your blue-plate special?

Translation: This is the girl.

The rest depended on Marge's response. If she had told him, "We don't do that here. What's printed on the menu is what we got," it meant that everything was called off. Instead, she said, "Salisbury steak." Which meant that everything was still a go and that he should leave Charlie at the diner.

What definitely wasn't part of the plan was Marge purposefully spilling tea on Charlie so the two of them could have a moment alone. He knows why she did it. She didn't think he was doing a good enough job and that Charlie might act in unpredictable ways because of it.

Turns out she was right.

He certainly didn't predict Charlie playing that damn song on the jukebox, revealing she knew if not everything, then at least enough. Nor could he have foreseen that she'd insist on getting back into the car with him. He only agreed to it because he knew he could easily bring her back in a few minutes. Besides, it seemed better than just taking off while she was still in the bathroom and never seeing her again. He thought it might be nice to drive a little and chat a bit more. A proper goodbye before he slapped on the cuffs.

Then Charlie stabbed him and now he's got five homemade stitches in his side, tape tugging at his skin, and a sweatshirt crunchy with dried blood.

So much for a proper goodbye.

When the diner comes into view a half-mile down the road, he sees that the place is dark and that the parking lot is empty. Yet there's still an unusual amount of traffic for this road at this hour. About halfway between the Grand Am and the diner is a Volvo sitting on the road's shoulder, its headlights off and the engine still. Far in the distance, a car with a broken taillight travels in the direction of the on-ramp to the interstate.

He pounds the brakes and cuts the Grand Am's own lights, curious to see what happens next.

When the car with the broken taillight fades from view, the Volvo comes to life and edges onto the road. As it drives off in the same direction as the other car, he spots an Olyphant University sticker on the rear bumper.

The boyfriend, he assumes.

Here to rescue Charlie.

Another assumption he makes is that this boyfriend of hers didn't come all this way just to tail some random car. That means the one with the broken taillight is Marge, with Charlie in tow.

He allows himself a pain-tinged smile.

Maybe he'll get his goodbye after all.

He waits until the Volvo is a good distance away before flicking on the Grand Am's headlights again. Then he resumes driving. For real this time, even though his rolling-and-steering approach hurt far less. He grits his teeth, grips the steering wheel, and endures the pain.

There's no other choice. He knows that he needs to keep up with the Volvo and that this night, already a clusterfuck to begin with, just got a lot more complicated.

INT. CADILLAC—NIGHT

Charlie's world is still blurred at the edges, even though the chloroform has all worn off. The blurriness now is caused by the Cadillac's speed. Everything out the window—trees mostly, but also occasional clearings and empty lots—passes by in streaks of gray.

She doesn't know where Marge is taking her. Nor does she know where they are anymore. Charlie thought they were headed for the highway, but Marge blew right through the interchange that would have taken them there, making it just another gray streak.

Now Charlie is left to fearfully wonder not only where they're going but what will happen to her once they arrive. It's the same feeling she got during her first time riding away from the diner. Terrified and confused and almost ill with unease. Torn between wanting to keep driving forever and just getting to the ending.

The main difference between the two situations, other than the person behind the wheel, is that then Charlie had a weapon. Now she has nothing.

Charlie looks at her hands, stained pink with blood. Yes, she's aware that Josh might still be alive and that she had acted in self-defense. It doesn't change the fact that she willingly drove a knife into another living person, and she fears the memory of that action will stay with her for the rest of her life.

Making it worse is knowing that a single flash of violence didn't change a thing. She's still being held captive, and Josh is still involved somehow. Marge never said more about that—and hasn't said anything since getting into the car—leaving Charlie to wonder what that means. The scenarios she's thought up are as plentiful as they are disturbing. Now she's not sure which frightens her more: what's already happened or what's yet to come.

In the front seat, Marge continues to drive in silence. She seems to be lost in her own world as she grips the wheel and stares out at the dark road ahead. She doesn't even sneak an occasional glance in the rearview mirror to check on Charlie.

Not that Charlie can go anywhere tied up like this with all the doors locked. All she can do is sit in fear, her arms and legs straining against their binds as she watches Marge drive them to only God knows where.

"Where are you taking me?" she says, angrier than Marge probably likes. She can't help it. A stinging sense of betrayal streaks her fear. She had liked Marge. She trusted her. Charlie had thought of her as kind and grandmotherly—not too different from Nana Norma. As a result, Charlie had gone out of her way to protect her when she should have been focusing on her own safety.

When Marge doesn't answer, Charlie tries again. "Tell me why you're doing this!"

Still no answer. The only sign that Marge can even hear her is a mean look she flashes Charlie in the rearview mirror. A scowl, but angrier.

Another thing Charlie can see is a change in Marge's hair. That high hairdo now sits slightly askew atop her skull.

A wig.

It shifts again when Marge abruptly cuts the wheel to the left, veering the Cadillac onto a side road half-hidden by trees. Up ahead, Charlie sees a large sign dominating the roadside. Two spotlights sit beneath it, both of them dark. Still, there's enough moonlight for her to make out what it says.

Mountain Oasis Lodge.

Charlie recognizes the name. It's the same lodge that was on the billboard they passed on the interstate. Like that ragged billboard, the sign has seen better days. The "O" in Oasis is missing, leaving only a phantom letter standing out against the sun-bleached paint around it.

Beyond the sign, a chain lies limp across the road. Attached to it, lying flat against the ground, is another sign.

NO TRESPASSING

Marge keeps driving, tires crunching over the chain.

The forest is thick here—a dense expanse of evergreens that climb the mountainside. Through the trees, Charlie gets glimpses of a large structure perched halfway up the mountainside. Accompanying them is the whoosh of rushing water from somewhere nearby. Soon the forest clears and the Mountain Oasis Lodge stands before them in all its decrepit glory.

The billboard on the interstate didn't do it justice.

The lodge is *big.* An ungainly stack of windows, walls, and exposed timbers that stretches five stories from stone foundation to slate roof. It sits atop a ridge, balanced precariously, like a set of Lincoln Logs about to crumble. Next to it, a wide creek flows past the eastern side of the lodge before tumbling over a cliff into a ravine fifty feet below.

It was all probably beautiful once. Now it just looks eerie. Sitting dark and silent atop the ridge, pale in the moonlight, the lodge reminds Charlie of a mausoleum. One filled with ghosts.

During the approach, the car crosses a bridge spanning the ravine at the base of the waterfall. The bridge is narrow, with only a low wooden railing to prevent cars from crashing into the drink, and so close to the waterfall that spray from the cascade spatters the windshield as they pass. Charlie looks out the window and sees dark water swirling roughly ten feet below them.

On the other side of the bridge, the road begins its ascent, taking a path so twisted it might as well have been carved by an apple peeler. Taking turn after winding turn, the Cadillac slowly climbs the mountainside.

Instead of another wooden railing, one bend in the road that comes close to the waterfall is lined by a fieldstone wall that follows the curve. When Marge steers through it, more spray smacks the windows.

After two more sharp turns, the Caddy reaches the top of the ridge. There the road bends again, this time curving into a loop directly in front of the lodge. In its heyday, there must have been a constant stream of cars circling this roundabout. Now it's just them, pulling under an entrance portico, where Marge slams the brakes and cuts the engine.

"Why are we here?" Charlie says.

"To talk."

Marge scratches her scalp, two fingers burrowing beneath the wig, making it slip back and forth atop her head. Rather than straighten it again, she yanks off the wig and tosses it into the passenger seat, where it sits in a furry clump like a dead animal. Marge's natural hair is bone white and sprouts from her scalp in thin, thistly patches a millimeter high.

"You're sick," Charlie says, shifting tones, hoping sympathy will soften Marge.

It doesn't. Marge grunts out a single, bitter laugh and says, "No shit."

"Cancer?"

"Stage four."

"How long do you have?" Charlie says.

"The doctor says weeks, maybe. Two months, if I'm lucky. As if any of this is lucky."

Despite being at what Charlie assumes to be their final destination, Marge makes no move to leave the car. Charlie hopes it means she's having second thoughts about doing whatever it is she has planned, possibly because they're engaged in conversation and not locked in silence. She takes it as a sign to keep talking.

"How long have you had it?"

"A long time, apparently," Marge says. "When the doctors caught it is a different story."

"Is that why you're doing this? Because you know you don't have much time left?"

"No," Marge says. "I'm doing it because I know I can get away with it."

She throws open the car door and steps outside, taking the satchel but leaving the wig. She then goes to the other side of the car and opens the rear door, aiming the pistol at Charlie's temple as she slides out.

With the pistol again at Charlie's back, Marge marches her to the lodge's entrance—a tall set of mahogany doors inlaid with twin windows of stained glass.

"Nudge it open," Marge instructs. "It's already unlocked."

Charlie uses her shoulder to push the doors open. Beyond them is total darkness.

"Step inside," Marge says.

Again, Charlie does as she's told. She knows not to try to put up a fight. Because Marge is right—she can get away with anything she wants. She's terminally ill. Already sentenced to death.

And if Charlie's learned anything from the movies, it's that few things are more dangerous than someone with nothing to lose.

INT. LODGE LOBBY—NIGHT

Inside the lodge, all is dark. Charlie can only see what's immediately beyond the rectangle of pale moonlight spilling through the open door. Still, she can tell the lobby is as big as the lodge's exterior suggests. Every footfall on the parquet floor echoes to the ceiling high above.

The whole place reeks of neglect, the odors inside heightened by the darkness. The smell of dust is thick and overpowering. There are other scents, too. Mold. Damp. Traces of animals that have gotten inside. Charlie's nose twitches. She tries to scratch it, but her range of motion is useless thanks to the rope around her wrists.

Behind her, Marge rustles through the satchel, never pointing the pistol away from Charlie. Eventually, she pulls out a large flashlight and flicks it on. As the light sweeps across the lobby, Charlie catches quick glances of dust-streaked floor, unadorned walls, support timbers vanishing into the gloom above them.

Marge nudges the pistol into Charlie's back, moving them toward the rear of the lobby. There's another entrance there—a set of French doors flanked by rows of tall windows. The glass on the

French doors is opaque with dirt on both sides. Drapes cover the windows next to the French doors, pulled completely shut, their fabric turned gray and fuzzy by dust. The result is such a scarcity of light that it might as well be another wall.

The area has already been prepared for their arrival. In the glow of the flashlight, Charlie sees a large canvas drop cloth spread over the floor. Atop it sit a wooden chair, a stool, and two kerosene lanterns.

Marge drops the satchel on the floor, does more shuffling through the contents inside, and pulls out a box of matches, which she uses to light the two lanterns. Their combined glow brightens the lobby considerably, revealing a massive space made all the more cavernous by how empty it is. What Charlie assumes had once been filled with armchairs, potted plants, and guests bustling about is now a wide expanse of nothing.

To the right, the front desk sits dust-covered and unused. Behind it are bare patches on the wall where paintings had once hung. A lounge sits to the left, now empty save for an oak bar and emerald-colored lighting fixtures that hang over spaces where tables must have been.

Closer to the back of the lobby, the front desk and lounge give way to wide halls that lead to the lodge's two wings, one on each side. Charlie tries to look down each one, searching for a means of escape, but she can't see beyond their entrances. Even with the flickering glow of the lanterns, they're nothing but tunnels of darkness.

Marge, apparently tired of rifling through the satchel, dumps its remaining contents into a clattering pile on the canvas drop cloth.

There's the bottle of chloroform, of course, and the rag already used to apply it.

What's worse are the other items now spread out on the floor.

A knife.

Bigger than the one Charlie had used on Josh.

A carving knife.

Marge removes it from its leather sheath, exposing a wide blade and an edge so sharp it looks like it could slice bone.

She sets it down next to a pair of slip-joint pliers.

Charlie's body clenches at the sight of them, her muscles sparking with the urge to run.

She doesn't care that Marge still holds the gun and that running is impossible and that she doesn't know where to run even if she could.

All Charlie and her twitching body and racing brain care about is getting away.

Now.

Right now.

She makes a break for it as Marge still kneels on the floor, heading toward the nearest exit.

The French doors.

Charlie jackrabbits toward them, hoping they're unlocked, prepared to smash through them if they're not. When she slams into them, the doors rattle but don't open. She rams a shoulder into them. A pane of glass pops out and shatters to the ground outside.

Through the open square it left behind, Charlie sees a stone walkway, a drained swimming pool, lounge chairs stacked like firewood. She doesn't know if the walkway leads to another part of the lodge, but she doesn't care. Anywhere is better than here.

Charlie tries to throw herself into the door again, but Marge is upon her before she gets the chance. She tugs on the collar of Charlie's coat, pulling her backward, yanking her to the floor.

A slap of pain hits Charlie as her head bounces off the canvas-covered floor. White spots float across her vision, obscuring the sight of Marge climbing on top of her, surprisingly strong and shockingly heavy.

Through the white spots, Charlie sees Marge tip the chloroform bottle against the rag before clamping it over her nose and mouth.

More white spots.

Gathering.

Growing.

Soon Charlie can see nothing but white as the chloroform casts its spell. Marge doesn't keep the cloth over her face long enough to knock her out completely. It only makes her weak. A rag doll being dragged across the floor.

Charlie feels her body being lifted into the chair. More rope is wound around her torso and the back of the chair, holding her in place. The white spots start to fade one by one, like stars at dawn. By the time Charlie can see clearly again, she's been completely bound to the chair.

Marge stands in front of her, the pistol replaced by the pliers.

Fear spreads like lava in Charlie's chest.

"Who are you, and why are you doing this?"

"I told you," Marge says. "We're here to talk."

"About what?"

Marge lowers herself onto the stool in front of Charlie. There's a hardness to her that goes beyond her spindly body. It's in the set of her jaw and the frown etched on her lips and the darkness of her eyes.

"I want to talk," she says, "about my granddaughter."

TWO A.M.

INT. GRAND AM—NIGHT

Driving—honest-to-goodness driving—has taken a toll on him. He's a sweaty, pain-wracked mess by the time he reaches the entrance to the Mountain Oasis Lodge. Sitting in the car next to the sign with the missing "O," he wants nothing more than a warm bed, a cold beer, and a couple of Extra Strength Tylenol.

He resumes driving because he doesn't like the situation. Marge told him all she wanted to do with Charlie was talk. Well, you don't need to bring someone to an abandoned hotel in the Poconos to talk. They could have done that in the diner.

Even if it was easier to talk in another location, there's no good reason that Charlie's boyfriend felt the need to surreptitiously follow them there. The Volvo passed the sign a minute ago, going slow, its headlights out to keep Marge from noticing it.

Something else is going on here, and he feels the need to check it out.

He owes it to Charlie.

She wouldn't be here if it hadn't been for his lies and tricks and half-truths. None of which he's proud of. It was all part of the job. At least, that's what he told himself when trying to justify it. But the truth is that none of it was kosher. He knew that but ignored it.

Because the job was simple.

That's what Marge told him when they spoke on the phone. She had called him out of the blue, saying she got his name from a friend whose brother is a cop in Scranton and that he came highly recommended.

"Never let a man get away from me yet," he said.

"How about a woman?" Marge said.

"Plenty of them have gotten away from me," he'd said, trying to make a joke about his woeful dating history.

Marge hadn't found it funny.

"This one's young. Twenty. She shouldn't be a problem. You think you can help?"

"I usually only track down fugitives," he told her. "At the request of law enforcement. What you're talking about sounds a lot like kidnapping."

"I prefer to think of it as chaperoning."

He would have hung up if Marge hadn't then given her offer. Twenty thousand dollars. Half of it wired to him beforehand with the rest paid upon delivery. God help him, he couldn't say no to that. Business had been slow the whole summer and his savings account was all dried up. He was a month behind on his most recent car payment and would be short on rent at the end of the month if another job didn't come his way.

"Give me the details," he said.

Marge told him about the murder of her granddaughter at the hands of a serial killer, sparing none of the gory details. Stabbed. Tooth pulled. Body dumped in a field.

"I'm never going to see justice done," she said. "Not while I'm alive. Unless I get to talk to one particular person."

That person was her granddaughter's best friend, who had seen the killer but couldn't recall a single thing about him.

"You think she's lying?" Josh said.

"I think she just needs someone to jog her memory," Marge replied.

The trouble, according to her, was that the girl had made herself scarce. She hadn't come to the funeral, and she no longer answered her phone.

"I need you to find her and bring her to me," Marge said. "I want to see if she can remember anything that might help find the man who killed my Maddy."

"Don't you think that's a job for the police?"

Marge sniffed. "I'm prepared to give you twenty grand to make that none of your business."

He agreed, and the rest is history. The job turned out to be not so simple, and Charlie *was* a problem, albeit one he can't keep himself from admiring. Now he's driving over a NO TRESPASSING sign into a situation he's really not physically or mentally prepared for.

Like Charlie's boyfriend, he cuts the Grand Am's headlights and lets the wan light of the moon guide him. Not the best idea. When taking the car across a bridge in front of a waterfall, a bolt of pain hits, causing him to swerve close to the wooden guardrail and almost crash into the ravine.

With the bridge behind him, he begins the slow, twisting drive up the hill to the lodge. His body sways with each hairpin turn, the stitches in his side straining. At the top of the hill, he parks the Grand Am just inside the circular drive leading to the front of the lodge and cuts the engine. Both the Cadillac and the Volvo belonging to Charlie's boyfriend are also there, parked under the portico, no one inside them.

Before leaving the car, he grabs the steak knife Charlie had stabbed him with. It's sat on the floor of the passenger side the entire drive, still wet with his blood. He wipes it clean with his sweatshirt.

Knife in hand, he gets out of the car, unsure of what will be waiting for him when he enters the lodge.

The only thing he knows is that it's his fault Charlie's in this predicament.

And now it's his job to get her out.

INT. LODGE LOBBY—NIGHT

Charlie stares at Marge, realization bubbling up from the addled depths of her brain. No wonder she thought there was something familiar about the waitress when she first came to their table. Charlie had seen her before tonight. Not in person, but in a photograph. A young looker posing poolside with Bob Hope.

"You're Mee-Maw," she says.

"We never had the pleasure of meeting," Marge says. "But I heard all about you, Charlie. My Maddy talked a lot about you. She said you were a smart cookie. I warned her about that. I told her, 'Watch out for the smart ones, baby doll. They know how to hurt you.' And I was right."

But Charlie wasn't smart. Not when it came to Maddy. She was devoted. Except for that one time.

And that was all it took.

One slip. One pissy mood. One mistake.

And everything changed.

Now she's being held hostage by a woman who wants to do God knows what, and all Charlie can think is that she deserves all of it.

"I'm so sorry," she says.

It's not a plea. She doesn't expect three words to give Marge a change of heart. It's just a simple statement, made with all the sincerity she possesses.

"My granddaughter's dead," Marge replies. "Sorry doesn't mean shit."

"I loved her, too," Charlie says.

Marge shakes her head. "Not enough."

"And Josh—I mean, Jake. Is he related to Maddy, too?"

"Him?" Marge says as she absently scratches her tufted scalp. "He was just someone I hired to get you here. Never laid eyes on him until tonight. He's not my responsibility."

She glances at the stain on Charlie's coat where she had wiped Josh's blood from her hands. When fresh, it had blended in with the red of the fabric. Now dry, it stands out, dark and incriminating. Seeing it causes Charlie's stomach to churn.

She stabbed an innocent man.

She likely killed him.

Knowing that she thought it was in self-defense no longer matters.

She is a murderer.

"That coat of yours used to be mine, by the way," Marge says. "I gave it to Maddy when she turned sixteen. It's how I knew who you were the moment you walked into the diner."

Charlie remembers being in the bathroom, watching as Marge checked the coat's label. At the time, she thought the waitress was looking to see if it could be replaced. Now she knows that Marge was really just confirming her identity.

"You can have it back," Charlie says, even though it's the only thing she has to remember Maddy by. "I *want* you to have it."

"I'd rather have my granddaughter back," Marge says. "Do you know what it's like to bury someone you love, Charlie?"

"Yes."

Charlie knows it all too well. Those twin caskets. Those side-by-side graves. That double funeral that she was so unequipped to handle that it rewired her brain. Every movie in her mind can be traced back to that horrible moment in time, and no amount of little orange pills will change that.

"I thought I did," Marge says. "I buried my husband, and it hurt like hell. But nothing prepared me for losing Maddy. Other than a doctor and a nurse, I was the first person to hold her. Did she ever tell you that? Her father—that deadbeat—was already out of the picture, so I was there when she was born. She came out a scream-ing, wriggling mess, but when the nurse put her in my arms, all I saw was her beauty. In a dark world, she was light. Bright and blaz-ing. And then she was snuffed out. Just like *that*."

Marge snaps her fingers, and the sound echoes like a gunshot through the cavernous lobby.

"My daughter went through a bad spell. There's no denying that. She was messed up after Maddy was born, so I took on the burden of raising her. For the first four years of Maddy's life, I was her mother. And that kind of bond? It never goes away. Ever."

She grabs the knife and holds it up, bringing it so close that Charlie can see her reflection in the blade.

"When I found out Maddy was dead, it felt like someone had jammed this knife right into my heart and plucked it out. The pain. It was too much."

Charlie thinks about four days ago. Filling her cupped palm with little white pills. Swallowing them all. Watching Gene Kelly twirl in the rain as her eyelids grew heavy. All the while hoping that it would bring an end to every rotten thing she was feeling.

"I felt that way, too," she says. "I wanted to die."

"Well, I *am* dying," Marge says. "Whoever first said life's a bitch, hoo boy, they really nailed it. Life *is* a bitch. A nasty one. Because that feeling I had? Of wanting to be put out of my misery? That went away the day we buried Maddy. As I watched them lower her into the ground, something in me just snapped. In its place was rage. Like whoever had yanked out my heart had plugged the hole left behind with a hot coal. It *burned*. And I welcomed the feeling. After we put Maddy in the ground, I looked at my daughter—my only child, who had just buried *her* only child. I looked at her and vowed that I would make the person responsible pay for what they'd done. I swore that I was going to find who killed my Maddy. I was going to find them and rip a tooth out of their mouth, just like what they did to her. And that tooth would become my most cherished possession because it was proof. Proof that the person who slaughtered my granddaughter got the justice they deserved."

Marge pauses to stare at Charlie. She stares back, knowing they're alike. Two women made mad by grief.

"The irony is that as soon as I found some sense of purpose again, I got a call from the doctor telling me about the cancer," Marge says. "My daughter's in denial. She keeps saying a miracle can happen. But that's bullshit. There's no miracle coming my way. My time's almost up. Which is why you're here."

She lowers the knife and picks up the pliers, letting Charlie know exactly what this is about.

Revenge.

The same kind she had fantasized about getting during those sleepless nights when both anger and those little orange pills kept her awake. It never occurred to Charlie that someone else who had known and loved Maddy would have that same thirst for revenge.

And that she'd be on the receiving end of it.

Yet Charlie also understands. Since she blamed herself for what happened to Maddy, it's natural for Marge to do the same. And since Charlie, at the lowest point of her guilt and grief, had tried to end it all, it makes twisted sense that Marge would want to end her as well.

"You've brought me here to kill me, haven't you?"

Charlie's amazed at how calm she sounds, considering all the fear churning inside her. It's how she felt as Josh drove them away from the diner. A combination of terror and inevitability.

Acceptance.

That's what Charlie thinks has come over her. A grim understanding that this is the way things are going to end.

"No, sweetie," Marge says. "I'm here for information."

Her answer doesn't make Charlie feel any better. Nor does the way Marge flexes the pliers in front of her, opening and closing them like a hungry bird's beak.

"I don't know anything," Charlie says.

"Yes, you do," Marge says. "You were there. You saw the man who killed my granddaughter. Now you're going to tell me who he is."

"I don't *know.*"

"You know something. You *saw* something. Even if you don't think you did. Maddy told me all about that, you know. Your delusions. How you sometimes see things that aren't there. But the man who killed Maddy, he was there. He was *real.* And your eyes saw him, even if your brain saw something else." Marge taps Charlie's forehead. "That information's in there somewhere. You're going to give it to me. Even if I have to pry it out myself."

"Maddy wouldn't want you to do this."

Marge flashes her another dark look. "Maybe not. But she's no longer with us, thanks to you. Now, I'm going to ask you a few questions about what you saw that night. And if there's something you don't think you remember, well, I'll make you remember."

Charlie stares at the pliers, still opening and closing. They make a little clicking sound each time they connect.

Click.

Pause.

Click.

"We'll start with an easy one," Marge says. "Just to get that memory going. Were you with my granddaughter the night she was killed?"

"Yes," Charlie says. "I was."

"Where?"

"A bar. I didn't want to go, but Maddy insisted."

"Why did she insist?" Marge says. "I know there's a reason."

"Because she didn't like to walk alone."

"Yet that's what she ended up doing, isn't it?" Marge says with a curious head tilt, as if she doesn't already have the answer.

"She did," Charlie says, knowing not to lie. If anything's going to get her out of this, it'll be the truth.

"Why is that?"

"Because I left her there."

"All alone," Marge says, not bothering to phrase it like a question. It's a fact. One Charlie has tried to grapple with for the past two months.

"I regret it," she says, her voice breaking. "I regret it so much. And if I could go back and change it, I would."

"But you can't," Marge says. "It happened, and you have to live with that. This is your reality now."

Charlie understands that. So much so that she wishes she could escape into the movies this instant. She longs for the soothing distraction of a film—even one that's just in her mind. If she could, she'd summon one, taking her away from her current state of uncertainty, fear, and, she suspects very shortly, pain. But that's not how they work. Even if the projector in her mind does click on, it won't change the reality that Marge intends to hurt her.

The movies can't save her now.

"What did you tell my granddaughter before you left her all alone?" Marge says.

Charlie swallows hard, stalling. She doesn't want to say the words aloud. Not because she fears what Marge will do to her when she does—although Charlie fears that plenty. She wants to stay silent because she doesn't want to hear them again. She doesn't want to be reminded of her last words to her best friend.

"Go on," Marge says. "Tell me."

"The police already told you what I said."

"I want to hear it from you. I want to hear the exact words you said to Maddy."

"I—" Charlie swallows again, her throat tight and her mouth dry. "I told her to fuck off."

For a long time, Marge says nothing. There's just silence, thick in the darkness of the lobby. The only things Charlie hears are the pliers opening and closing.

Click.

Pause.

Click.

"For that," Marge finally says, "I should rip your tongue out. But then you wouldn't be able to tell me about the man in the alley. What did he look like?"

Charlie twists in the chair. "Please don't do this."

"Answer the question, sweetie," Marge says, holding the pliers open now, the space between the tips exactly the size of one of Charlie's back teeth. "It'll be easier for both of us if you do."

"I didn't get a good look at him," Charlie says.

"But you *saw* him."

"I saw a figment of my imagination. It was different than the real thing."

"Or maybe it was the same."

"It wasn't," Charlie says. "He looked like something out of a movie. He wore a hat."

Marge leans in closer. "What kind?"

"A fedora."

"And his clothes?"

Charlie closes her eyes, silently begging her memory to conjure what she saw that night. Not the movie in her mind, but the reality she failed to comprehend. Nothing comes to her. All she sees is the same dark figure that's haunted her for two months.

"I didn't see them."

"Yes, you *did*," Marge says, angrier now. An anger so palpable Charlie can feel it in her bones. "Now remember."

"I can't." Charlie's voice is a desperate rasp. "I can't remember."

"Then I'm going to make you."

Marge lunges for her. Charlie bucks in the chair as Marge draws near. Its legs rattle against the floor, creaking from the strain. But Charlie can't force herself from the restraints.

Not like this.

Not with Marge upon her now, pliers in hand, the tips still opening and closing.

Charlie closes her eyes and, in a last-ditch move to save herself, thrusts all her weight to the left, trying to topple the chair, even though the effort is futile. Her tooth can just as easily be yanked out while she's on the floor.

Marge uses one hand to steady the chair. The other shoves the pliers between Charlie's lips without hesitation. Charlie turns her head, but the tips of the pliers hook the corner of her mouth, like she's a fish caught on a line. Marge keeps up the pressure, first twisting the pliers then knocking them against Charlie's teeth.

A scream forms in Charlie's lungs, filling them. She doesn't want to scream. She knows it won't help. Yet here it is anyway, rising in her chest, choking its way up her throat, parting her jaws.

Marge finds the opening and stuffs the pliers through it.

Charlie bites down on them, her teeth grinding against metal.

Marge tugs on the handles.

The pliers open, parting Charlie's jaw like a car jack.

She tries to scream again, but the pliers are inside her mouth now, snapping open and shut until they close around her tongue.

Instead of a scream, another sound erupts from Charlie's throat—a strange, grotesque grunt that continues as the ridged insides of the pliers dig into her tongue and Marge keeps pulling, pulling, pulling. So hard Charlie fears she'll rip her tongue right out. The pain it creates causes more white spots, and Charlie knows their appearance means she's going to pass out again. Not from chloroform but from pain.

The pliers slip from her tongue with an agonizing rasp and latch onto a molar at the back of Charlie's mouth. Marge yanks, and Charlie lets out another brutal grunt that's quickly drowned out by the pliers scraping tooth enamel. A horrible sound that echoes against the inside of her skull.

But then another noise comes.

Distant.

Glass shattering from somewhere else in the lodge.

Marge hears it, too, for the pliers release her tooth and go slack inside Charlie's mouth.

There's more noise now. A door opening somewhere and a crunch of glass.

Marge looks behind them. She drops the pliers to the floor and removes the pistol from her apron pocket. Then, without speaking, she stands, grabs one of the lanterns, and leaves to find the source of the noise.

Charlie—in pain, bound to the chair, white spots still swirling across her vision—can only watch as Marge vanishes down one of the lodge's two wings. The glow of the lantern she carries forms a bubble of light around her. It isn't until both Marge and the brightness turn a corner and disappear that Charlie sees someone else.

A figure emerging from the darkness in the opposite direction.

Josh.

Seeing him prompts a dozen disparate thoughts in Charlie's head. Astonishment that he's there. Relief that he's alive. Worry about what he might do to her in retaliation for stabbing him.

Half of his sweatshirt is crusted with blood. The other half looks damp with sweat. Josh moves toward her, the stab wound making only half his body work properly. The other half drags behind him. Still, when his half-good, half-limping form draws near, Charlie flinches.

After what she did to him, she expects the worst.

But all Josh does is scan the lobby before whispering, "Where is she?"

Charlie jerks her head toward the wing Marge disappeared down.

Josh puts his hands on her shoulders, almost as if checking for signs of damage. "Are you okay? Did she hurt you?"

Not an easy question to answer. The throbbing pain inside her mouth where the pliers had scraped and clawed tells her that yes, Marge hurt her. But not as much as she could have. Not yet. To save time—and to spare her aching mouth—Charlie just shakes her head.

"Good," Josh says.

He pulls something out of his pocket.

The knife.

The same one Charlie had plunged into his side.

Unlike her, Josh puts it to better use by cutting through the rope wound around her wrists. He does it carefully, sawing through the rope in a way that won't cut her. Charlie can't believe what she's seeing.

Josh is saving her.

Using the very knife she tried to kill him with.

"I'm getting you out of here," he says as the rope binding Charlie's wrists finally falls away.

Josh moves behind her, trying to undo the rope wound around her torso and the chair.

"I'm sorry," Charlie says, relieved to find that the pain in her mouth lessens when she speaks. "I'm sorry for what I did to you."

"I'm the one who's sorry. I never should have let you get into my car. She told me she just wanted to talk to you. I didn't know she was going to do something like this."

"And I didn't know you were a—"

"Bounty hunter?" Josh says. "I figured that."

"Why didn't you tell me?"

"Because I couldn't. You're not a fugitive. And this wasn't a law enforcement gig. You're just a college student some old lady hired me to bring to a diner in the middle of fucking nowhere. A private job I took because I needed the money. I could lose my license if anyone found out."

"So everything you said in the car—"

"Was all just a way to get you here as easily as possible," Josh says. "I was never planning to hurt you, Charlie. Using force would have been a last resort. So I had to get creative. But messing with your head like that was a shitty thing to do, and I'm sorry."

Charlie would have been less forgiving under normal circumstances. But it's hard to stay mad when the rope around her arms drops away from the chair and into her lap. Because her hands are free, Josh lets her try to unloop it from around her as he comes around front again and starts sawing at the ties around her ankles.

He's almost through one strand when Charlie notices the glow of a lantern over his shoulder.

Marge.

She stands on the other side of the canvas drop cloth, kerosene lantern in one hand, pistol in the other.

Seeing Josh there, about to set Charlie loose and ruin her plan, breaks something inside the woman's grief-rattled psyche. Charlie sees it happening. An internal snapping that jerks her whole body.

And before it passes, Marge raises the gun, aims, and fires.

EXT. LODGE—NIGHT

Robbie almost used the front doors. After quietly steering his Volvo to a stop behind the dented Cadillac, he intended to just storm into the building, tackle that old waitress if necessary, and retrieve Charlie.

But then he thought about the gun.

He knows the waitress has one. He saw it poking against Charlie's back outside the diner.

And he's watched enough movies with Charlie to know things usually don't end well for characters who simply burst through the front door. Especially if the bad guy has a gun. And since the only weapon Robbie has is the same tire iron he'd used to knock out the Caddy's taillight, he opted for an alternative route.

Now he clambers through the woods to the right of the lodge. His plan is to find a back way into the building that will let him sneak up on the waitress. But this side of the building isn't landscaped. It's just a strip of rocky, tree-choked terrain sitting between the lodge itself and the rushing creek that leads to the nearby waterfall, which is deafening in its roar. Robbie can't hear anything else, which is good in that it masks the sound of his approach but bad in that it does the same to anyone who might be trying to sneak up on him.

The darkness doesn't help. The trees here are mostly evergreens with full branches that blot out the moonlight and crowd the ground with shadow. Wearing only sneakers, Robbie's feet slip often on the snow that had fallen earlier. Never a good thing when you're mere yards from water. One false step could send him tumbling into the creek, at which point it would be over. Sure, Robbie was the star of the swim team and now a coach, but not even an Olympic gold medalist would be able to overpower the pull of that waterfall.

As he trudges through the snow and the dark, always keeping an eye on the rapids to his right, Robbie knows it would have been easier to use the pay phone he saw outside the diner to call the police.

It also would have been foolish.

He'd already tried calling the police once, and that didn't help. Then there's the fact that, had he waited in the diner parking lot for the cops to arrive, he'd have no idea where the waitress had taken Charlie. He certainly wouldn't have known this place existed if he hadn't followed the Cadillac here.

Making his way to the rear of the lodge, Robbie knows deep down that he made the right decision. It's better for him to be here, where he can actually do something, than back at the diner, waiting for cops who may or may not believe him.

But he also knows he needs to be cautious. Not just in his movements, but in his thinking. He's a smart guy. He's studying to be a math professor, for God's sake. He can deduce his way out of this. Slow and steady. That always wins the race.

But then a noise erupts from deep inside the lodge.

A gunshot.

Robbie's sure of it.

Not even the angry roar of the falls can disguise that sound.

Hearing it, he knows instantly that slow and steady are no longer going to cut it.

He needs to be fast.

And even then it might already be too late.

INT. LODGE LOBBY—NIGHT

In the echo chamber of the lobby, the gunshot is as loud as a fire-cracker.

It's followed by a splat of blood hot on Charlie's face and a grunt from Josh.

Soft. Surprised.

He lists to the right and hits the floor with a thud that sounds nothing like the way a body lands in the movies. It's a pitiful noise. Both soft and loud at the same time. Like a sack of laundry landing on a bed.

Charlie looks down and sees Josh facedown on the floor, a bullet hole and widening splotch of blood in the shoulder of his sweatshirt. More blood oozes out from under him, soaking into the canvas drop cloth.

Frantic, Charlie bends forward and tugs at the rope around her ankles. She needs to help Josh. If he's not already beyond help. He doesn't move when she looks his way, nor does he make a sound.

On the other side of the canvas, Marge stands with the pistol still raised. Her face is a mask of surprise, as if she, too, can't believe what she's just done. Like Josh before her, she leans precariously to the side.

Although she manages to remain upright, the lantern in her hand falls from her grip and smashes onto the floor.

Kerosene spills from the toppled lantern. A quicksilver stream that twists across the canvas.

It makes it all the way to the drapes at the windows before the fire arrives. At first, it's a streak of blue flames rushing over the path laid out by the kerosene. The fire starts to glow orange as it digs into the canvas, forging its own path over the drop cloth and, soon, the drapes.

They ignite in an instant, the flames climbing the fabric toward the ceiling. Within seconds, all the drapes are engulfed. One set falls away, dropping to the floor in a flutter of fire, smoke, and ash.

A new fire springs up where it lands, spreading across the drop cloth. Once it's chewed its way to the edge of the canvas, it gets to work on the parquet floor.

When another section of drapes falls, a third patch of fire forms, with the same result.

Charlie knows it'll just keep happening until that whole area and beyond are engulfed in flame. And when the fire reaches the other kerosene lantern, the situation will go from bad to worse.

Looking to Josh, Charlie sees a growing wall of fire rolling his way.

"Help us!" she yells to Marge, who's backed away from the flames, stunned.

Lost in a daze, Marge either doesn't hear her or refuses to listen.

Charlie pulls the final bit of rope from her legs and goes to Josh, who remains silent and motionless. Without thinking, she grabs him by the ankles and begins to drag him away from the fire. Their progress is marked by a streak of blood on the canvas that's quickly devoured by the flames trailing them.

Soon they're off the drop cloth and sliding across the lobby's parquet floor. Not safe from the flames. Far from it. But away, which is all that matters right now.

Marge has also made her way toward the front of the lobby, staring at the growing fire with an agonized look. The pistol's still in her hand, still extended, and for a surreal moment Charlie thinks she's going to try to shoot at the flames. But then Marge swivels, aiming the gun right at her.

Charlie raises her hands.

"Please," she says. "Please don't do this. He needs help."

Off to the side, the fire gets larger. Both the chair and the stool now burn, flames leaping from the spot where Charlie had been sitting minutes earlier. All but one set of drapes has fallen away from the windows, revealing more flames reflected in the glass and making the blaze seem even bigger. Smoke spirals toward the ceiling, accumulating at the peaked roof and exposed beams.

Charlie sees all that wood above and thinks one thing: this fire is only going to continue to grow.

"Please," she tells Marge. "Let me go. Let us both go."

Charlie thinks she might be getting through to her. Marge looks genuinely torn over what to do. She even starts to lower her arm, the gun barrel tilting toward the floor.

But then the last of the drapes falls, taking the curtain rod with it. An end of the rod smashes through the window, and the sound of shattered glass makes Marge change her mind. Again, Charlie sees it. Another internal snap.

She raises the pistol.

As Marge pulls the trigger, Charlie feels a hand wrap around her ankle, jerking her downward. She hits the floor as the bullet passes overhead, inches away. Beside her is Josh.

Still alive.

Eyes open.

Mouth opening to form a single word.

"Run."

INT. LODGE—NIGHT

Charlie sprints toward the first place she sees: one of the lodge's unlit wings, the entrance hazy with smoke. She hurtles through it, hacking out a cough before throwing herself into the unknown black void of the hallway.

Once there, she hurries through the darkness, still twisted up in rope. A length of it clings to her waist and flaps behind her as she runs. She doesn't know what's down this hallway. Away from the fiery lobby, she can't see a thing. She lets instinct be her guide, hoping it doesn't fail her.

The wall of windows continues here, their curtains shut tight. Charlie senses them rustling in her wake as she moves. And although they're still intact for now, she knows it's just a matter of time before the flames also reach them.

The whole lodge is going to burn.

There's no doubt about that.

For Charlie, the only question is if she can find a way out before it does.

Or before Marge catches up to her.

Charlie didn't stick around to see if Marge followed her down this part of the lodge. She doesn't think so. She assumes she'd sense a presence.

So she runs.

Blind.

Arms thrust out in front of her, fingertips brushing the walls, feeling for a door.

She finds one where the hallway makes a sudden ninety-degree turn, veering off in another direction as Charlie keeps moving straight ahead, colliding not with a wall but with a swinging door.

Not knowing where else to go, Charlie pushes through it, into another room. Thin gray light trickles through a set of doors at the other end of the room. Charlie bolts toward it, managing three long strides before colliding with something cloaked in shadow in the middle of the room. She slams into it with her hip, pain rushing up her side.

Charlie stops, regroups, takes in surroundings that are barely visible in the pale light coming from the doors across the room.

She's in a kitchen. A big one. Like in a restaurant. There's a wide stovetop, a stack of ovens, a fridge big enough to fit three people standing up.

The thing she collided with is an island in the middle of the room. Her fear-warmed hands leave palm prints on the stainless-steel surface. Charlie's watching them disappear when she hears a noise.

Nearby.

Footsteps.

Moving purposefully toward the door Charlie just came through.

She knows it's Marge. It has to be. She's come looking for her like Charlie should have known she would. She feels suddenly foolish for thinking she could escape so easily.

Charlie drops to the floor and slides under the kitchen island. Holding her breath, she listens as Marge enters the kitchen, the soles of her shoes squeaking on the floor.

Squeak.

She's closer now.

Squeak.

Closer still.

Squeak.

Marge's shoes come into view. White sneakers. Sensible waitress shoes. The toe of the left one is spattered with blood.

Charlie stays completely still, even though her body begs her to run. If she remains silent and motionless, maybe Marge will think the room is empty. Maybe she'll go away. Maybe Charlie can escape.

But Marge takes another step.

Squeak.

And two more.

Squeak, squeak.

She's right beside Charlie now, the blood-spattered sneaker inches from her nose. Flat on her stomach with one cheek against the floor, Charlie's heart thunders in her chest so hard she can feel it reverberate through the cold tile beneath her.

She fears Marge can sense it, too, because the sneakers don't move. They remain where they are. So terrifyingly close.

Charlie doesn't move.

She doesn't breathe.

She stays that way until the sneakers move on.

Squeak.

Squeak.

Squeak.

Then . . . nothing.

After another minute of silence, Charlie allows herself to exhale.

After two minutes, she moves.

And after five minutes, each second counted off in her head, she slides out from under the kitchen island.

Charlie rises into a kneeling position, intending to peer over the island at the rest of the kitchen.

The first thing she sees are a pair of sneakers, one stained with blood.

Charlie looks up to see Marge smiling down at her from her perch on the kitchen island. In her hands are a pair of pliers, dripping blood.

"Found you," she says.

Charlie screams, backs away, slams into another counter.

As a fresh wave of pain courses through her, she sees that the kitchen island is empty.

There's no Marge.

There's no anyone.

"No," Charlie mutters to herself. "No, no, no, no. Not now. Please not now."

But it's too late.

It's already happening.

At the worst possible moment, the movies in her mind have returned.

INT. BALLROOM—NIGHT

Charlie bursts through the doors on the other side of the kitchen.

She's in a ballroom now.

Maybe.

She sees mirrored walls, gilt trim, polished floor under a chandelier festooned with cobwebs, fully aware that none of it could be real. Including a set of French doors on the other side of the room that appears to lead outside.

Charlie hurries toward them, watching, waiting, wondering if it's all going to disappear and change into something else.

When she reaches the center of the dance floor, directly beneath the chandelier, Charlie catches her reflection in one of the mirrored panes on the wall.

A mirror on the other side of the room picks it up.

A reflection of a reflection.

Which is caught on the original wall again, bouncing yet another version of herself onto the mirror across from it.

Charlie stares at dozens of different versions of herself. Doing exactly what she's doing. Mimicking her motions. Spinning under the chandelier like tops.

She stops moving.

The other Charlies do the same.

Because Marge has also entered the ballroom.

Charlie sees her in the mirrors. Not just one Marge but many, all pointing that dainty, retro pistol right at her.

All the Marges pull their triggers.

One of the Charlies shatters into a hundred pieces.

Another shot rings out, this time across the ballroom, and a second Charlie is hit, a spiderweb of cracks covering her face.

Then another is shattered.

And another.

Charlie moves to the French doors.

Fast.

Panting.

She pushes through the doors and out of the ballroom.

EXT. ALLEY—NIGHT

Charlie staggers outside, trips, tumbles hard onto cold asphalt.

Before climbing to her feet, she peeks through the French doors into the ballroom she's just vacated.

Marge isn't inside.

The room is empty.

All the mirrors are intact.

A movie. Just like she thought.

But then Charlie stands, turns away from the ballroom, and her heart stops.

She's outside, but it's not the kind of outside she thought it would be.

Instead of in the lush woodlands that surround the lodge, Charlie finds herself outside the bar she was at the night Maddy was killed. It's exactly the same, from the beer and puke smell outside to the Cure cover band inside.

And there, right in the middle of the alley, is Maddy, looking the way she did the last time Charlie saw her.

Standing with a dark figure.

Bathed in slanting white light.

Head lowered as she lights a cigarette.

This time, though, she casts a glance Charlie's way, over the shadowy man's shoulder, looking straight at her.

Then she smiles.

Such a glorious smile.

She could have been a star, Charlie knows. She had the looks for it. Her beauty was unconventional, incandescent—perfect for the big screen. But it was Maddy's personality that would have sealed the deal. She was badgering and blunt, charming and chaotic. People who admired such traits—people like Charlie—would have adored her.

Now none of it will happen, and Charlie can't help but feel sorry for those who missed out. Most of the world never got to experience Madeline Forrester.

But Charlie did.

She experienced it and loved it and misses it dearly.

"I'm sorry," she says, even though she knows Maddy isn't really there. Her appearance is just another movie in her mind. It doesn't matter. Charlie still feels compelled to say it. The last words she wishes she had uttered when Maddy was still alive. "You weren't an awful friend. I'm sorry I said that. I didn't mean it. You were an amazing friend. You made me feel—"

"Alive?" Maddy says.

"Yes," Charlie says.

And not just alive. In-a-movie alive, which is far superior in every way.

"I know," Maddy says. "I've always known. Right until the end."

The man standing with her remains frozen in time, still unknowable with his turned back, bowed head, hand cupped around the lighter's flame. Charlie knows that even if she steps closer, like a director entering the frame, she won't be able to see what he looks like. He'll be a shadow no matter how close she gets.

So it's Maddy she looks at, sparkling in the spotlight. She's so bright that the shadowy figure in the fedora fades away. Darkness banished by light.

Maddy stands alone now, ridiculously tall in her high heels and clutching a Virginia Slim.

"Do you miss me?" she says.

Charlie nods, holding back a tear in the process. "Of course."

"Then stay."

Charlie would like that. If she could, she'd live in this movie for as long as possible. But she knows she can't.

"You're not real," she says to Maddy. "You're just a movie in my mind."

"But isn't that better than real life?"

"It is. But I need to live in the real world."

"Even if it's scary?" Maddy says.

"Especially if it's scary."

Right now, she needs complete knowledge of her surroundings. Not only where she is but who might be nearby.

Clarity.

That's what the situation requires. Her life depends on it.

"But this might be the last time you ever see me," Maddy says.

Charlie feels more tears coming. She keeps them at bay, determined to make this make-believe goodbye the complete opposite of the real-life version.

No anger.

No tears.

Only love and joy and appreciation.

"Then make it memorable," she says.

Maddy strikes a pose, standing in profile, one hand on her hip, the other elegantly extended as the smoke curls from the cigarette between her fingers. It is, Charlie thinks, perfect.

"What a dump!" Maddy says.

Charlie smiles and closes her eyes, knowing that when she opens them, Maddy will be gone for good.

"I think I adore you," she says.

EXT. LODGE VERANDA—NIGHT

Just as she suspected, Maddy is gone when Charlie opens her eyes. Instead of in the alley, she finds herself on a stone walkway outside the Mountain Oasis Lodge. Cold night air slaps her face, bringing much-needed clarity.

The movies in her mind are over.

Possibly for good.

Because of the fieldstone beneath her feet, Charlie suspects she's near the veranda behind the lodge. She saw a similar walkway earlier when trying to escape through the French doors in the lobby. Further cementing her theory are dark plumes of smoke drifting toward her from around a corner of the building. With them are the snap, crackle, and pop of something burning.

She rushes down the walkway and rounds the corner, the smoke getting thicker and the sound of burning louder. Soon Charlie's at the same pool area she spotted earlier, although now it looks much different.

Smoke rolls through the area, streaming in from the nearby lobby. Through the throat-choking haze, Charlie gets undulating glimpses of the wall of windows. Just behind them, large tongues of flame lick at the air. From what she can see, she thinks the blaze has expanded to the rest of the lobby. Flames crawl along the front desk and scale the support timbers rising to the ceiling. Inside, a piece of the roof breaks free and crashes to the floor, sending up a cloud of sparks. A wall of heat hits her, making Charlie take several steps back.

That's when she notices the French doors.

They're not just broken, like most of the windows.

They've been opened.

And while Charlie hopes it was Josh who did it, she suspects it was someone else.

Marge.

Outside.

With her.

Charlie moves backward through the smoke, her sneakers shuffling over the stone walkway until, suddenly, it drops away.

She spends a moment teetering on the lip of a concrete ledge, her arms pinwheeling in a desperate fight to keep balance.

One of her feet slips, flying out from under her.

A scream escapes Charlie's lips as she topples, clawing at the air, falling into what she now realizes is the empty swimming pool. She closes her eyes, bracing for impact against the bottom, but instead of her body slamming against cold concrete, Charlie lands in several feet of rainwater that's gathered at the bottom of the pool. The water—black with dirt, slick with algae—consumes her.

For a moment, Charlie's lost, unsure if she's still falling or now floating. Her eyes are open, but all is dark. Caught mid-scream, her mouth is filled with water and slime and filth. Some trickles down her throat, choking her.

She stands, emerging from the swill, coughing up the parts of it that made it to her lungs.

Then she looks around.

She's in the deep end, standing in about four feet of water. On the other side of the pool, a ladder clings to the concrete, rusted yet usable.

Charlie wades toward it, moving through water that's akin to primordial ooze. Rotting leaves float on the surface. Nearby, a dead mouse does the same.

At the ladder, Charlie struggles to climb its rungs. Her hands are too wet and the soles of her shoes too slippery. Adding to the trouble is her wool coat, sodden with rancid water. It's heavier now, like lead, weighing her down as she scales the ladder.

Still, she climbs.

Feet slipping off a rung once.

Hands screeching off the railing twice.

She keeps climbing until her eyes breach the edge of the pool, revealing the same stone walkway that had dropped out from under her earlier.

Charlie also sees smoke, drifting over the pool like lake mist.

And in that smoke, right at the top of the ladder, is a pair of white sneakers.

Although there's no blood on them, like there was in her imagination, Charlie knows they belong to Marge and that this time it's not a movie in her mind.

A second later, she feels the barrel of a pistol cold against her forehead.

"Keep climbing," Marge says. "We're not done yet."

She backs off, giving Charlie just enough room to crest the ladder and step onto the walkway. The two of them stare at each other, Charlie drenched and streaming dirty water, Marge's face darkened by smoke.

"Where's Josh?" Charlie says.

"He's safe."

"I don't believe you."

Marge's shoulders rise and fall. "I don't care."

Beside them, a low rumble rises from inside the lodge. Another chunk of roof—bigger than the first—crashes down. The walkway under their feet shakes. Smoke and sparks roll over them—a wave so dense it blots out Charlie's vision and makes her head swim.

When it clears, she sees Marge still across from her, the pistol now aimed at her chest.

"And what about Maddy?" Charlie says, getting a flash of the most recent movie in her mind. Maddy in full glamour mode. "You care about her, right? She'd hate it if she saw us like this."

Marge starts to speak, changes her mind, goes silent again. She can't argue with Charlie's reasoning. Both of them know it's true. If she were here, Maddy would be sickened by what she saw.

"I can't just let it go. I have to do *something*." Marge keeps the pistol pointed at Charlie. "I swore—"

"That you'd get revenge? Hurting me won't do that. It won't bring Maddy back. She's gone, and I hate that fact. It makes me sad and angry, but most of all, I just miss her. I miss her so much. Just like you do."

"It hurts," Marge says, her voice cracking. "Missing her—it hurts so bad."

"I know," Charlie says. "It hurts me, too."

"And this uncertainty. I don't know what to do with it. I need to know who killed my Maddy."

Charlie does, too. But she also knows life doesn't always work that way. It's not the movies, where plots are often tied up in a tidy bow. In the real world, you may never learn what caused the crash that killed your parents or who murdered your best friend. It's hard and it hurts and it's so unfair that sometimes it makes Charlie want to scream. But it's life, and everyone must go on living it.

"Let me go," Charlie says. "Let me go and we can get through it together."

"I can't. I'm sorry, sweetie. I need to learn as much as I can. That all depends on you now. You can tell me what you saw—*who* you saw—right now. Or we can do it the hard way."

Marge cocks the pistol.

Behind her, Charlie sees something flitting through the smoke. A lightness amid the dark.

Robbie.

Creeping through the smoke, a tire iron clutched in his hand.

Charlie's eyes widen, tipping Marge off to the presence behind her.

As Marge spins around, Robbie lifts the tire iron and brings it down hard against her shoulder.

The gun goes off.

A horrible bang.

Robbie grunts and falters backward.

Marge collapses outright, crumbling to the ground, the pistol falling from her grip and skittering across the walkway.

Charlie swoops in, picks it up, thrusts it out in front of her. It's the first time she's ever held a gun, and she hates the feel of it in her hands. Her arms quake, the gun barrel unsteady as she points it at Marge.

Behind her, Robbie sits on the walkway, his right hand pressed to his left shoulder. Blood trickles out from beneath his palm. Charlie gasps when she sees it.

"Are you hit?"

"Grazed," Robbie says. He starts to let out a low, disbelieving chuckle but stops midway. Eyes widening, he gasps and says, "Charlie, watch out!"

Charlie instantly understands what's happening. Marge is on the move. At first, Charlie thinks she's coming for the gun. She is, but not in the way Charlie expects.

Marge crawls toward her, not stopping until the pistol is inches away from her forehead.

"Do it," she says, looking up at Charlie with a pained, pitiful expression. "Pull the trigger. Please. Put me out of my misery. I was going to do it anyway. Right here. Tonight."

Charlie steadies the gun and thinks about all the damage Marge has caused that night. She deserves to pay for what she's done. Not just to her, but to Josh and to Robbie. All in a misguided quest for information.

Then she thinks of Maddy and her habit of calling her mee-maw on the phone every Sunday. Charlie pictures her doing it. Sitting in the jade silk kimono she preferred over a bathrobe, the phone cord wound around her finger, laughing at something her grandmother had just said. The same woman who made her laugh now kneels in front of her, begging to die, and Charlie can't bring herself to do it.

"No," she says. "Maddy wouldn't want that."

Charlie tosses the pistol into the pool. It lands with a splash and disappears in the black water.

Marge says nothing. She simply stares at the spot where the gun now rests, a vacant look in her eyes.

Charlie moves past her, going to Robbie, who still has a hand pressed to his shoulder. Blood runs down his sleeve and drips from his elbow.

"We need to get you to a hospital," she says, helping him to his feet.

"First, we need to get away from this place."

Another rumble erupts from inside the lodge, followed by the sound of timber cracking. Charlie knows what it means. The support beams holding up what's left of the room are about to fall.

And they don't want to be here when it happens.

The two of them hurry along the back of the building, leaving the walkway and entering the woods to put more distance between them and the lodge. When it comes time to round the corner of the building, Charlie pauses long enough to check on Marge.

She sits next to the pool, watching the fire that will in all likelihood consume her should the lodge collapse.

Which it's about to do in a matter of minutes.

But Marge doesn't look scared. In fact, Charlie thinks she looks at peace, bathed in the orange glow of the flames. Maybe she's thinking about Maddy. Maybe Marge even sees her. A movie in her own mind.

Charlie hopes that's true.

She even wishes it as Robbie grabs her coat sleeve and tugs her until Marge fades from view.

THREE A.M.

EXT. LODGE—NIGHT

It's all so loud.

That's what Charlie thinks as they trudge out of the woods and head to Robbie's Volvo.

The roar of the fire. The roar of the falls. It's deafening, those twin sounds, like a pair of beasts in the thick of battle. It even looks like they're fighting. Charlie sees the burning lodge to her right, the frothing head of the falls to her left, and, in between, a spot where the rushing creek reflects the flames.

Yet through that din, Charlie thinks of Josh.

He's here. Somewhere.

"We need to get Josh."

"Who?" Robbie says.

"The guy I was riding with. He's here."

"Where?"

Charlie doesn't know. Not where he is or even if he's still alive. Marge could have been lying about that.

"He was shot," Charlie says.

"So was I," Robbie says, jerking his chin toward his wounded shoulder. "And we're running out of time."

Charlie eyes the fiery lodge. Tall, fingerlike flames break through the roof and reach toward the sky, bringing with them sparks that pinwheel through the air and drift down around them like pulsing orange confetti.

Robbie's Volvo is parked right behind Marge's Cadillac. Although the portico the cars sit under remains untouched by fire, it won't really matter if the lodge collapses. Charlie knows Robbie is right.

They need to leave.

Now.

At the car, Robbie leans against the hood.

"Are you okay?" Charlie asks, when it's obvious he isn't.

"I'm fine," Robbie says as he hands her his car keys. "You're going to have to drive, though."

Charlie had assumed that, even though she's not in the best condition, either. She's dizzy from the smoke and her chest is tight and the flames and waterfall are too loud and she thinks she's going to faint.

Still, she dutifully guides Robbie into the passenger seat before rounding the front of the Volvo and sliding behind the wheel. It's not until she's fully in the driver's seat that the realization hits.

She hasn't driven since the day before her parents were killed.

INT. VOLVO—NIGHT

Four years.

That's how long it's been since Charlie sat in the driver's seat of a car.

Four long years without turning a steering wheel or tapping a brake.

That's about to end right now.

It has to.

Charlie coughs. A sharp, stabbing hack that makes her double over. But she feels better afterward. Letting out that last bit of smoke and being in the car, where it's calm and quiet, boosts her consciousness. She's no longer dizzy, although the weakness remains.

But she can do this.

There's nothing to be afraid of.

Driving a car is just like riding a bike. Her father told her that.

Charlie starts the car, flinching at the muffled roar created by the engine rumbling to life. At the same time, another deep rumble emanates from inside the lodge. Next to her, Robbie says, "Charlie, we need to get out of here."

She touches her foot to the gas pedal, hitting it too hard. The Volvo lurches forward and smacks into the Cadillac's rear bumper. The car shudders.

She slams down on the brakes, puts the Volvo in reverse, starts driving backward. Then it's back to drive again. This time, when Charlie presses the gas pedal, it's with more caution. The car eases forward, letting Charlie steer past the Cadillac and out from under the portico.

"We need to get further away," Robbie says.

"I'm trying."

Charlie keeps the car moving, rounding the circular drive in front of the lodge and heading toward the twisting road that will take them to the bottom of the waterfall. After that, Charlie has no idea where to go.

"I don't know where we are."

She hits the brakes again, puts the car in park, and reaches for the glove compartment in front of Robbie, searching for a map. The glove compartment door drops open, and a small box tumbles out, almost landing in Robbie's lap.

He tries to catch it but is slowed by his gunshot wound. That leaves Charlie to grab it and pull it toward her.

It's a jewelry box.

Black.

Hinged.

Big enough for a single engagement ring.

Heat spreads in Charlie's chest. She'd suspected, back in the recesses of her mind, that Robbie might try to propose before she left. When he didn't, she was more relieved than disappointed. Guilty and depressed and lost in her own world, she wasn't ready for such a commitment.

But now—after this long, horrible night—Charlie wonders if she might have been wrong about that.

"Robbie, I—"

"Wait!" he says.

But Charlie's already opening the box, excitement blooming in spite of herself, the hinge sounding out a light creak as she lifts the lid and things start rolling out of it like dice. That's what Charlie thinks they are as she cups her hand to catch them.

Dice.

Three startlingly small dice the color of ivory.

It's not until they're rattling in her palm that she understands what they really are.

Teeth.

Angela Dunleavy's tooth.

Taylor Morrison's tooth.

Maddy's tooth.

"Robbie, why do you have these?"

She knows the answer.

Robbie took them after killing Angela.

And Taylor.

And Maddy.

Staring at Robbie with her dead friend's tooth still in her hand, Charlie feels something break loose inside her chest.

Her heart.

There's now an empty space where it used to be. A void, inside of which the sound of her last heartbeat still echoes. Then it, too, is gone, and she feels nothing.

Charlie thinks it means she's dying. And wouldn't that be a relief? Surely better than having to endure *this*.

Yet she remains alive, her heart still gone but her head spinning and a stark ache in her gut that feels like the inside of her body trying to gnaw its way outside.

The nausea, when it comes, is too fast to stop. The bile rushes up and out, and soon Charlie is bent forward, vomit dripping off the steering wheel.

She wipes her mouth with the back of her hand and says, "Why?"

Charlie says it softly. Barely a mumble. So soft she's not sure Robbie even heard her. So she says it again, shouting this time, the word smacking off the window and echoing through the entire car.

"*Why?*"

Robbie says nothing. He simply stares into the open glove compartment, looking at something else inside that Charlie had missed until that moment.

A pair of pliers.

Dried blood stains their tip.

Seeing it conjures an image of that night outside the bar. Robbie approaching Maddy, who smiles because she recognizes a friendly face. He comes in close, his head lowered, hand cupped around her lighter. Seeing it is so terrible Charlie has to close her eyes and shake her head to make it go away.

"I can't believe I didn't know it was you," she says, still shocked and nauseous and waiting for her missing heart to finally stop its stubborn beating. "Did you know I was there? That I saw you?"

"Not until later," Robbie says, as if that will make it easier for her to bear. "But by then I knew that you also hadn't really seen me. That something else was going on in that head of yours."

Charlie drops the teeth back into jewelry box and snaps the lid shut, unable to look at them any longer. The box itself slips from her hands as she wails, "Why Maddy?"

"Because she was too brash," Robbie says, spitting out the last word like it's a curse. "Always loud. Always demanding attention."

"Is that why you killed the others, too?" she says. "Because they were too loud? Too brash?"

"No. Because they thought they were special. They thought they deserved the attention they were constantly begging for. And they're not special, Charlie. I've been waiting a year for you to figure it out. Most people are stupid and useless and pathetic. And those deluded enough to think they aren't deserve whatever punishment they get."

Charlie recoils against the driver's-side door, terrified. "You're sick."

"No," Robbie says. "I truly am special. As are you. Remember the night we met? In the library?"

Of course Charlie remembers. It was her own personal romantic comedy, which means it was likely different from how she remembers it. Now she looks at Robbie, trying to see if she recognizes any part of the man she encountered that night.

She can't.

He's a complete stranger to her now.

"I thought I was going to kill you that night," Robbie says. "Sitting with you at the library, then the diner, then walking you home. The whole time I kept thinking about what it was going to feel like to kill you."

The matter-of-fact way he says it feels like a punch to Charlie's solar plexus. For a few seconds, she can barely breathe.

"Why didn't you?" she says.

"Because there was something about you I was drawn to. You were so—"

"Innocent?"

Robbie shakes his head. "Clueless. You watch your movies and you think that makes you smart. Like you know the way the world works. But all it's done is warp your brain. You have no idea what the world is like."

He's wrong about that.

Charlie knows what the world is like.

Parents leave in the morning and never come back.

You fight with your best friend and tell her to fuck off and then have to live with knowing that's the last thing you ever said to her, when what you really should have done is thanked her for being by your side and understanding you and loving you for who you are.

After seeing too much of this senseless, brutal, cruel world—far too much for someone her age—Charlie chose to retreat into other worlds. Ones that can't hurt her.

Life has failed her time and time again.

The movies have never let her down.

"But then there was a moment at the diner when you completely tuned out—just for a minute. That's when I knew you were different from the others. Special. Like me."

"I'm nothing like you," Charlie says, spitting the words.

Something takes hold of her.

Rage.

The same kind Marge had talked about. White-hot and seething.

It's the kind of rage that makes Charlie, like Marge before her, want to do unthinkable things. The only difference is that Marge had directed it at the wrong person.

Now Charlie has a chance to do it right.

She shifts the car into drive and lets it start to roll.

"What are you doing?" Robbie says.

"Driving."

"Where?"

"Away from here."

Charlie glances in the rearview mirror. Sitting in the back seat, right behind Robbie, is her father.

"Remember, never drive more than five miles over the speed limit," he says in that father-knows-best voice Charlie couldn't stand when he was alive but misses like crazy now. "Cops won't bother you. Not for that."

Her father pauses, locking eyes with Charlie in the rearview mirror.

"But sometimes," he says, "sometimes your only choice is to drive like hell."

Charlie nods, even though her father's not really in the back seat. Even if it was just a movie in her mind, it's still good advice.

As her father's voice echoes in her head, Charlie doesn't just press down on the gas pedal.

She floors it.

INT. VOLVO—NIGHT

The Volvo takes off down the winding drive like a bottle rocket, its rear tires squealing on the blacktop.

When the car nears the first turn, Charlie doesn't tap the brakes. Instead, she lets the car keep picking up speed on the approach before cutting the wheel to the left at the last possible moment.

The Volvo fishtails around the bend before regaining a grip on the road as it straightens.

"Slow down," Robbie says.

He reaches for the steering wheel with his left hand, getting the briefest of grips before Charlie slaps it away.

"Charlie, *slow down.*"

They reach another sharp turn, and Charlie does the same as before, jerking the wheel, sliding through it, on the thinnest edge of control.

The pliers slide from the glove compartment and plink to the floor.

It distracts Charlie just enough for Robbie to lunge for the steering wheel again. This time, he grabs it tight, giving it a pull. The car almost jerks off the road.

Charlie lets go of the wheel with her right hand and swings at Robbie, her knuckles connecting with his cheek and whipping his head sideways.

"Fuck you," she says.

The Volvo approaches a third turn. The one with the stone wall close to the waterfall. They come in fast, screaming around the turn, the roar of falling water all around them. Charlie cuts the wheel a second too late and the driver's side of the Volvo scrapes the wall, grinding against the stone wall. Sparks spray past Charlie's window.

In the passenger seat, Robbie yells, "Are you trying to kill me?"

"Isn't that your plan for me?" Charlie says.

Although the Volvo is now flying down a straight section of road, up ahead is the last bend before they reach the bridge. Instead of slowing down, Charlie hits the gas.

"Tell me, Robbie," she says. "Your plan now is to kill me, right? Because I know who you are. I know what you've done."

The turn is closer now.

A hundred yards away.

Just beyond it is a cluster of trees so dense that the car will be smashed to bits if it crashes into them.

"Admit it," Charlie tells Robbie.

The turn sits before them.

Now fifty yards away.

Now twenty-five.

"Admit it!" Charlie shouts. "Or I'm going to drive this car straight into those fucking trees!"

"Yes!" Robbie yelps, gripping the dashboard for support as Charlie hits the brakes and, with a death grip on the wheel, skids the Volvo around the corner.

"Yes what?" she says.

"I'm going to kill you."

Charlie slams the brakes. The Volvo slides to a stop.

When Robbie speaks, his voice is unnervingly calm.

"I don't want to do it, Charlie," he says. "I need you to know that. I *love* you. You might not believe me, but it's true. And I'm sorry for what I have to do to you. We could have had a wonderful life together."

Charlie can't bear to look at him, so she stares out the windshield. Just down the road is the bridge at the base of the waterfall. A short rickety span crossing the ravine. Beneath it, black water churns. It's nothing compared to the fear rushing through Charlie's body. Her terror is twice as dark and twice as volatile.

She only thought she was scared earlier. Leaving the diner with Josh. Being tortured by Marge. That wasn't even a fraction of the fear she feels now.

Because now she wants to live.

Really live.

The way Maddy had lived. The way she had tried to get Charlie to do. Maddy saw what Charlie couldn't: that she had spent the past four years being an audience member to her own sad existence.

Movies are my life, she had told Josh. It should have been the other way around. Charlie should have been able to say, *My life is like the movies.*

And now that she realizes it, she's terrified Robbie is going to take away her chance to do something about it.

With her fists around the steering wheel and the car humming under her, Charlie stares at the bridge over the ravine. In that moment, she understands that she's in charge of her own destiny.

She's Ellen Ripley.

She's Laurie Strode.

She's Clarice Starling.

She's Thelma *and* Louise, kicking up dirt in a final fuck-you as they choose freedom over life.

Their choice. No one else's.

Now it's Charlie doing the choosing. Robbie can't be the one in control.

She reaches for her seat belt, pulls it across her chest, snaps it into place.

She takes a deep breath.

Then she slams the gas pedal against the floor.

The Volvo streaks toward the bridge, shuddering, out of control. Tires screaming. Engine screaming. Robbie screaming. All of it blending into a single scream that's part human, part machine.

The car thumps onto the bridge, roaring over it.

Halfway across, Charlie yanks the wheel to the right and the Volvo careens toward the bridge's wooden railing.

A second later, the car smashes through it.

Wood scrapes against metal. An earsplitting friction.

The bridge beneath the tires disappears and the car seems to take flight, although Charlie knows that what it's really doing is falling.

Arcing over off the bridge and crashing toward the water below.

Charlie lurches forward, her chest pinned against the steering wheel a moment before she's jerked backward by the seat belt.

Robbie, on the other hand, is thrown like a rag doll against the dashboard.

When the car hits the water, Charlie's head snaps against the back of the seat. The impact sends a shudder through her body. And as a rush of water engulfs the car, a wave of darkness does the same to Charlie until both she and the car sink beneath it.

INT. VOLVO—NIGHT

Water on the windshield.

That's what Charlie sees as she regains consciousness.

A line of it runs right across the glass. Above it is night sky and streaks of stars. Below is murky water illuminated by the Volvo's headlights. Charlie guesses it's about fifteen feet deep and that the Volvo, pitched forward, will be reaching the bottom sooner rather than later. Water gushes into the car from below, already up to her lap.

Charlie looks to the passenger seat.

Robbie's still there, wide awake and watching. The slam against the dashboard has left him bruised and bleeding. A large red mark covers half of his face. Blood trickles from his right nostril.

"Is this what you wanted?" he says. "To kill us both?"

"No," Charlie says. "Just you."

She unhooks her seat belt, not worried about getting out of the car. She knows what to do. Wait until it fills completely with water, which alters the pressure against the side of the car, then open the door and swim out.

She knows because she saw it in a movie.

The water, up to her chest now, keeps rising. As the car fills, it makes a worrisome groaning sound and tilts even farther forward. The Volvo's headlights sweep across the bottom of the ravine before flickering and going out.

In that newfound darkness, Charlie doesn't see Robbie's bent elbow coming right toward her face. She's only aware of it after the fact, when his elbow slams into the bridge of her nose.

The blow is hard.

A firecracker of pain.

Charlie's head smacks against the driver's-side window.

She sees stars as Robbie leaps on top of her.

"Shh," he says. "It'll all be over soon."

Then he grabs Charlie by the hair and shoves her head underwater.

INT. VOLVO—NIGHT

Robbie keeps Charlie's head submerged, although he doesn't want to do it. Not this. Not to her. Not while she's kicking and thrashing and flailing just below the surface.

She's special. Exactly like him—even though she refuses to admit it. And people like them are rare. They hide their specialness under a bushel, only revealing it to others who are special.

Robbie thought Charlie knew this.

He assumed she knew they were kindred spirits.

But some people don't realize they're special—a problem Robbie never had. He knew from an early age who he was. A genius. Athletic. Golden. One look in the mirror and it was clear he was a rarity.

Charlie, though, is different. She doesn't know how blessed she is. What a gift she has—being able to disappear into fantasy whenever reality gets too painful. People would pay for that kind of ability.

She's not like Katya, the girl from his neighborhood who strutted up and down the sidewalk like she was hot shit when she was really just trash. Her family was the poorest in the neighborhood, their house a wreck, the parents always screaming at each other in the front yard. But Katya thought that she was better than everyone else. It didn't matter that she was chubby and showed too much skin and was so loud Robbie could hear her coming from two blocks away.

The police still think she ran away from home because he'd buried her body so deep in the woods it's never been found.

Charlie's not like Angela, who threw herself at him while working at that bar. As if Robbie would ever deign to fuck someone so worthless. Special girls don't need to show off in too-tight shirts and too-high skirts. To get his attention, they don't need to write their number on a napkin and slip it with a wink into his lap.

He offered her a ride back to campus when her shift was done. After she was dead, he took her tooth because he regretted burying Katya so deep and wanted something to remember Angela by.

Charlie's not like Taylor, who mocked his purchases at the bookstore she worked at, trying to flirt by pretending she was smarter than him when she clearly wasn't. "I bet I read more than you," she said, as if he cared a whit about any aspect of her life. A common mistake among people who aren't special—that they're worthy of care.

But he pretended to be interested. He waited around after she casually told him her shift was ending soon. By the end of the night, he had a second tooth in his collection.

And Charlie's definitely not like Maddy, that attention whore. From the moment he met her, he couldn't stand her. Dressing like that. Talking like that. Doing any pathetic thing she could just to be noticed.

That Robbie found her like he did was a happy accident. He'd been roaming the streets, looking as he always did for those who were special like him and judging the many who weren't. He headed down the alley, lured by the awful music coming from inside the bar.

And there she was.

Clutching her gaudy purse and fumbling with her lighter.

She whined to him about her awful night, even though he didn't care. But then she mentioned Charlie, how they'd fought, how she was worried she'd fucked up their friendship for good.

That was when Robbie knew what he had to do. Get rid of Maddy. Have Charlie all to himself.

He'd spent the past year getting to know Charlie, learning from her, even loving her. He had planned their life together. Marriage, kids, careers. They would grow old and be special together, and everyone would envy them.

With that in mind, he didn't hesitate to kill Maddy, even as she begged for her life.

But now it's led to this.

Now he's making Charlie go away as well. He has no other choice. Keeping her alive is too risky. His specialness outweighs hers.

One small consolation is that he'll be able to take a tooth. Something to remember Charlie by. The jewelry box that contains the others bobs in the water near his shoulders, as if waiting for a new addition.

His right arm strains to keep Charlie submerged. His spine bends and twists to keep his head above water. His legs press against the seat and the dashboard, giving him leverage.

Under the water, Charlie goes still.

There's no more kicking, no more thrashing, no more flailing.

All is calm.

But as Robbie starts to pull his hand away, something cold clicks around his right wrist.

Looking down, he sees it's now encircled by one end of a pair of handcuffs.

Then, with a horror so deep it pierces his soul, he hears another click.

INT. VOLVO—NIGHT

Charlie hadn't forgotten about Josh's handcuffs. They were always present in her thoughts, cold and flat in the front pocket of her jeans. She just didn't know when—or how—to use them.

It wasn't until Robbie pushed her under the water that she finally knew.

And as she clicks the other end around the steering wheel, Charlie's glad she waited.

She emerges from the water into a car that's almost completely filled. There's about eight inches of air left. Just enough for Charlie to tilt her head back and speak.

The same can't be said for Robbie.

Thanks to the handcuffs, he can't keep his mouth above the surface. The waterline is now even with his nose as he uses those big, Bambi eyes to stare up at her. Mere hours ago, that expression would have melted Charlie's heart. Seeing it now, she feels only anger.

Robbie keeps looking at her, though, beseeching. It's clear he thinks she has a key to the cuffs.

He's wrong.

Even if she did know where the keys are, she sure as hell wouldn't use them to set Robbie free.

"That was for Maddy," Charlie says, knowing he can still hear her.

She holds up the pair of pliers she'd grabbed off the floor while underwater.

"And this," she says, "is for Marge."

MORNING

INT. HOSPITAL—DAY

It's quiet inside the hospital. Everyone from the nurses to the clerks to the volunteers in their candy cane pinafores works in a subdued hush, even though it's not very busy. There's only one other non-employee at the help desk—a middle-aged man slumped in a chair by the door with a vacant look in his eyes. Charlie hopes he's just tired, but she doubts it. He has the appearance of someone back-handed with bad news. Charlie suspects she looks the same.

She had been here earlier, before being taken to the police station. A frantic ambulance ride straight from the Mountain Oasis Lodge—the speed necessitated by the other person in the ambulance with her.

Charlie's injuries were minor. Some scrapes, bruises, and a broken nose from when Robbie elbowed her in the face. Now a fat strip of medical tape sits across the bridge of it. When Charlie first saw it in the mirror, she couldn't help but say, to no one in particular, "*Chinatown*. Roman Polanski. Nineteen seventy-four. Starring Jack Nicholson and Faye Dunaway."

The nurse who'd done the taping didn't get the reference.

"You need to see it," Charlie told her. "It's a classic."

Then it was off to the police station, where she described her long endurance test of a night—leaving out the bits she didn't think the cops needed to know. They weren't particularly concerned about the details of why Charlie was at the lodge and how it caught fire and what the others were doing there. All the cops really cared about was that the Campus Killer had not only been identified but that his corpse was found drifting in a sunken Volvo, handcuffed to the steering wheel.

Charlie didn't fudge the truth about that. "It was self-defense," she said, and she meant it.

Mostly.

In return for her information, Charlie was told how someone driving along Dead River Road saw the lodge in flames, went to the diner, and called 911 on the same pay phone Charlie had used earlier. When first responders arrived, they found her drenched and shivering on the side of the road leading up to the lodge.

Charlie ended up being the first person they found. She wasn't the last.

It's this last person she's here to see, having been driven back to the hospital from the police station. She's dry for the most part, although Maddy's coat is still damp and in dire need of dry cleaning. Charlie could use a good cleaning herself. Her hair is a mess, swimming pool swill still sticks to her in spots, and she smells like a wet dog that's rolled in something dead.

Now she's at the door to a hospital room, taking a steadying breath before entering.

Inside, Marge lays in a hospital bed, looking ten times smaller than she did mere hours ago. She's hooked up to an oxygen tank. A clear tube runs under her nose and loops around both ears.

Charlie had hoped she'd be asleep, but Marge is wide awake and propped up by several pillows. Beside her is a tray table, the breakfast on top of it untouched.

"You should have pulled the trigger," she says when Charlie steps into the room.

Charlie stops a few feet from the bed. "Hello to you, too."

"I mean it," Marge says. "I'm probably going to die in this place. I might never leave this hospital bed. That's what the doctor said."

"Doctors have been wrong before."

It wouldn't surprise Charlie if Marge stuck around for longer than two months. She's still got some toughness to her. She must, or else she wouldn't have lasted through the night. Firefighters found her still sitting by the swimming pool, long after the lodge had collapsed in on itself. Although suffering from smoke inhalation, second-degree burns from flaming debris that hit her during the collapse, and the onset of hypothermia, she was still kicking.

"I'm assuming the police came by," Charlie says.

"They did. I was surprised by what they had to say. I didn't know we went to the lodge just to reminisce. And that the fire was an accident. And that I apparently hadn't shot anyone, let alone two people."

"What they don't know won't hurt them," Charlie says.

Marge starts to reply, grasping for the right words. When they refuse to arrive, she simply says, "I'm sorry. What I did was—"

"I'm not here for an apology," Charlie says. "And I'm sure as hell not here to seek *your* forgiveness."

Marge peers up at her, curious. "Then why are you here?"

"To say that we're square."

Charlie approaches the tray beside the bed. She reaches deep into her pocket, pulls out something small and ivory, and sets it down on the breakfast tray.

Marge stares at Robbie's tooth, the corners of her mouth twitching upward into what Charlie can only guess is a smile. Sinking back into the pillows, she closes her eyes and lets out a long, satisfied sigh.

"Good girl," she says.

INT. HOSPITAL ROOM—DAY

Charlie's final stop is another hospital room, just a few doors down the hall from Marge's. Unlike her, Josh is sound asleep and lightly snoring.

No, not Josh.

Jake.

True to her word, Marge had indeed moved him someplace safe, dragging him out of the lobby and putting him in the back seat of the Cadillac. When the portico fell with the rest of lodge, the roof of the Caddy bent but didn't break. A couple of firefighters found him inside and unconscious as they were loading Charlie into the ambulance. Josh was loaded in right along with her. Charlie held his hand the entire way to the hospital.

Now she sits by his bed, watching him sleep. When he wakes, his eyes flutter open in a way that Charlie can only describe as cinematic. And even though she shoved a knife into his side, he still smiles when he sees her. Not even pain can dim that megawatt grin.

"You stabbed me," he says.

"You kidnapped me."

"I also tried to save you."

Charlie gives a nod of thanks. "You did."

Josh tries to sit up, groaning with effort. Most of his body has been wrapped in bandages. Some are for the stab wound. Others are for the gunshot wound. And still others might be from when Charlie accidentally rear-ended the Cadillac while he was inside.

"*The Mummy*," she says. "Nineteen thirty-two. Boris Karloff."

"I've heard of him," Josh says. "Some film nerd told me he was in *The Secret Life of Walter Mitty.*"

Charlie grins. "That film nerd must be a very smart girl."

"She is," Josh says. "Although she must not be too smart to be sticking around this place."

"I just came by to thank you for saving me." A lump forms in Charlie's throat. She swallows it down. "I-I'm not sure I deserved it."

"You did," Josh tells her. "You need to stop being so hard on yourself."

"I know." Charlie pauses. "And you need to find a different job."

Josh laughs until it starts to hurt. Clutching his side, he says, "That I do. I think I'd make a great chauffeur. Maybe I should move to Hollywood. Be a driver to the stars."

"Sounds like a good plan to me."

"Speaking of driving." Josh gestures to his clothes, neatly folded on the nightstand beside the bed, almost as if they'd just come from a cleaner who'd forgotten to tackle the bloodstains. "Reach into the front right pocket of my jeans. There's something inside I want you to have."

Charlie does, dipping her hand into the pocket and finding a set of car keys. She pulls them out by the plastic fob, the keys jingling together below it.

"It's yours," Josh says.

"I can't take your car."

"You need to get to Ohio somehow. Besides, you're only borrowing it. Go home, spend some time with your grandmother, bring it back to me. I'll probably still be here." Josh touches his side. "And when you do, maybe we can, I don't know, go see a movie or something."

Charlie curls her fingers around the keys, a sign she's considering it. Not just borrowing Josh's car, but all of it. For one, she feels indebted to him. He came to her rescue, in spite of what she'd done to him. That needs to be acknowledged and appreciated.

Then there's the fact that she likes this version of Josh. It's the one she got brief glimpses of during the long, strange trip of the previous night. Now that all suspicion is gone, she thinks it might be nice to meet the real him.

But the bedrock truth is that surviving the night has left Charlie feeling lonelier than ever.

Maddy's gone.

Robbie, too.

Now more than ever, Charlie's in need of a new friend.

"Maybe," she says as she stuffs the keys into her coat pocket. "As long as I get to pick the movie."

EXT. LODGE—DAY

Charlie has to take a cab to get to the Grand Am, which is still parked at the base of the ridge where the Mountain Oasis Lodge had once sat. The cabbie, kind enough not to mention the way Charlie looks and smells, only gets as far the sign for the lodge before being stopped by a police barricade.

Forced to walk the rest of the way, Charlie eventually gets to the bridge in front of the waterfall. The chunk of railing she'd taken out with the Volvo is now covered with police tape—clearly a symbolic gesture and not an adequate replacement.

The Volvo itself still sits in the grass beside the ravine. Although Robbie's body had been removed and carried away hours earlier, Charlie gets a chill when she sees the car. It reminds her not only about how close she had come to death but about how little she knew Robbie.

And how, when pushed, she was capable of anything.

As she crosses the bridge, Charlie wonders if there had been warning signs that she missed. She assumes there were. She also assumes it'll take years of therapy to figure out what they were.

That and maybe some little orange pills.

Charlie knows that the movies in her mind need to stop. She can't spend parts of her life in a dream state. She suspects that's one of the reasons she had so spectacularly misjudged Robbie. He was too handsome, too smart, too perfect for real life. The flaws were there, but she had overlooked them in favor of preserving the movie-version boyfriend she wanted instead of looking for the real-life one she needed.

That's the tricky thing about movies. They can be wonderful and beautiful and amazing. But they're not like life, which is wonderful, beautiful, and amazing in a different way.

Not to mention messy.

And complicated.

And sad and scary and joyful and frustrating and, very often, boring. Charlie knows the night she's just had is the exception rather than the rule.

She reaches the Grand Am, which had been left unlocked. Sliding behind the wheel, Charlie grabs the keys Josh gave her and starts the car. She then grabs a cassette and pops it into the stereo. She presses play and a familiar song starts to blast through the speakers.

"Come as You Are."

Charlie bobs her head in time to the music. She can't help herself. It's a great song.

As the music plays and the Grand Am's engine hums and the sun rises over the mountains, Charlie shifts into gear.

Then she drives like hell.

Fade out.

Screening room.

The middle of the afternoon.

The middle of somewhere.

The lights come up on the audience of movers and shakers scattered throughout the theater. Charlie doesn't know who half of them are or why they're here or what they think of the movie they just watched. But she knows the important ones.

The director, a Tarantino wannabe wearing a thrift-store bowling shirt and a ten-thousand-dollar watch. He kept his tinted eyeglasses on the entire screening.

The actress, a few years older than Charlie was at the time but far prettier. So pretty that it was impossible to hide. Throughout the movie, she was radiant in her sadness, radiant in her madness, radiant in her rage. Rather than feeling jealous about that, Charlie's delighted that a better, more beautiful version of herself now exists. The world will see it and, hopefully, think that's what she was really like back then.

The leading men are the opposite. They just can't compare to their real-life counterparts, even though both are bona fide teen idols. The bad boy on that hit WB show leaning into type as Josh and the good boy from that other hit WB show playing against it as Robbie. Having seen the real deals, Charlie can't help but be unimpressed.

After a smattering of applause, the director stands and turns to her, rubbing his hands together and giving her a smile that's meant to be warm but comes across as predatory. Charlie knows the score. He thinks exploiting her ordeal is going to solidify his career. Maybe it will. Charlie's long given up on trying to understand modern moviegoers.

Her main focus now is preserving the past, which is part of her job duties as an archivist at the Academy of Motion Picture Arts and Sciences. She loves what she does. Getting to be a gatekeeper of honest-to-God film history is her dream job. She even gets to attend the Oscars every year, although way back in the cheap seats. And when she goes home at night, she leaves it all behind. No more movies in the mind for her. Those ended the night depicted in the real movie she just watched.

"What do you think?" the director says.

He wants her to say she loves it. Charlie can see it in his eyes, which blaze bright even behind those tinted lenses.

But here's the rub: she doesn't know how she feels.

Charlie's issue with what she just watched is that it ironically does everything she normally likes about the movies. It's life, made bigger, if not better. The trouble lies in the fact that it's her own life that's been enlarged. This isn't the story of that night. Not the true one. And she has a hard time seeing past the liberties that were taken.

For one, it was spring. There was no chill, no picturesque snowfall, no red coat, although that Charlie can forgive because the color pops beautifully on-screen. Most of the locations were also invented or altered. There is no Olyphant University—that was changed because the real college wanted nothing to do with the production. The Skyline Grille was less of a diner and more of a truck stop, its Formica tables colored a sad brown, its booths worn dull by the backs of slumped patrons.

As for the Mountain Oasis Lodge, Charlie almost burst out laughing when it appeared on-screen. It was so over-the-top as to be absurd. The work of a production designer with a lot of money and a penchant for exposed timbers. The real lodge was a glorified motel—one central building with a smattering of cottages forming a horseshoe shape around the swimming pool.

But some of the embellishments she likes very much. The fire—which didn't happen—added some much-needed punch to the third act. The waterfall—which didn't exist—added a great backdrop to the scene of the sinking Volvo.

That, by the way, did happen. Right down to the satisfying click of the handcuffs around the steering wheel.

Yet Charlie's favorite part of the movie was the denouement, mostly because it showed what could have been. Marge died at the Mountain Oasis Lodge. According to police, she climbed into the pool, fished out the gun, and pulled the trigger.

There was no hospital room conversation.

No unspoken truce between them.

No triumphant moment with a tooth.

Watching all of that on-screen made her wish it was true. In this instance, she doesn't mind the Hollywood ending. In fact, she cherishes it.

Movie magic. It's a palpable thing.

And Maddy would have loved it.

Which is why Charlie smiles back at the director and says, "I adore it."

After that, she's free to go.

The screening room is located in a downtown building and not a studio lot. A shame, really. Charlie loves it when she gets to visit them for her work. They're magical and mundane at the same time. Factories where dreams get made.

The upside about her current location is that a Lincoln Town Car is waiting for her outside. Rather than climb into the back, she slides into the front passenger seat.

"Hey," she says.

The driver flashes her a killer smile. "Hey yourself."

That part of the movie, as improbable as it may seem, is true. Josh did let her borrow his car. Charlie drove it straight to Ohio and Nana Norma. When she returned the car two weeks later, Josh did indeed ask if she'd like to go to the movies.

Her answer was simple: "I never say no to a movie."

They went. Josh paid for the tickets.

They went the next night. Charlie returned the favor.

By their third movie, Josh had learned that she preferred to sit in the middle of the sixth row. By the fourth, Charlie had learned that Josh liked to put Raisinets in his popcorn. By their fifth, she finally learned to start calling him Jake.

That was six years ago.

"How was your day?" she asks.

"Good," he replies. "I got to take Sharon Stone to the airport."

"How'd she look?"

"Like a Hitchcock blonde."

"Exactly what I wanted to hear."

He waits a beat before asking the question she knows is at the forefront of his thoughts. "And how was the movie?"

"Not bad. Not great, but certainly not terrible. It was a typical movie. But real life—" Charlie exhales a sigh of contentment as she reaches for her husband's hand. "Real life is so much better."

END CREDITS

While it would be appropriate to compare writing a novel to a long, lonely drive through darkness, it's not quite the truth. Getting a book published is a team effort, and I have many people to thank for helping me reach my destination.

To Maya Ziv, for being a fantastic editor and, even more, all-around joy.

To Emily Canders, Katie Taylor, Christine Ball, and literally everyone at Dutton, for helping me do what I do. I'm so lucky to have found such an amazing creative home, and I'm astounded daily by all your enthusiasm and support.

To Michelle Brower, for being an incredible agent, a fierce advocate, and a wonderful human being.

To everyone at Aevitas Creative Management, for keeping the business side of things running like clockwork and letting me focus on the writing.

To Mike Livio, for, well, everything.

To the Ritter and Livio families, for their encouragement, support, and bringing quiet normalcy to a sometimes crazy world.

To Sarah Dutton, for being the best first reader a writer could ever have.

To Ben Turrano, for answering my many questions about driving a late-eighties Pontiac Grand Am.

To the filmmakers whose work inspires me and that I return to again and again—Alfred Hitchcock, Orson Welles, Billy Wilder, Steven Spielberg, David Fincher, Vincente Minnelli, Wes Craven, Brian De Palma, Walt Disney.

Finally, *Survive the Night* is a love letter to the movies, yes, but also to a specific time period. In November 1991, I was a senior in high school, which was a particularly fraught, magical, memorable time in my life. And if you'll forgive one final bit of nostalgia, I'd like to thank the people who were so special to me then: Jenny Beaver, Jason Davis, Christine Fry, Marta McCormick, Marsha McKinney, John Paul, Sarah Paul, Brian Reedy, Jeff Richer, Seema Shah, and Kelly Jo Woodside. Thank you all for the many night drives.

ABOUT THE AUTHOR

Survive the Night is the fifth thriller from Riley Sager, the pseudonym of an author who lives in Princeton, New Jersey. Riley's first novel, *Final Girls*, was a national and international bestseller that has been published in more than two dozen countries and won the ITW Thriller Award for Best Hardcover Novel. Sager's novels *The Last Time I Lied, Lock Every Door,* and *Home Before Dark* were *New York Times* bestsellers.